BITTERSWEET

Sue Robertson Danells

Old Crow Books

FOREWORD

In twenty-fifteen, a man's body was discovered on Saddleworth Moor. He lay on his back, his head at the top of the slope, his feet perpendicular down the hill, and his arms across his chest. He had died of strychnine poisoning with a vial found close by which, on examination, had contained the liquid. It was concluded that he had taken his own life. His body revealed no evidence of who he was.

An author's imagination is sparked by such reported events and by life experiences, not only personal, but from those of people they have known along the way. This novel, while entirely fictional, was inspired by a knowledge of the events it portrays.

PART 1

AT BALLYWALTER
NORTHERN IRELAND

Nineteen Twenty-Nine

Domestic Turmoil

CHAPTER1

Patrick and Orla Blair

The Ards Peninsula is that piece of land which lies at the most easterly point of Northern Ireland about thirty miles from Belfast. Its long-hooked finger almost encloses one half of Strangford Lough and is bordered by the Irish Sea. Strangely, many of its early inhabitants had not been Irish at all, but Scottish folk who sailed the short passage in the early seventeenth century to take advantage of the good corn-growing soil when their own harvests failed.

The land was fertile, and much use had been made in centuries past of the wind to drive windmills. By the end of the eighteenth century seventy-five percent of windmills in Ireland were located on the Ards Peninsula but after about eighteen seventy a decline in the grain industry left most of the land to be used as pasture.

One such family to have made the journey two hundred years before, went by the familial name of Blair. They were a proud family despite who they had become. Through the decades stories passed down were exclusively about their heritage; about the important Scottish clan they had belonged to; about the Blair crest which meant so much to them; about the lands they had owned until the middle of the eighteenth century when the important line of heritage ended. It was then that the lower ranking of the clan began their journey across the dangerous Irish Sea to settle on the Ards Peninsular.

Perhaps it was the nature of their fall that they instilled into their children a desire to maintain the family name at all costs, for it was this need within them which influenced the way they were raised. Boys were prized for their one ability to further the Blair name. Girls less so. They were married to anyone who would have them but whatever occurred, the mingling and gradual dilution of Scottish blood continued until they were all in reality, Irish.

This did not diminish the fact that their souls remained Scottish, that their heads continued to be filled with the need to father sons, that their lives were predicated on achieving this. Patrick Blair was no exception.

Patrick Blair married Orla Flynn, she being just seventeen, her husband twenty-two, and they settled in the small town of Ballywalter on the coast of the Irish Sea. This was about as far south on the peninsula as they wanted to be, since they were, as with all Blairs, Presbyterians. Any further south would have seen them too close to those whose religion they disagreed with.

Patrick and Orla had many children over the years, but miscarriages, still births and infant mortality ensured that only six lived, and of those six, five were girls. The youngest to survive was Ailill and being much cherished, was cossetted more by his father than his mother who often worried that her son might turn into his father one day, for her bruises and scars were testament to the way the hearts of Blair men smouldered with anger.

CHAPTER 2

Ailill Blair

Ailill sat at the table just as his mother spooned food onto his plate, his father already waiting to begin. He saw the fresh bruise blooming at his mother's right eye, the one on her left almost gone now. He smiled at her, thanked her for his food and bowed his head. He was ashamed of his inability to confront his father. The atmosphere in the small room was so thick, Ailill could not bring himself to speak so ate as quickly as he could.

'Don't eat so fast,' said his father. 'You'll get the stomach cramps.'

'I'm fine,' he said but the look on his father's face reminded him of his place at the table, and when the meal was done, Patrick laid a large hand on Ailill's arm to prevent him from leaving.

'You're comin up twenty-one ... no prospects

yet of marriage ... when are you goin to bless us with a daughter-in-law?'

'I've got my eye on a girl.'

'No good havin your eye on her! What've you done about it?' His voice rose. 'All family's waitin for you to produce the next bairn ... male mind you.'

'I know! I know ... I'm not like you Pa. I don't want to marry because I have to ... When I'm ready ... OK?'

'Ach! You'll do as I say in the end.'

Ailill raised himself but looked at his mother, whose face was so sorrowful he sat again. He did not want to leave her with his father in this mood. He saw the tension in her body, knew she was afraid, knew he could not protect her. After a while she told him to go wash and freshen himself and he was glad of it, although far from washing, he went out to his shed at the bottom of the garden.

Aillil was a tall man, almost lanky, with thick dark hair which grew to his shoulders where it sat and curled. His eyebrows were long too, with a tendency to stick out towards the outside corners, the eyes themselves, two distinct colours. His right was a rich blue, the left a deep chestnut, its darkness more pronounced in the shadows of his deep-set features. He was quite a handsome man in spite of these quirks of nature. His weather beaten face was rugged from time spent in the air at the lime kilns where he worked. The smell from the fertilizer soaked into his clothes and wafted after him.

Ailill remembered the stories told to him by his father almost every day at bedtime. As a child he had been enthralled by them, imagining battles and all sorts of wonderful adventures. He loved his father when he was young, looked up to him, thought him funny because he always joked about the big important man he would become. He had sisters then too, older than him, but sisters who looked after him, cared for him when his mother was out or unwell,and he'd loved them but he wasn't very old before they all married and disappeared from his life. Ailill had never seen the way his father treated the women of the family until he became a teenager. It was only then that he started noticing his father's anger towards his mother, the way Orla shrank from him so different from the way Patrick behaved towards him. Now with this never-ending battle about marrying and producing a son, Ailill could not take much more.

Away from the stifling atmosphere of the house, Ailill would normally continue with his furniture making which always granted him the space to forget. He was working on a chair for his mother. Today he sat in the corner with a piece of rough wood which he rolled in his hands, the splinters catching his skin, and thought of the girl. She was not in any way pretty, but as his father would tell him, she had good child-bearing hips. What drew him to her was her beautiful soprano voice, like an angel, or perhaps a lark high in the sky. He had first heard her in the village when she and her father sang in the square at Christmas and he had hidden among the crowds. He was captivated by the music.

His father would have him marry anyone and quickly. His mother knew better than to marry without forethought. She had never spoken of it to him, but he knew what she endured. Maybe if his father had genuinely loved her things might have been different. By the time daylight had faded, Ailill had decided that this girl might just be the one for him; that he would talk to her father for permission to walk out with her.

CHAPTER 3

Ballyferris Northern Ireland

Bridget Niall

Mary and Fearghal Niall were at home in Ballyferris, Northern Ireland, with their remaining two children, the others safely married. Bridget was the older of the two girls but it was Cora who was about to be wed.Bridget and her father were practicing the songs they would sing at the event. Fearghal and Bridget were well known in the small sleepy town, for they sang in many a public house, as well as at the Market Square on special occasions. Between songs they caught up on all the local news, laughing mostly, as they so often did.

'I had a visitor the other day,' said Fearghal. Bridget and Cora turned towards him when he fell silent.

'And who would that have been?' Cora said

cheekily.

'That young man, Ailill Blair ... yes ... came to ask me something ... and I'm duty bound to let you know.

When he said nothing else, Cora exclaimed,

'We won't know till you tell us Pa.'

'Yes ... well he came asking after you Bridget,' and stopped again seeing the surprise on her face. She had little experience of men folk. The mention of her name with that of a man made her uncomfortable, the thought that she had been asked after confused her. Already her stomach tightened. She became flushed with embarrassment.

Unlike her sister, Bridget was not pretty. In fact she was extremely plain with little about her to encourage but she was happy, and calm. She was pensive, her thoughts unlikely to be shared with many, and she was creative with needles. Cora was none of these things.

'Will you tell us what he wanted, Pa? For I'm sure I don't know what he'd be asking after me for.'

'He wanted permission to walk out with you, but your mother's not so sure I should give it.'

'Why?'

'There's many rumours about 'em. They say his father's violent towards his mother ... those who know 'em even say it runs in the family. I'm not liking thoughts of you with him,' she said.

'The girl's not been asked after by any so far ...

she's getting on Mary ... maybe Ailill's different ... you know not like old Patrick ... but there's only one way to find out ... I think we should let 'em,' said Fearghal.

Bridget listened. She was resigned, even at her relatively immature age, to being a spinster; living with her parents; looking after them in their old age. She wanted children and loved her nieces and nephews, harbouring a secret hope that one day someone might want her. She had seen the man in town a few times, even spotting him at some of their singing nights. She knew his name because someone had called him but he was a complete stranger to her. She wondered how it would be to walk out with him unsure if she wanted to.

'What did you tell him?' she asked.

'I told him straight away that if he didn't rid himself of the smell on him, it'd be a no, but that he should come back in a weeks' time.'

'Alright,' said Mary ... he lays one finger on my girl, Fearghal, and you'll go after him!'

'So I will.'

CHAPTER 4

The Date

Ailill called at the house for Bridget one fine summer evening smelling fresh and sweet. Wearing her finest dress, she went with him to the annual fair on Market Square. They were awkward with each other on the walk, neither knowing how to break the ice so when Ailill said he always tried to hear her sing, she was both surprised and instantly gratified.

'Oh! It's kind of you. You like our singing, then?'

'I do Bridget. You have the sweetest voice I ever heard.'

She looked up at him, saw his face redden, and felt the heat rise to her own. In the pause that ensued, she noticed his eyes. Unable to avert her gaze, she realised she was staring at him.

'Your eyes,' she said. 'They're different

colours!'

'They are.'

'How?'

'I was born with blue eyes mam says, but the left turned brown. I don't know how ... I'm used to it now ... don't even think about it. Does it bother you?'

'No ... it's just unusual ... a little strange perhaps but I could get used to it.' As she said it, she realised it was rather presumptuous. 'Sorry.'

'You don't need to be.'

The fair was not a big event, but sufficient to have an evening of fun so that they might relax a little. There were stalls of food, games to play, huge swings in the shape of gondolas and even one of those rides with horses that go up and down. Organ music played loudly across the square. Laughter, shouts and sounds of people enjoying themselves found their way into their hearts.

Ailill had a look at the peep show, and they both tried to knock Aunt Sally from her perch. When Bridget saw the stall where you could hook a prize, Ailill paid for her to have several goes but she was unlucky, all her prizes falling off at the last minute. It made her laugh and he thought that when she did, her face was quite beautiful.

By the end of the evening Ailill had won two china dogs and a cat, which he gave her as a keepsake saying they would remind her of their time at the fair. Bridget took them, carefully wrapping them in her basket. It flustered her so she could only say thank you knowing her face blushed.

'What's he like?' Fearghal asked. Bridget felt herself colour, the heat rising from her neck into her cheeks as she glanced at her mother across the table.

'He's polite and we had fun,' was all she said. The truth was she found herself unable to say much about him. She only knew that she had enjoyed being with him and hoped he would want to see her again.

'Is that all you can say girl?'

'Well ... I think him very handsome ... his eyes are unusual colours ... one's blue and the other brown.'

'How so?' her mother asked.

'I don't know. They just are.'

'I don't like the sound of that ... maybe the devils in him. What do you think Fearghal?'

'Saw it when he came to the house. Don't think it's anything to do with the devil though ... nothing to concern ourselves with,' he said giving his wife a furrowed look.

'Well ... I hope you're right. Did he say anything about seeing you again?'

'No. But I hope he wants to. I think him kind.'

At home, Ailill slumped into the chair opposite his father.

'Good time son?' Patrick asked.

'A good time Pa. The fair was fun … we had plenty to do and see … I won some things for Bridget.'

'Is that it! The fair was fun! What about the girl?'

'Her name's Bridget, Pa.'

'Well, what about her?'

'I like her …'

'I like her,' his father mimicked. 'Will she give bairns?'

'I don't know! I don't care!' Ailill shouted, moving forward in the chair as if to leave. 'I liked her enough to want to walk out again … can't that be enough for you? Has everythin always got to be about bairns and family name? How do I know what lies ahead?'

Patrick almost leapt across the room pushing his son back into the chair and stood over him, his menacing face only inches from Ailill's.

'You dare talk to me like that. You dare shout at your own father. Remember whose house you live in … whose bread you eat … whose bed you sleep in! Remember your birth right when you want your own way. I expect a grandson … and before you're too old to manage it.'

Patrick barely stopped himself from striking his son, so angry was he with the boy's attitude but managed to move away. He glared at him, all his inner malice marked on his face. Orla had come downstairs after the noise. It would not end well if she saw him harm Ailill.

'What's amiss?' she said.

'What's amiss is our pathetic son … sometimes I'm ashamed he's a Blair. Time he went and lived somewhere else, Orla. Time he took himself off … wed this girl and only come back when there's a boy to show for it.' He turned towards the stairs, taking hold of his wife to follow him, but she held her place and said,

'You go up. I'll not be a while.'

'You alright Ailill?'

'Yes. Will he hurt you now?'

'If he does, he does. I've grown so used to it I hardly feel it anymore. Perhaps he's right though … perhaps it's time for you to find a home somewhere away from him … somewhere you can take a wife one day … somewhere you'll be happy.'

'What of you then?'

'I think … maybe he'll calm a bit … this thing inside him … it's taking over … if you could give him a grandson … well, he might go back to the man I married.'

Ailill wasted no time in finding somewhere he could call home. It was a small almost derelict cottage, the owner not having bothered with it for years and Ailill negotiated a low price for the rent in exchange for making it habitable. He toiled all daylight hours after work; made it watertight; hung new doors; sealed windows; repaired the stairs, and then ensured the hearths in each room were ready for use.

In fair weather and, if his mood permitted, Patrick would help out. Ailill was wary at first but began to enjoy being with his father, who never mentioned bairns, nor marriage for that matter. It was as though the man he worked alongside was not the father he knew at all, and he sometimes wondered if the spell would break.

In the outhouse at the back, Ailill made furniture. A bed to begin with, wide enough for two and long enough to stretch out properly, so his feet were not cramped in the mornings ... he was a tall man ... much too tall for the bed at home. His head was full of plans for the place, not just for him but for Bridget, for they had been courting, and he had decided that he would marry her.

Not long after Ailill began his renovation, he found a stray in the garden, a malnourished Irish Setter, his rich red coat matted. The hang dog-look melted Ailill's heart, for he loved all animals and hated to see them abused. He gave him scraps of food from his plate and gradually a bond was formed between them so they went everywhere together. He called him Murphy.

CHAPTER 5

A Wedding

A year after their first evening at the fair there was a wedding in the small town of Ballyferris, Ailill and Bridget declaring their vows and exiting the small church as man and wife. Bridget had brightly coloured wildflowers in her golden hair, her good luck handkerchief tucked into her sleeve and almost missed seeing the boot as it sailed out of the crowd and over her head. It was late in the day as they made their way from Bridget's home. Ailill guided the horse skillfully, Bridget's chest of belongings rattling in the cart, Murphy between them. But for all the good luck traditions, Ailill had still not heard a cuckoo and he feared it did not bode well for them.

Bridget had never been out of Ballyferris. She knew her home was to be in Ballywalter now but had little idea of where that was so in the silence she said,

'Ailill. How far is it?'

'A bit further yet.'

'But we've gone a long way already.'

'It just feels a long way because you haven't been there before. It's not far really.'

'How will I visit home, or get to where Pa and I sing?'

'I'll take you. Don't fret about things like that now,' and he took her hand, squeezed it, felt the warmth of it in his and smiled at her, his eyes creasing at the corners.

She felt the road become uneven as they passed through Ballywalter. She saw the houses go by but the horse kept going. Even in the darkening skies she could tell there were no further dwellings so she began to fret. Where was he taking her?

'Haven't we just passed Ballywalter?' she asked but there was no reply so she asked again a little louder.

'That's the main town, but we're still in it. Our home's on the edge,' he said.

When Bridget first set foot on the road again, she was surprised to realise that 'on the edge' of town was no exaggeration. She could hear the sea to her left, waves crashing onto rocks, and the breeze that had followed dusk whipped her hair, taking with it the flowers she had so carefully looked after all day.

Ailill hurried her inside where he lit the lamps

and stoked the fire he had made that morning. In the dim light the room gradually came into view. Bridget saw the size of it, larger than she could ever have imagined. Stairs rose from the back. Chairs so new and beautiful and a fireplace almost grand. The furnishings she had made with the help of her mother and Cora, were on the chairs, their bright colours comforting and homely.

'What do you think, Mrs. Blair?' It was the first time she had heard herself referred to as his wife. She liked the sound of it; the fact of it.

'It's beautiful, Ailill. I never thought to live in such a place. You've laboured much to make it so lovely.'

'We both have. Come on let's get your chest upstairs while the water boils and you can see the rest of it.'

The narrow stairs were only just wide enough to take the chest but with some pushing and shoving they managed to make it to the small landing, Murphy leaping up and down the stairs swishing his tail in their faces. There was a door at each side of the landing and Ailill opened the one to the right. Bridget gasped at the size of the bed already adorned with the mattress, linen and quilt she had prepared for them; the cupboards and chests of drawers that lined the walls; the little chair beside the window. She looked up at him and put her hand on his arm, drew his mouth to hers for the first kiss in their own home.

Very quickly she put away some of her clothes, found her nightie to lay on the bed and then went to the room opposite. It was about the same size she judged and though there was no furniture it was clean. Downstairs again Bridget was eager to see the kitchen and she could tell then that although there were only four rooms, they were all about the same size, two below and two above.

In the middle of the kitchen stood a fine table with four chairs, placed two at each of the long sides. Against the inside wall, a wonderful dresser rose up almost to the ceiling and filled the space from the internal door to the front wall of the house.

'Ailill, you haven't made all this furniture in the brief time you've been here, have you?'

'Not all myself. I had help from a friend at work and you know Pa came too. I didn't know what a good carpenter he was. I suppose it's where I get it from.'

'Well … there was I thinking we'd struggle to have wonderful things and all along you've made it happen for me.'

'I wanted us to start right, Bridget. Not to have to worry … I want …'

'What?'

'I want us to have a family. To be a family

without the strife I've known all my life.'

'And we will.'

'Please be gentle with me,' Bridget said as she lay on the soft feather mattress.

Ailill kissed her lips tenderly, stroked her soft skin, her spine shivering with the sensation. She found the scar on his chest almost hidden by black hair, but visible to her touch. She tried to let go, to relax, but his newness, the newness of it all made her body tense so he coaxed her, showed her how to touch him and her natural instincts responded. Afterwards he lay with his arms about her so she could snuggle into him and discover the fit of their bodies.

CHAPTER 6

The Harbour

Bright morning sun lit up the bedroom. Bridget opened her eyes to find him gone. She could smell him on her, feel the stickiness of him and as she moved, found a new soreness. Cora had warned her it would hurt … this first time but said it would not last, and Bridget remembered how they had laughed at her sister's telling of it.

She found her nightdress and walked to the window at the back of the room, the eastern side of the house, drew the curtains and opened the window. She was anxious to see where she was, where she would be for the rest of her life. She let her eyes rove across the garden past Ailill's shed, finding a little track which ran along their rear fence to the cliff edge. The sea, only a few yards away, was as clear in the sunshine as the sky was blue; soft lapping waves against the cliff. Below the surface black, rugged rocks were visible for as far as she could see along the coast and they continued out to sea for some distance. Turning to her left she found what looked like a little harbour with three small boats moored, fishing boats she thought.

Bridget moved to the other side of the room where the window was not quite as large, though she could still hang out of it for a good look. The road they travelled yesterday ran past north to south and she was able to see why the last part of their journey had been so rough. It had no top. It was potholed with deep gullies at either side. The view here was of miles of pasture, hedges dividing some of it into distinct fields but mostly land that went on north, west, and south as far as the horizon.

Not another home in sight. Not another person. Bridget listened, no sound of human existence, only animals grazing. This must be the last house in Ballywalter. Will it be only him and me now? What does this new life really hold for me? Not wanting to dwell on such thoughts she made her way downstairs, finding Ailill at the kitchen table.

'Mornin Mrs. Blair.' He got up to give her a hug and kiss. 'How're you feelin? You know …' and he looked down towards her lower body.

'Fine,' she said, embarrassed in the light of day and seeing Murphy's tail wagging furiously bent over him to pet his head. 'Hello Murphy! How are you this fine morning?'

'Porridge? I don't know if you like it, but I have it every mornin ... sets me up for the day.' He fetched a bowl and set her breakfast on the table opposite him. He wanted to look at her.

'You should have woken me. I'm normally up much before this.'

'Aye, well ... tomorrow you'll be makin it. I've to be at work by seven.'

'It'll be a pleasure, Mr. Blair. Ailill ... I looked out of both bedroom windows and ... there aren't any houses ... Just sea on one side ... fields on the other.' She took small mouthfuls of porridge between speaking, not sure if she wanted to know what he might say.

'Peaceful isn't it.'

'Yes, it is, but are there no other people to be friendly with? I'm so used to having people around ... not sure how I'll manage with no-one to talk to all day ... to mull things over with ... or laugh with ...,' and Bridget hesitated seeing the smile fade from his face.

'You'll have me after work and at weekends. I said I'll take you to Ballyferris to see your folk and when you want to sing. Won't that be enough for you? And soon ... well ... there'll be bairns to look after,' and as he said this, his eyes looked up into hers, but his head stayed bent over his food. Bridget could find no humour in his voice.

Where Lagan stream sings lullaby
There blows a lily fair
The twilight gleam is in her eye
The night is on her hair
And like a love-sick lennan-shee
She has my heart in thrall
Nor life I owe nor liberty
For love is lord of all.

Bridget donned her old apron and sang her way through the morning chores followed by Murphy, always with her now. She had grown to love him dearly, her only companion through the long days without Ailill and when the cleaning was finished and evening meal prepared, they went together on their daily walk along the cliffs, sometimes when the tide was low along the small beach too. Miles she would walk, the fresh air brightening her spirit if it were low and if it were not, simply energising her. She had let her hair grow longer since marriage, Ailill saying he liked running his fingers through it so today, with the stiff breeze, it blew in all directions and whipped across her face. Murphy had brought his old bit of rope and wanted her to throw it. She loved to watch as he raced over the sand after it and then ambled back for another go.

'Come on Murphy! Here!'

Instead of going straight home, Bridget went past their house to the end of the little path at the bottom and turned right onto the unmade road towards the harbour, Murphy running ahead. She did not often visit it but now she wanted to see if there were any fishermen about, to chat with. Only one boat was moored, its owner carting boxes of fish onto shore.

'Well. Hello Murphy,' said Paddy, as the dog bound towards him to lick his face. 'What brings you here today, Bridget?'

'Looking for a bit of company. How are you? Is the fishing still good?'

'Aye. The weather's been on our side these last few weeks, so we've all made some money.'

'That's fine. Can't be so good in these winds though.'

'You get used to it. Done it all my life … doesn't mean I haven't been in the sea trying to hang onto the boat though,' he said, laughing.

Bridget was unsure of his age but thought he must be at least in his sixties. He had tousled white hair that looked as if it had not been cut for many a month and a very bushy beard to go with it. His thick fisherman's jumper only just managed to cover a bulging belly. Bridget thought it must be all the drink he took. She had seen him tip the bottle from her bedroom window.

'How's the fella? He still in the lime pits?'

'He is.'

'Stinks a bit!'

'I'm used to it now,' she said, thinking that the smell of fish was no better. 'I'll need to be getting his dinner ready. Bye Paddy. Come on Murphy.'

With everything cooking for their meal, Bridget wrapped the cakes for taking to Ballyferris, put what they would need into bags and then sat in her favourite chair and took up her needle, Murphy by her feet. It was not long before Ailill arrived. She jumped up to greet him, almost tripping over the dog, and Ailill caught her, holding her in a hug that she always looked forward to.

'Smells good in here,' he said, releasing her and going straight to the sink. 'I'm hungry!'

'I went to the harbour ... saw Paddy ... he asked after you,' said Bridget between mouthfuls.

'Olden or Youngen?'

'Olden,' she said. 'The wind was fair blowing but it was warm ... we stayed out almost all the afternoon.'

'Needn't take young Murphy out again then. How's old Paddy doin?'

'He says the fish are plentiful these last few weeks. There's a belly on him now ... too much drink!'

'Aye. He's a fisherman ... they're all the same.'

The late sun was still shining through the window as they settled for the evening, and tentatively, Bridget asked,

'Ailill. Can I go with you tomorrow … to your parents?'

'No.'

Bridget stiffened. The answer came quickly … too quickly and she was not sure if she should continue. After a pause, she looked at him, smiling and asked,

'But why not? I've baked a cake for them too this week, and it would be nice to see them.'

'No! No Bridget. I've told you … it's not a good idea.'

'So, when will I go with you?' He paused before answering and for a moment she thought he would say nothing.

'You're my wife. I've said no. That should be enough for you.'

She saw a new expression in Aillil's face. He got up to stoke the fire, prodding it with an unnecessary force. To his back, she said,

'But it isn't Ailill …'

Before she could say any more, he stood and faced her, his demeanour threatening. She shrank back in her chair, for the first time seeing a man she did not recognise.

'You'll come when there's a bairn … I'm goin out to the shed … somethin to finish.'

'Wait. I'll come down with you,' she said, desperate to know why he had reacted so.

'No! … It's a surprise,' he said, turning to her with a hint of a smile but Bridget saw a darkness behind his eyes, his left one indiscernible in the fading light. Then he was gone, Murphy too and left on her own Bridget struggled to understand what had happened. She lay her head back, her mind replaying it, but still she was unable to find an answer to his behaviour. For the first time since she'd known him a fear she didn't understand crept into her heart.

CHAPTER 7

The Night of the Crib

Bridget took up her sewing. She had no heart for it tonight but as the needle passed slowly between cloth, she wondered if the surprise Ailill was making might be a box for all her bits and pieces so her mood improved. When he had not returned to the house until later than usual, Bridget packed her things away and went upstairs, which was also unusual for she always waited for him so they retired together.

Tonight was different. She felt it in her bones and her head ached from over thinking. Before climbing into bed, she looked from the window. The night was black but within the shed a lamp burned and she could see the shadow of him bent over his work. Bridget imagined her husband putting the finishing touches to a beautiful workbox and knew she would always treasure it.

'Bridget!... Bridget,' louder this time so her name came to her through the first drifting of sleep. 'Come down. I've somethin to show you.'

Something large covered in a cloth stood in the centre of the room. Beside it, Ailill, sat in a chair, his face lit up with pride.

'What is it?'

'Take the cloth off.'

Bridget knew immediately that it was too big for a workbox so gingerly lifted a corner, peeping underneath.

'Come on woman,' Ailill said, as he tugged at it revealing something altogether unexpected. His face beamed now and he asked, 'What do you think?'

'Er ... It's a crib.'

'Is that all you can say?'

'It's beautiful Ailill.' And so it was; possibly the most beautiful rocking crib she had ever set eyes on. 'But it's a crib! Who's it for?'

'Who d'you think it's for? For you ... for our bairn.'

'There is no bairn Ailill. Why make a crib when there's no bairn for it?'

'You'll need time to make all the things to go in it ...' he said, with a hint of anger. 'And there will be a bairn ... no harm in being ready ... I thought you'd be pleased.'

But Bridget was hardly listening. She had bent down to touch the wood, to feel it's smooth finish. She ran her hand over the side and found something carved there. Her hand traced the edges and when she looked to examine it, saw that it was a name.

'What's this Ailill?'

'It's the name of our bairn,' and he sounded incredulous that she would even have to ask.

Bridget turned to him, held out her arms and said as softly as she could,

'Ailill. There is no bairn. There may never be a bairn. How can we know? If there is, it's just as likely to be a girl. You know that Ailill. And if it is a boy, you did not think to speak to me of a name first?'

She had not let him interrupt her even though the fear rose in her breast with the change in her husband's demeanour. When she finished, he pushed her so hard she stumbled backwards landing on the floor.

'You're wrong Bridget. There will be a boy and he will be called James, after James of the great clan we come from.'

Stunned, Bridget lay still, afraid to move, afraid to speak, afraid of this man she loved and thought she knew. But this was all too much. His preoccupation with having a bairn, she could manage but a great clan? James, the assumption of any bairn being a boy. Ailill took the crib and went toward the stairs.

'Come on. To bed now.'

Murphy ran after him as Bridget sat up, wondering how she would lie beside this man she did not recognise. He waited for her letting her go before him, the crib an almighty force between them and to her amazement, Ailill placed it lovingly at the window of their bedroom. It was too much.

'It would be better in the other room for now,' she said tersely, as she climbed between the sheets.

'It stays there,' he replied, 'where it will be a reminder of your duty.'

It was like being stabbed through the heart. How could he have changed so much in only a few hours? She did not want to watch him ready himself for bed. She did not even want to look in his direction.

Ailill took Bridget's arm, not gently as she was used to but with a grip that hurt, as he pulled her towards him.

'I'm tired Ailill. Please let me sleep.'

'After.'

He forced her to lay flat. She tried to fight against him but he held her down, his hands on her shoulders, his fingers digging into her flesh, causing her to yell out.

'You're hurting me Ailill ... Please stop ... Please Ailill ... don't do this,' but he raised his fist, so she stilled herself with the fear of it.

He pushed her legs apart as far as they would go and when he entered her she believed she might be split in two, such was the pain.

When it was over, his weight lifted from her, Bridget turned on her side and slid towards the very edge of the bed, her back to him, curled into the tightest ball she could manage. She squeezed her eyes shut, clenched her fists, and prayed she would not cry.

CHAPTER 8

A Confidence

Ailill lay on his back, then his side and his back again, wide awake and feeling the distance between them thought of what he had just done. *How could I have behaved like that to this girl I love? Do I love her? Yes*, came his own reply. He was acutely aware of how she lay, closed to him, shutting him out, not angry or tearful that he could detect. He remembered those words to her, 'your duty'.

It was her duty. He had always believed, regardless of his father's influence, that a wife should bear children and the thought of not having them filled him with a deep sense of premature loss. He went to the kitchen, made himself a drink and sat at the table with his thoughts. They were jumbled. He was unable to sort them, to understand where his behaviour had come from, what it was inside him that had erupted in that moment, how he could have let it happen after all the years of hating his father for his cruelty against his mother.

Bridget found him there when she came down with the linen bundled beneath her arm. His head on the table, soft snoring issued from his nose and she hated him. By the time she'd made her tea and started the porridge he was watching her with something so poignant in his face, her heart melted.

She sat opposite him wanting to touch him but found that she could not. The pain of it was too raw. There was a brightness in his blue eye. A brightness that should not have been there this morning. A brightness that seemed to her to be delusional, as if he would deny the act. When she looked into his brown eye there was only darkness, and it was as though each eye portrayed a different half of him. She feared him, or at least this new knowledge of him, having to steal herself to speak,

'Are you so needy of a bairn, Ailill, that you would have one born out of anger … out of rage … out of violence? You would be happy for a bairn to be born from pain … from my pain?'

He said nothing but at least his head was bowed.

'Are you not sorry, Ailill?' Getting up, he left her in silence but for the slamming of the front door.

'No tellin Bridget,' Ailill said, as they were welcomed by Mary and Ferghal, Cora waiting behind to greet her sister. Bridget tried to move normally but the pain and soreness of her body made it difficult and though they had a pleasant day once Ailill had departed to see his own parents, Ferghal said,

'You look frail girl … what's amiss?'

'Nothing Dad. I fell yesterday so walking's a bit painful.'

'Has he hurt you? My God … if he lays one finger on you Bridget … I swear I'll go for him.'

'No need to worry Pa. He's a good man. You should know that.'

'How did you fall?' asked her mother and Bridget thought quickly enough to say that it was on the slippery kitchen floor so the subject came to a close.

In bed, Bridget was thinking about what Ailill had done to her, wide awake when the door squeaked open and Cora's face appeared beside her.

'You didn't fall, did you?'

'No Cora. He took me last night against my wishes …'

'Tell me.'

'It was awful … he wasn't himself at all … like there was some other man inside.'

'Why Bridget? He's always been tender towards you … he loves you; I know he does.

Why would he do something like that?'

'His mind seems preoccupied with having a bairn. Sometimes it's all he talks of ... I'm sure it has something to do with his father.'

Bridget told Cora what had happened. She trusted her sister to keep it secret, and it was good to be able to share it.

'Perhaps you can't have bairns.'

'Oh. I know I can ... I've had three that were lost in the first few months,' she said, her eyes now overflowing. Cora gathered her up hugging her tightly, making Bridget wince but she endured it for the warmth and love emanating from her sister. 'I haven't told him about them ... I'm waiting to be sure before I do.'

'What will you do?'

'I married him, Cora. I must bear it ... and hope I can give him what he wants.'

'And if you can't?'

'I don't know. There's time yet. I'm still young. As long as Pa never gets to know ... I think he might do something dreadful.'

They stayed like that for a while, Cora taking it all in; Bridget thankful she was not alone, and then Cora asked tentatively,

'Bridget? ... why do you not go to see his family?'

'That's how it all started last evening. He said when there's a bairn to show, he'll take me ... perhaps he's ashamed of me.'

'And perhaps there's something amiss in his

home! Please don't keep things from me in future. What will you do with the crib?'

'I'll dress it ... you know ... for when it's needed. It's the most beautiful crib you'll ever see ... and it rocks. I'll have to be very careful now not to make Ailill angry, but I think it'll be hard.' Bridget sat back on the bed before she added, 'after last night ... I don't know if I can trust him ... and what's worse is that I'll never be sure how he might react to what I say or do.'

'You have to look after yourself, Bridget. We should get some sleep now, otherwise we'll be yawning all day tomorrow.'

Cora kissed her sister on the cheek and crept out. Bridget snuggled into the bed, falling asleep easily now that her burden had been shared.

CHAPTER 9

Acquiescing

Only his mother was at home when Ailill arrived, having left Bridget with her family. Orla came to him taking him into a deep hug, feeling the quiver in his body and looked into his eyes.

'What is it son? '

'Nothing Mum,' he said, pushing her away gently.

'Ailill,' she said, pointing a wooden spoon in his direction ...' you lie to me at your peril. What have you done to make you shake so? You seem different today.'

'I told you. There's nothing wrong. Perhaps I'm hungry. Where's Pa?'

'How's Bridget? Is she going to come and see us soon?'

'Mam ... you know Pa won't have her here until she's carrying. You'll just have to wait ... like me.'

Orla frowned, walked into the kitchen to check on their meal, her mind conjuring up an array of reasons for her son's distance, the change she detected .

'Have you hurt her Ailill?' she shouted, and even as she said it she knew and did not want to hear the answer, did not want it to be true but there was no reply. It was all the answer she needed. *How could he? What is the matter with Blair men?* 'Shame on you Ailill,' she shouted.

Her worst fears had come to pass. All those years she had prayed for Ailill to be the one who might break the thread, who might show them all how to love without violence, without control. *Had he not witnessed what that sort of love does to people?* Orla wept for her son, her daughter-in-law, for herself, for the knowledge of this deeply inherent flaw now in her. Her tears flowed freely dripping from her chin into the stew pot.

On Sunday night, Bridget curled up with her back to Aillil thinking only of what would be on his mind. The bed creaked as he tossed and turned. *Don't touch me. Don't touch me. Don't touch me.* Her mind repeated it like a mantra as though by doing so she could ward him off, until she felt herself drifting down heavily, sleep carrying her away from him.

Ailill lay on his back staring at the ceiling. He thought of his mother, of how he had disappointed her. But it was worse than that. He had betrayed her, betrayed her trust in him to know what was right and wrong between husband and wife. He closed his eyes against the memories of what his father had instilled in him from such a small boy pushing them all aside. *She's yours now. She's to obey you, to do her duty. You must make her Ailill. You own her.* It was all he could do to stop himself from taking her there and then but her regular, shallow breathing confirmed she was asleep. *Bide your time Ailill. She'll come round in the end.*

Bridget came to think of that night as "the night of the crib", all her memories located either before or after. Early memories faded as she accepted the loss of the man she loved and tried to live with the man he had become. Murphy became her only comfort but even the long walks they still took were not joyous as they had once been. Bridget no longer sang of young men and women finding love, her heart unable to feel them. She was empty, cold most of the time and when she allowed her thoughts the space to wander it was always the shivering that made her realise where they had gone.

All tenderness had disappeared that night. Ailill taking her now whenever he felt the need. He did not spare her feelings nor concern himself with the physical aftermath, for he knew only to mark her where clothes would hide his deeds. He was only ever in the house to eat, sleep and abuse her, the rest of his days spent either at the lime pits or in his shed. Some evenings she would watch him from the bedroom window bowed over his work, shadowy and when night began to draw in, almost unworldly.

She often wondered what exquisitely crafted pieces he made, where he stored them, what he did with them, for he never showed her. And as she stood there, the crib, barren of its furnishings, remained between them, a sentinel, watching her, mocking her for her failure to fill it.

It occurred to Bridget that if she could conceive, if she could give him what he most wanted, he might ... just might revert to her Ailill. After all, she considered, change can happen both ways so she determined to be compliant. In the end she wanted a bairn too. A bairn would give her new hope, someone to focus on, to love and cherish and maybe they would become a proper family like the one she had dreamed of.

Murphy rose from her feet, tail wagging furiously and went to the door. He could sense Ailill coming home from way down the road and sniffed the air crying for his master. Bridget went to the kitchen to finish dinner. She always had it on the table ready for him as was her obligation. He had made that quite clear. She deliberately left the crib in the living room with her sewing bits and pieces thinking it would at least,begin the conversation.

'What you doin?' Ailill asked, pointing towards her work.

'Oh. I thought I'd make a start furnishing the crib. As you said, it's better to have it ready for when we need it.'

'Does that mean ....'

'No. I'm sorry ... but we will need it ... one day ... and then it'll be done.'

Bridget waited for his response, her stomach tight with fear of ensuing anger, but he said nothing until he had started his dinner.

'That's good, Bridget. You'll make it beautiful. I want a bath after this, so put the water on.'

Yes. She would do anything necessary to avoid his wrath but was dumbfounded by his dismissal of this powerful thing between them. Not another word was uttered that evening though he allowed her to scrub his back, wash his hair and towel him down, which he had not asked for in a long time.

'Will you put your night clothes on now?' Bridget asked. 'It's getting late. Maybe we could have an early night.'

He looked down at her with something of the old Ailill behind his eyes, held her face and kissed her gently. In her surprise, she said,

'How I've longed for you to kiss me like that, hold my face as you used to. I've missed you so much.'

Aillil said nothing. She watched him take her sewing from the crib. She saw as he lifted it up, the side level with his face. He kissed the name, so beautifully carved into it and Bridget's knees almost gave way. She held on to the door, her heart racing.

'Upstairs then.' His tone was harsh. In an instant his eyes changed in stark contrast to how they had been just a moment ago, his lips hard set.

'D'you think you can soften me with your likin the crib now? D'you think I don't know what you're doin? How you're tryin to trick me with your lovey dovy stuff … gettin the crib out and all that?'

As he spoke, Aillil pushed her roughly towards the stairs, chased her up and threw himself on top of her, winding her so that she choked, even as he pressed himself into her. She heard Murphy whine at the door.

CHAPTER 10

A Long-Awaited Visit

It was two full years they had been married and about eighteen months of violence by the time Bridget felt it safe to tell him.

'Ailill, we're having a bairn,' she said, looking at him as they sat at breakfast.

She wanted to see his reaction, to know how her news would be greeted, for even at that moment Bridget did not feel safe in his company. He looked up, met her eyes, all the fierceness of the last months draining away from him so that his face became as she had once known it, soft, loving and kind. He took both her hands in his.

'Are you sure … can it be true?'

'Yes. It's true. You'll be a father.'

'When?'

'I think I'm four months gone … so about five months,' she said, now feeling the broadness of her own smile.

Ailill stood and came to her lifting her into a hug. He kissed her cheeks, her mouth, her chin, and placed his hands on her belly, rubbing it gently.

'I told you Bridget. I told you didn't I ... we'd have a bairn ... we'd need that crib I made. I'm so happy ... you've made me so happy ...' and tears glistened at the corners of his eyes so that she felt the old love for him as she wiped them away.

Bridget followed him to the bedroom. Saw him standing before the crib as though he were worshipping it, a strange reverence clouding his face.

'James Blair.'

Her stomach contracted.

'Please Ailill ... it might not be a boy ... you must expect that it may be a girl ... don't get your hopes up ... please.'

'I'm quite sure it'll be a boy. I can feel it, Bridget. Ma and Pa will be so pleased.'

Bridget let his comment hang in the air unwilling to challenge him further, afraid that if she did, his demeanour might revert again

'Does it mean I can visit them with you at the weekend?'

'I'll think about it. Might be better if I tell them first.'

Bridget was at a complete loss to understand what lay behind all this business about the importance of a boy and not being able to see his parents, but knew from past experience that he would not divulge any of his family peculiarities and said no more. Ailill did take her though, after three weeks of knowing. It was a strange time for Bridget. The atmosphere in the home a peculiar mix of joy and tension, unsettled her so she did not understand quite how to behave.

Orla and Patrick were strangers to her even after these years of marriage to their son, and so different from each other she could hardly imagine how they married in the first place. Bridget took an instant dislike, against her better nature, to Ailill's father. Almost before the front door had closed Patrick had his hands on her belly looking at it like a wolf might look at its prey, saliva dripping from its chin, tongue hanging out in anticipation. Her entire body shivered under his intrusive glare, and though he congratulated her, at no time while she was there did he speak to her of anything but how she should keep Ailill happy.

Bridget removed herself to the kitchen where Orla was busy with dinner and offered her help, the two women chatting easily about all things baby. They sat at the kitchen table with a cup of tea, Bridget feeling herself warm to this woman.

'He's hurt you hasn't he,' Orla said.

'No.'

'But I know he has Bridget. Please tell me.'

'I can't ... I can't speak of my husband to

others.'

'I'm not others, am I? I'm his mother ... I know him ... or I thought I did ... I hoped all the time he was growing up, that he would be different ... but he isn't, is he?'

'What do you mean, different?'

'From his father ... from all the other Blair men I've known ... but I was stupid Bridget ... I should have warned you before you married him ... I should have ...'

'Should have what?'

'Sometimes I think ... I think ... it would have been better if he hadn't lived.'

'Please don't say that. Ailill is wonderful in some ways. And I was happy until it started.'

Orla took Bridget in her arms cradling her head, wanting only to remove all the pain they had both known and would know in the future. With her arms outstretched on Bridget's shoulders, Orla studied her daughter-in-law's face.

'Don't put up with it, as I have. Don't let him treat you like a chattel, for it will surely break you in the end.

'Why did you stay if it was so bad?'

Orla moved to the stove, held onto it her body frozen with the question she had so often asked herself.

'I stayed for the children, Bridget. I suffered it for their sakes, so they should have two parents.'

Orla turned to look at her.

'I should have known that his ways would hurt us all in the long run.'

For much of Bridget's pregnancy Ailill was a model husband, looking after her needs and taking on chores when they became too difficult for her. A lightness returned to their home so they walked together, laughed together, lay next to each other peacefully, Ailill never attempting to make love to her in case it would hurt the baby. He continued to work in his shed, secretly making Bridget knew not what, but she paid no mind to it. Nothing would cause her to upset this equilibrium.

As Bridget's time drew near, Cora came to stay with them and Bridget was glad of her for she brought with her that wonderful nature Bridget loved. Cora scurried about taking on as much as her sister would allow and performing everything with her inimitable good humour.

The two women sat of an evening sewing, or knitting for the new bairn, admiring each other's work while laying out garments and storing them away in readiness. Ailill was pleased to have his sister-in-law there. It meant he had more time to be in his shed and sometimes Cora would join Bridget at her bedroom window to watch and wonder what the draw of it was. They would laugh to think that whatever secrets lay inside, Ailill would rather be out in the cold than by the fire with them.

The two sisters had just packed away before their final cup of tea of the evening when Ailill burst through the door carrying a large object under his long arm, Murphy attempting to get through the door before him. It made the girls jump so unexpected was it and they both placed their hands on their hearts to still them. Ailill put the object in front of the fire, his face full of happiness, his blue eye full of light.

'What is it?' asked Cora.

'Take a look Bridget,' he said, and her spine tingled at a memory. A memory that in recent months she had locked away but the very fact of its shape and size had instantly brought it to the fore. Bridget stepped forward, drew away the cover without any hesitation, for she could not believe it would be what she thought it was.

'A crib? Ailill? Who is it for this time? I don't know of anyone in need of such a thing.'

For us ... for our bairn ...' he said.

'But we have a crib ... a beautiful one you made long ago ... much better than this one.'

'That's for James, Bridget. This one's for if it's a girl.'

Cora looked horrified as she turned towards Bridget and then Ailill, not believing this little scene, not believing that Ailill could be so insensitive.

'I've seen the one you made before,' she said. 'Why is this one not as beautiful?'

'Well ... if it's a girl it won't need anything as

good as if it's a boy,' he said, as if the entire world knows it, understands it, agrees with it. Anger flared in Bridget's body. She remembered Orla's words and wanted to gouge her husband's eyes out in that terrifying moment, to take the left dark orb and destroy it, for she believed now that there was some kind of force behind it.

'Take it out!' she yelled. 'I'll not even consider it until it's as beautiful as the other, and even then, I won't use it. The one I've got is the one I want, whatever our bairn is.'

Bridget grabbed Cora's hand and headed for the stairs, but Ailill caught her, looked at her with such hatred she thought he would harm her there and then in front of her sister. He steadied himself, backed away and did as she said. Cora ran into her bedroom, Bridget following and they sat breathless on the bed.

'Are you alright?' Cora asked, and though she was shaking, Bridget managed to smile and tell her sister she was fine. 'How often does he hurt you?'

'It's been a lot but since I've been carrying he's changed. He's the man I married again ... that is until tonight. I don't know what's going on in his mind, Cora. He can turn in a flash like he's two different people. When I look at him now, it's his blue eye I see ... it's like the right side of him behind that beautiful blue eye is pure and loving ... the left side ... sometimes I can only see malice there ... a sort of growing evil. If this bairn's a girl … ', Bridget turned to look at Cora, her fingers playing with the quilt on the bed, so that it was scrunching up, 'I don't know what I'll do … I don't know how he'll be with her … or me.'

'Try not to think of that now.' Cora went to the window, looked down at the shed, and tried to imagine what this man was like to live with. Her husband was so different, evenly tempered, kind … and yes he was angry at times, but he had never hurt her, and although she knew something of what Bridget had put up with, it was only then, in that terrible moment, she came to understand the magnitude of Ailill's double nature. And what was all that about girls not needing pleasant things like boys? Who ever heard of such a thing! All her children received the same care and attention. They were all loved equally.

She did not know what to do so went to make a hot drink for them both while Bridget changed into her nightclothes. Cora was anxious. She worried about her sister. She did not want her to be on her own with Ailill, so thought to get word to their mother to come and help. The bairn would not be long.

They heard Ailill's footsteps on the stairs, a tail banging on the wall and finished their drink quickly. Bridget thought she would be better already asleep but there was a knock on the door and Cora called for him to come in.

'Goodnight, Cora. Are you coming to bed?'

he said, looking in Bridget's direction, perhaps seeing her wide eyes at the surprise of her husband actually being pleasant. Bridget kissed Cora's cheek before getting off the bed and walking the three steps across the landing to their own room. She wanted to say something. Something that would ease the tension between them because her nerves twitched, but instead crawled between the sheets, folding herself into that safe position she had long since taken. Ailill was quick to climb in beside her. He lay on his side too, facing her, drawing himself into her shape and put his right arm over her waist. It was gentle. It made Bridget's heart skip a beat. She had not known him like this in bed for so long. Ailill placed his mouth to her ear and said in the smallest of whispers,

'I'm sorry Bridget. I should not have brought the crib in while Cora was here … I should not have held you so roughly.'

For some seconds, Bridget was unable to speak. She was not sure she had heard correctly.

'Do you mean it Ailill?'

'Yes.' But as he spoke, Ailill took her elbow and squeezing it hard pulled her onto her back, putting his face so close to hers that she could only see his eyes.

'Don't you ever speak to me like you did tonight … not in front of other people … not when we're alone … not ever. Do you hear me, Bridget?'

His anger threw drops of spittle towards her, but his own was so close, his grip on her so tight there was no room for her to avert her face from him. She cried out with the hurt, with the humiliation, with the terrible transformation in him so unexpected and frightening.

CHAPTER 11

Fish For Supper

Cora waited until she was sure Ailill had gone to work before leaving the bedroom. She did not want to see him, to see him with her sister.

'Did you sleep well?' Bridget asked, as Cora sat wearily from her disturbed night.

'Not really … and neither did you, I imagine.'

'Oh. I slept quite well.' Cora looked at her in amazement.

'Don't lie to me Bridget. Please don't pretend that all was well. I heard you cry out … why would you do so if he hadn't hurt you?'

Bridget carried on with Cora's breakfast, set it in front of her and sat down her hands clasped tightly, her face towards her lap.

'I pretend, not to you Cora … but to myself. Today's another day. It might be better.' She turned to face Cora before adding, 'If I pretend that what's happened has gone … if I put it out of my mind … well, then I think it helps me. I don't dwell on it. It's the dwelling on it that makes it all seem worse.'

'Surely it can't be much worse!'

'It can Cora. It has been … and I know it will be again, so I have to find ways to manage it.'

'Bridget, you can't live like this. You don't deserve it. Why don't you leave now … this minute? Go back home.'

'Because he's my husband. I married him with wide open eyes and I took a vow to love, honour and obey him.'

'This isn't the man you married! This isn't the Ailill we welcomed into our family … why should you be obliged to honour your vows?'

'He *is* the man I married Cora. I just didn't know all of him then.'

Bridget rose to wander about the kitchen, easing her back with small movements of it side to side and bending slightly to pet Murphy who wagged his tail against her legs. Cora sat still, mortified to think she could not persuade her sister of her need to leave this vile man.

'I wrote to Mam in the night,' said Cora. 'I've asked her to come and be with us.'

'Do you think that's wise?'

'I believe we'll be safer if there are three of us. Mam won't take any nonsense … she,' but Bridget did not allow her to finish.

'I don't know Cora. For one thing it might

make it worse for me ... you know ... after you've gone ... if Mam riles him. And then ... well I've been keeping all this from Mam and Pa. If Mam comes to stay, she'll know ... she'll tell Pa, and he'll most likely come for Ailill.'

Cora was silent for a moment not quite knowing how to say her next words.

'Bridget. Since I've been here, there have been times when Ailill has been almost pleasant, but now I see he can't control himself. I don't feel safe with just the two of us. I want Mam to come for me as well as you ... so I'm going into Ballywalter to post it.'

Cora left Bridget no room to object and in truth she understood how Cora must be feeling and how much their Mam was needed.

'Well. Since you're going, will you call on the old midwife to let her know it won't be long before she's needed?

'Of course. You'll be alright here?'

'I'll perhaps take a walk. See if Paddy's boat is in this afternoon. Here. Take this,' she said, finding some money from her tin in the cupboard. 'See if there's anything you'd like from the butcher for dinner tonight.'

The day was fair for the time of year so after banking up the fire, collecting her coat and making sure all was right in the house, Bridget walked the short distance to the harbour. She was hoping to see Paddy. He had become a friend for her, always making time for conversation, always able to bring a smile to her face. They often sat on the wall side by side, the fishy aroma no longer abhorrent to her. Paddy was down on the boat as she approached and seeing her, waved to attract her attention.

'Hello Paddy.'

'Hello there Bridget. It's a fine day for a walk, but you look as though you shouldn't go far my girl.'

He had taken to calling her 'my girl' in recent months and Bridget liked it. She thought it had an air of fondness about it.

'Just here and back,' she said.

'Lay this blanket on the wall and sit yourself down. I'll just finish these last three boxes and join you.'

She lowered herself gently, wondering how she might get up again but the thought vanished quickly enough. There were half a dozen little fishing vessels moored up, all bobbing up and down as the breeze rippled the sea towards land. Bridget thought she had not seen so many fishermen at work together for a long time and let her eyes wander over their burly shapes clad in waterproof coats, with hats and scarves and long waders right to their thighs.

Fish lay everywhere along the harbour walls, all with unusual colours, some tiny, others huge. As Paddy climbed up to sit with her, another head popped up from their small cabin and she was surprised to see Paddy Youngen. He would normally be at their fishmongers in town by this time of the day but his father had needed him so the young lad who worked for them had been left to do all the selling. He sat the other side of Bridget, and said,

'There's a pretty sight for sore old eyes.'

'Thank you,' she said. 'But should you be telling that to a married lady?'

'Perhaps not,' he said, 'but it's true, so what's the harm?'

Exhilarated from her walk, not to mention Paddy youngen's words, Bridget laid the fish they had given her by the sink and saw to the fire. Less than an hour later, Cora burst through the door windswept and ruddy cheeked laying her purchases on the table.

'How did you get on?' Bridget asked.

'Look what I bought for dinner,' she said unwrapping the paper. 'There's a really nice fishmonger in town and I just fancied some for dinner.'

Bridget burst out laughing and pointed to the sink.

'Paddy Olden gave them for our supper!'

CHAPTER 12

Deceived

Bridget's and Cora's mother, Mary, arrived a few days later stopping outside the house in a cart laden with her case and gifts for her daughters. It was very cold, the rain coming in with blasts of frigid air from the Irish Sea, but even so they ran out to greet her before she could even get to the ground. Cora hugged her mother, crying on her shoulder, her relief evident. Bridget waited her turn with Murphy at her side. The driver took everything from the cart and placed it at the front door before leaving. Bridget went to make tea while Mary and Cora lugged it all inside.

'You haven't told her, have you?' Mary asked Cora in a whisper.

'No, but she might have guessed, seeing four wheels under that paper! I'll take your case upstairs so we have a little more space. I try to make sure all is tidy before Ailill gets home.'

'And what mood is he in, these days?'

'I never know. He's two different people … we don't know which one he'll be at any time. It's wearing me out never mind poor Bridget. I've tried to persuade her to go home with you … you know, for her safety but she won't have it.'

Bridget came through with the tea and some special biscuits she had Cora buy for her mother. They sat round the fire, Bridget's eyes wandering often to the thing sitting in the centre of the room, hoping it was what she thought it might be. She saw Cora look at their mother, a smile playing on her lips.

'Go on child! Take the paper off … see what your Pa and me bought for you.'

Bridget tore it off to reveal a wonderful pram which she looked at for ages. It was a substantial size with large wheels, a deep body, hood, and apron, and it was her favourite colour, a dark blue with silver trim.

'I don't know what to say. It's beautiful!'

'It's not new, but it's in good condition and we've given it a good scrub, so it's ready to use. Look inside.'

Beneath the apron she found a mattress, pillow, blankets, and an exquisite quilt.

'Oh Mam,' she said, tears welling,' it's more than I could ever have hoped for. Did you make the quilt? It's so beautiful! Cora … come and see. Ailill said I couldn't have a pram … said not having one would keep me in the house ... so he'd know where I was.'

She looked at her mother as she said it knowing there was pleading in her face.

'Now I can take the bairn out for walks. I can even go into Ballywalter.'

She had quite forgotten in her excitement that she should not speak of such things to her mother, but then thought she would know soon enough.

Mary settled herself in with Cora's help.

'The house is lovely,' Mary said. 'A lot of room and they've furnished it nicely. I like the soft covers. We did well, didn't we?'

'Aillil made the furniture,' Cora said.

'He's good for something then,' her mother replied. They both laughed bringing light relief to the bedroom.

Bridget was well on with dinner so mother and daughters chatted comfortably round the kitchen table catching up on news, laughing at the stories Mary told of their father.

'He misses you, Bridget. So do all the people who go to his singing. Won't you think about going back to it after the bairn's born?'

'No. I don't think so. I can't seem to find the singing in my heart anymore. Besides, there'll be little time with a bairn to look after ... you both know that.'

Only a few days later, Ailill paced the floor listening to the sounds in their bedroom and those of Cora doing things in the kitchen. Mary and the old midwife were with Bridget. He could not stay still. This was the moment he had waited for all these months, and it seemed to him that his dreams would be fulfilled; that his father would be happy; that he and his family would be able to visit without the anxiety he had experienced since he and Bridget married.

He did not want to hear his wife yelling in pain, wanted it to be over, covered his ears against it. Cora brought him a cup of tea and a sandwich, saying he would need to keep up his strength now. He smiled at her for her thoughtfulness.

Had the day been kind, he would have gone outside to the shed perhaps but rain fell in large drops soaking everything and making rivulets in the road. He studied the pram, admitting to himself now that it was a fine thing for his James. He would be proud to walk out with Bridget, their bairn snuggled down under the quilt's warmth.

It was not long before he heard someone on the stairs. It was Mary, her face beaming from ear to ear.

'You're a father Ailill!'

'Where is he? Can I go and see him?'

Aillil looked up the stairs. He heard the baby cry and took a step towards the bedroom.

'You've a little girl and she's just beautiful.'

'What did you say?'

'You have a little girl.'

'No! It can't be. Have you checked?'

'Don't be ridiculous,' Mary said. 'Go up and see Bridget and the bairn.'

Cora was hovering at the kitchen door watching the scene. Coming forward, she said to Ailill,

'Bridget needs you, and there'll be other bairns. You just need to wait for your James.'

Ailill's face was thunderous as he turned and left, slamming the door after him.

'Ailill! Ailill! Where are you going? He's mad,' said Mary, as she rushed out of the door, followed him across the garden, called all the while but he did not look back. In the kitchen again, she looked at Cora, her face a picture of puzzlement.

'I told you. I really fear for my sister now. She should leave him … he's not in his right mind … he could do anything. '

'He'll calm down surely. When he sees her and realises his responsibilities. He'll come to see it's not the end of the world.'

'I wish I had your faith,' Cora said, as she turned to go upstairs.

Ailill shut himself inside his shed, put his arms on the bench and wept into his hands, his shoulders shaking with the strength of his sobs. The world had played a cruel trick on him. He would not countenance going up to see this bairn. He would not even go to see his wife, for had she not delivered him the one thing he absolutely did not want. How would he tell his father? How would he come to terms with being so blatantly set against?

Everyone would laugh at him now, having said so often it would be a boy. He did not believe he could carry on. When he lifted his head, he saw the toys he had made for his James. He reached out, picked them up in turn; the little train with its carriages; the horse-shaped rattle he had worked so long and hard to get right; the bricks in their bright colours for James to build with. He fondled them, held them to his chest, loved them for what they represented, the continuance of the Blair line.

He was not seen for two days. Mary and Cora assumed he was going to work and then spending the nights in the shed but they cared not, for while he was not there, they had some peace. It was not so for Bridget. She cried most of the time. She was weary from the birth, afraid for their future, slept only fitfully listening out for him to come home. Bridget wept for the loss of what might have been. Being pregnant had given her hope. Now she was so alone it was as though she'd been transported back to the night of the crib.

She named the bairn Siobhan and thought if only Ailill would take one look at her, he would see how she took after him. She already had a full head of dark curly hair just like his. Her mother and sister did everything they could to help her through her sadness, making sure she ate well and fed Siobhan as often as needed. They carried Siobhan downstairs to give Bridget space to rest and while they had her, they swooned over her and cuddled her so she would know she was safe.

CHAPTER 13

A Pile of Sticks

Bridget was sleepy when she heard the front door slam and the creak of the stairs and knew he had returned. He appeared at he door with the other crib which he placed on the floor. Bridget could see he had made an effort to finish it in white paint, all the rough edges now smooth.

'Pick the bairn up,' he said.

'She has a name Ailill. She's Siobhan. Please let us sleep a while.'

'Pick – the – bairn – up!'

'Ailill. You're being unreasonable. When she wakes, I'll pick her up and feed her, then you can take the crib away. I know that's what you've come for.'

He said no more but as he left, he allowed the door to slam hard causing Bridget to jump and Siobhan to wake with a startled cry. Bridget collected her daughter in her arms, soothed her and then lay her in the middle of the bed. She took the furnishings from the forbidden crib, placing them delicately in the one she was allowed to use.

The stopper in her bottled emotions burst, the pain, the hate, fear, disappointment and weariness, spewed from her hearted through her veins into every tiny crevice of her body. She felt it in her breasts, souring her milk and she wept, her anger knowing no bounds in the instant she stood and kicked Ailill's crib with all the force she could muster. Once she had begun, there was no stopping. She watched as the pieces flew in all directions until only a pile of sticks remained of his beautiful handiwork.

The sound brought Ailill rushing upstairs. He stood in the doorway stunned into silence at what she had done. Before she had time to react, he grabbed her hair with one hand, her arm with the other, pulled her through the door and down the stairs. She felt each part of her body as every tread dug into her. She could hear her own cries, her own tortured screams, echoing rom the ceiling. Her chest hurt with the wind taken from it.

'For the love of God Ailill! Stop,' shouted Mary, and she reached out to take his arm.

'Don't you interfere, old woman.' He brushed her away, so that she stumbled backwards and

Cora ran upstairs to Siobhan, bringing her down to safety.

Before Bridget realised it, Ailill had dumped her out on the hard gravel road, gone back to the house and slammed the front door behind him. With pale faces, Mary and Cora watched him run upstairs then slowly descend, a bundle of wood in his arms, tears dripping from his nose. When he left the house they ran out to find Bridget. She sat in the middle of the unmade road, a lump of hair in her hand, her face completely white and Murphy licked her, whined, and protected her. Cora was afraid that he would not let them near but Murphy knew they would not hurt his mistress.

In the warmth of the house Bridget allowed her mother to check for any broken bones while Cora fetched warm water and a cloth to soothe her grazes and broken skin. Bridget was ashen faced but there were no tears. With one hand she stroked Murphy as he sat beside her. With the other she felt the tender place on her head where the hair was missing.

'Where's Siobhan?' she asked.

'She's in the crib upstairs. She's fine ... too young to know of any upset,' said Cora.

'I must get her ... I really don't want her to be on her own,' Bridget said, rising from the chair.

'You stay where you are young lady,' said Mary, 'Cora, go and get her.'

'She's so beautiful Bridget. You have a gorgeous

little daughter,' Cora said as she put the bairn in her sister's arms.

'You know what's really sad?' Bridget said, 'she's so like her father already,' and the thought caused a tear to rise. 'She has such bright blue eyes, but at least they are not different colours!'

'And let's hope it stays that way!' Her mother replied.

CHAPTER 14

Slow Motion Potatoes

Bridget watched drizzling rain run down the windowpane and looked across the grass to the little road that ran to the harbour. Mary and Cora had left a week ago after being sure that Ailill had returned and that his anger had dissipated. Mary had taken him aside, the sisters not really knowing what was said between them but believed he was getting some sort of ultimatum regarding his behaviour. At any rate, he had been much better, Bridget finding it in her heart to forgive his cruelty. It was considerably more difficult for her to forgive him for his attitude towards his daughter. He had not once referred to her by name, calling her instead the bairn, and he utterly refused to look at her, never mind hold her but Bridget had decided to stay with him in hopes that they could make their life together work.

With all the chores completed, Bridget wanted to get out of the house, where she had been for so long. She wanted to feel the wind in her hair, the rain on her face, and she wanted more than anything to introduce her baby to Paddy. She tucked Siobhan well down in the pram, wrapped her tightly in blankets, laid the quilt over her and fastened the apron. With the hood up, there was no sign of a baby in there. This would be their first journey out together, Bridget so proud as she negotiated the step onto the path and wheeled her baby down the road.

By the time they reached the harbour, there was little rain and no Paddy. In fact, there were no boats at all for her to gaze at. She walked round the harbour wall without hurrying the crunch of her boots on the gravel a reminder of how long she had been shut away. She lifted her face to the wind, tasted the salt on her tongue and let them soak into her heart, her soul. All the time rocking her baby in time with the lapping of waves.

She sat on the wall and waited for what seemed hours, checking all the time on Siobhan who stayed soundly asleep. Grey fluffy clouds swept past. She searched for dark vessels bobbing up and down on the waves but there was nothing between her and the horizon so she had to accept that today would not be the day.

Instead of going straight home, Bridget

walked a while up the road towards Ballywalter seeing no sign of human life but plenty of grazing animals. It made her think of all the wonderful times ahead, showing them to Siobhan, sharing the pleasure of the fields and the sea. She loved the feel of this amazing pram she had been given, the way it bounced on its springs, its smooth travel on the large wheels and felt herself smiling at her fortune. It was not until they reached the first house, their neighbours, although not close at all, that she turned round to head home. On passing the harbour road she heard her name called.

'Bridget wait!' It was Paddy Youngen, running up the road, all arms and legs. The wind blew his cap so he had to turn to retrieve it, his hair blowing in the breeze. It made Bridget laugh to see him. She waved as he drew close, reaching her breathless.

'Pa saw you crossing. How are you?'

'I'm well, thank you.'

'Can I have a peek at the little one?'

'Of course. We came down to find you. I wanted to introduce you to her, but there was no-one there,' she said, as she pulled back the apron and blankets to expose Siobhan's tiny head.

'This is Siobhan.'

Paddy went to touch the child but thought better of it. 'I've come off the boat,' he said, smelling his hands. 'Don't want to sully her. There'll be time enough for me to hold her if that's alright with you.'

'I look forward to you meeting her properly … your pa too.'

'Well … I suppose I'd better get back to help him. See you soon Bridget.'

'You're a good man Paddy,' she said, and watched him run back.

The excursion left Bridget feeling relaxed and newly energised so that while dinner was cooking she fed Siobhan and laid her in the crib upstairs before tackling the dirt now splashed along the sides of the pram, its wheels no longer white. When she was satisfied, she sat in the chair by the fire to wait for Ailill. It occurred to her that she might take up some sewing again now that life was returning to some normality but for now, the warmth of the fire after the exhilarating walk lulled her into a comforting sleep. Paddy's gangly running came to mind. She thought he must be older than herself but it was difficult to tell, his sea swarthy face may hide a younger man.

Bridget woke as Ailill's footsteps sounded on the gravel road. She had no idea how long she had slept, but it must have been a deep sleep for her not to have realised how much time had passed. Getting up quickly, she went to the kitchen, thankful to find the dinner still cooking in its juice. She had encountered Ailill's temper before when the meal was overcooked or dried up and always did her utmost to ensure that whatever time he arrived, their meal was acceptable to him.

'Dinner smells good,' he said, making her smile, for it was not often that he commented on such things.

'It won't be long. I'm just going to check on Siobhan. She's been sleeping a while now.'

'Be quick then. I'm dyin of hunger tonight.'

He was sitting at the table, knife and fork in his hands ready to be waited on when she returned. She suddenly felt pressured. In her rush to dish up, she dropped the potato pan spilling hot water down her legs and over the floor. She watched potatoes roll across the kitchen in slow motion, mortified after such a wonderful day that she had given Ailill a reason to admonish her.

'Don't just stand there you stupid woman! Get the rest on a plate and I'll eat while you clean up.'

'You might help me, Ailill. I've scalded my legs.'

'I'll show you where the potatoes rolled,' he said, smirking.

With the kitchen cleaned, Bridget washed her legs with cold water, seeing that already a large blister of skin was forming on her right shin and no longer feeling hungry herself, offered what was left to her husband. She watched him stuff it into his mouth as though he had not eaten for days, gravy dripping down his chin, slurping noises accompanying each mouthful, enough to put anyone off their food. She was disgusted by this display of manners he was putting on just for her. She wondered what to do to soften him, knowing that if he remained in this mood her evening and night would be terrible.

'We went out for our first walk today, as far as the house towards Ballywalter. Siobhan looks so comfortable in her pram.'

'Huh. So would I be if I had all that molly coddlin. That's a big pram. How long's it goin to be there? It takes up all the space.'

'Until she no longer needs it, I suppose. You should try to be grateful for the gift. Without it I wouldn't be able to go anywhere … I'd be stuck inside.'

'Don't go tellin me what I'm to be grateful for,' he said, pointing his knife towards her. 'Anyways it suits me to have you at home … don't want you gettin ideas.'

Bridget could not listen to it anymore. She would never be able to outwit him, or say the right things because he always turned it around towards himself, as though he was the centre of the world. She left the table, cleared away the debris and went up to feed Siobhan. This was a peaceful time. Bridget always took longer than was necessary so she could cuddle her daughter, talk to her, and watch all her little movements.

Ailill was snoozing in the chair by the fire

when she came down. As Bridget laid Siobhan in the pram, she began making small crying noises, and it was not often she cried. Bridget thought she must have wind pain but before she was able to pick her up, Siobhan cried out in long baby sobs. Ailill lifted his head a fraction and said,

'Can't you shut that noise up?'

'It's probably a bit of cholic. She'll be better in a while,' though even propped up on Bridget's shoulder, the crying continued, until eventually several loud belches sounded.

'Thank God for that,' Ailill moaned. 'Take the bairn away. A man can't get any rest with that goin on.'

Bridget rocked the pram bringing peace to the room again, collected some long-forgotten sewing and made herself as comfortable as her tense body would allow. She did not want the night to come. She did not want to have to go to bed. She knew, even as the peace settled, that the night would bring only pain.

CHAPTER 15

The Library

Ailill did honour his responsibilities towards Bridget and the bairn, at least his financial responsibilities. He gave her more housekeeping than before to provide for them, and she, having always been thrifty, was managing to save a little each week, hidden in a tin at the back of the kitchen cupboard. As she sewed, her mind turned to all the pain she had endured over the last two years, to the way she had changed since her marriage, or at least since Ailill began this ridiculous obsession about having a son.

She was never an extravert like her sister but always had a measure of confidence, much of which came from her singing ability. Although timid as a child and still shy, she had always been able to speak for herself, offer opinions and discuss them in company she felt familiar with. *Where has that girl gone? Who have I become?*

There were times when she believed Ailill really did have a streak of madness in him, that there were two different people dwelling in his brain, for when he was not angry, he was loving and caring and yet he would have nothing to do with his own daughter. Bridget wondered how she would protect Siobhan, because deep inside she knew that one day his temper would get the better of him.

It occurred to her that other women might suffer the same beatings and if so where were they, how did they manage. She wanted to talk to them, to share her pain, to hear about theirs. She thought of Orla. Orla was her mother-in-law though. It would be impossible to talk to her even if she could, for they hardly ever saw Ailill's parents now. *Why do men do these things? Ailill must know I would do anything he asked, so why does he have to be so cruel? Is there something I've done to turn him into this person? Will he break me completely?*

Bridget was constantly conflicted between having to hide her situation and needing an outlet, a sharing of the condition. Her head was too often full of hurt and pain with nowhere to store it, to leave it behind, to find space for pleasure. She knew people had seen her bruises and cuts, had seen her limping occasionally.

Women would generally look with measures of sympathy. Men sometimes looked at her as if she deserved it.

She had heard talk during her visits to town. Men spoke of the partition and Catholics as being the enemy, for Ballywalter and its towns to the north and west were Protestant, as was her family. She saw anger in men's eyes when they spoke of it. She heard of skirmishes between the two vastly different religious groups but she had no understanding of it beyond knowing not to go too far south. Were men just angry whatever the cause.

She had heard of the Suffrage movement too and the movement's fight against the inequality between men and women, its achievement in gaining the vote for women, Bridget had no political persuasion. She cared neither for the vote, nor who governed her, as long as the people of Ireland could be spared conflict. And as for religion, she was even less caring. We all worship the same God so why can we not live peaceably together? Her thoughts had tired her. It was not often she dwelled on such matters but tonight her mind had wandered to all manner of things. Deciding to walk to Ballywalter the next day, Bridget packed away her things, made a nightcap for them both and prepared Siobhan for bed. Her day was marred, but the thought of it brought a picture of Paddy to the forefront, turning his hat round in his hands as he spoke to her, leaning over the apron to see the new-born, but most vivid, was the smile on his face when she had told him he was a good man. The heat rose in her cheeks as she poured the tea.

Spring became early summer, each day warmer than the last. Bridget found it hard to believe that her daughter was already heading for her fourth birthday this coming winter as she watched her play in the garden. Bridget was hanging washing out, being frequently distracted by Siobhan, the sound of the sea lapping against the rocks and her thoughts.

Walking to Ballywalter regularly had slimmed her figure, the undesirable effects of pregnancy gone and she had spent many hours making herself new dresses, of which she now had several to choose from. She felt good in them, liked wearing them as they strolled along the beach. She believed they suited her and whether they did or not, they made her feel as though she had taken some care in her appearance.

Ailill had said more than once that it was unnecessary to look good when there was nobody to notice. But there was. Most weekdays Paddy would be waiting for them at the corner where their house met the little track to the beach. They would go miles together, Siobhan on Paddy's shoulders, or between them holding hands for a swing. Stones, shells and other bits would end up in the bag Bridget took with her.

Moments of silence were rare. They talked about so many things they shared an interest in, or maybe even gossip from the town but mostly they laughed, a sweet pleasure Bridget only knew when they were together.

If Paddy was not waiting for them Bridget felt cheated of some wonderful sense of fulfilment, as though the beach was lacking a critical constituent. In summer, Bridget's and Siobhan's skin would tan so that they looked almost like a family. In winter, Paddy would sometimes take Bridget's arm to steady her, steer her away from a fast-rising tide. She thought of him now, hurried with the washing and made them both ready.

Bridget's time was as divided as she knew Ailill's mind to be. During the days she found peace and tranquillity in her routine. She had even begun to sing again yet could not place when it started; perhaps it was because she sang 'Golden Slumbers' to Siobhan each night; perhaps it was the sheer delight of Ailill being out of the house all day. At night, her world was transported to somewhere, a place far away where hell fires burned, where pain reduced her to a weeping coward, and the breath was forced from her lungs. Most nights, before sleeping, she prayed not to wake up. In the mornings she was thankful she had for she could not bear the thought of leaving her daughter knowing she would be at the mercy of her father.

That winter, when it finally arrived, was

particularly cold with heavy snow even on the coast. Ice refused to thaw in the weak winter sun. Bridget kept the fire banked up, the kettle filled on the stove and she found some old rugs for the floor so she and Siobhan could sit and play. While Siobhan slept, not so often now during the day, Bridget sewed or knitted but all the time her hands were busy, her mind was free to roam. She found it difficult to think of pleasant memories and even when she could, her thoughts always returned to those places of unhappiness.

With the worst of the weather behind them Bridget began her walks to Ballywalter once more, finding a new lending library had opened. She had never been one for reading, but the books on the shelves fascinated her. Some were so large she wondered how anyone could hold them. They had beautiful leather spines with titles engraved on them. Others were tiny by comparison. She found the print difficult to read in those. She chose two novels with the help of the librarian, although unsure if she would actually reach the ends of either.

Snuggled beside the fire the following afternoon, her legs curled up in the comfy chair, Bridget began reading. This book would be the first of many, for she discovered that in reading she could not only stop thinking, but she could be taken to other worlds, where wonderful things happened, or where she could identify with the feelings of characters. After their meal was done, she would escape back into the words, the pages, and not even notice Ailill coming and going. Reading led her from the frosty winter weather to the beauty of spring.

CHAPTER 16

Paddy Youngen

'**Hello** Paddy,' Bridget called as she approached the corner. 'How are you today?'

'Fine lass. And how's the little beauty?' he said, opening his arms to gather Siobhan, who always ran to meet him.

'A lovely balmy day. Exactly right for a stroll. I've got buckets and spades for Siobhan to play with. She wants you to build a castle with her.'

'Yes, I do,' said Siobhan. 'Will you help me, Paddy Youngen?'

At six, the child was quite at ease with Paddy, always adding the 'youngen' as though it was his surname. She had learned all her numbers and letters and Bridget was teaching her to read so Siobhan always had books from the library as well. They found a spot along the beach, Paddy laying down his fishy smelling blanket, and they sat to enjoy the heat. While Siobhan filled her buckets with gravely sand, Paddy fetched sea water to make a moat. Bridget watched him bending low to collect it, his feet and shins bare, the sea reaching his mid-calf as the waves rolled gently in. Something in her stirred.

She knew she was falling in love but could not be sure it was because he represented an escape, or if it was the man himself. Paddy ran across the stones, flopped onto the blanket and splashed her with his wet hands. For a few seconds there was laughter, until Paddy stopped and looked at her for what felt like a long time.

'Bridget,' he said, his face serious, 'why do you stay with him?'

'Oh Paddy. He's my husband. How would I manage on my own with Siobhan? Where would I go? He keeps a roof over our heads and food in our stomachs. All I know is this life. Maybe what's out there would be even worse.'

Paddy looked out towards the horizon unsure if he should say what was on his mind. Once said, once she knew, it could never be taken back and it might cause her even more pain.

'We know he hurts you … we've heard you cry out when we walk past at night. He's not right in his head, Bridget … there are rumours in town …

'What rumours?' she asked quietly, wondering as she asked if she really wanted to know.

'He goes to the pub after work … people say he talks about you … says unkind things.'

'Well Paddy. He's been coming home from the pub later and later recently … always smelling of the drink.' She paused. 'What sort of things do they say?'

Paddy gazed at her. She had raised her legs, clasped her hands round her calves and rested her head on her knees. It was as though she was hiding, as though by curling up she would not hear what he might say. Her blonde hair fell from her shoulders, leaving soft bare skin. He wanted to kiss her there. His whole body ached to kiss her there, to hold her and protect her, to whisk her away from this foul man.

'Tell me,' she said softly. 'It's better I know.'

'He says you're barren …'

'And that little girl's in our imagination, is she?' She pointed to Siobhan, her softness fleetingly gone, her anger uppermost.

'He says she's not his …,' and he waited as she turned to him.

'What do you believe Paddy?'

'I know she's his … I don't trust anything he says, Bridget, and you've only to look at her to see the likeness.'

'I don't care for what others think … only you Paddy. As long as you know the truth.'

They both lay back shielding their eyes from the sun, listening to Siobhan running backwards and forwards with her buckets, the sea gently hissing on the stones, and each other's breathing.

'I love you Bridget … there. I've said it. I love you.'

'Paddy,' she said sitting up, tears falling slowly across her cheeks, 'you can never have me … I'm married. And you wouldn't want me either … I'm damaged from Ailill's constant beatings … there'll never be any more bairns. There must be so many girls who would love you if you gave them the chance.'

'Nobody out there I would give a chance to,' he muttered. 'I'm not asking you to love me … only to be by my side.'

'But I do love you, Paddy! A vow is a vow though. Maybe we should stop walking together.'

'No! No, no Bridget. You'll not rid yourself of me so easily! We can stay as we are … we don't have to speak of it … knowing it is enough for me.'

'Is it Paddy?'

'Bridget … I'll wait for you until the Earth crumbles.'

CHAPTER 17

The Man in the Moon

'I can't cope with this anymore,' Bridget shouted at Ailill. 'If you keep finding new ways to hurt me, I swear I'll leave you.'

'You won't,' he shouted back, 'you're mine … I own you now … and you should watch out because if you do, I'll be huntin you down.'

An argument was rare but on this occasion Bridget was unable to stay calm. He had pulled more hair from her head, threatened her with a knife, and left finger marks on her throat. He was very drunk. He stayed longer and longer at the pub, arriving home so inebriated, sometimes he simply collapsed before the front door was shut. She did not mind those times. He left her alone then. It was when he returned still able to stand, to take his anger out on her and either take her forcefully or beat her, that she lived in fear of.

He repeated those words, *I own you*, but now they were slurred, though she understood the threat. She had to think of Siobhan as well as herself. Ailill had never hurt his daughter. He had never even touched her or picked her up and as Bridget thought about it, she believed he had never spoken to Siobhan. About her, yes, but not to her. Bridget knew this new threat put them both in danger. He came towards her again, hand poised but Murphy growled at him and moved to sit in front of Bridget. His hand found Murphy instead, hitting him so hard, he yelped loudly, sinking to the floor.

This was too much for Bridget. She turned to run upstairs, taking Murphy with her. Ailill put his foot out to trip her, causing her to fall against the corner of the wall. By the time she reached Siobhan's room, pulled Murphy inside behind her and closed the door, Ailill was at the top, banging on the door. When he had given up, Bridget said,

'I'll see if Paddy will fix a bolt on your door. We may yet need to have your bedroom as a safe place to be.' Siobhan hugged her mother, seeing another bare circle of scalp and cried into her shoulder.

'It'll be alright,' Bridget said, willing it to be.

Siobhan was ten when she began to wake in the night, sometimes crying, at others screaming and as time passed, her nightmares became more terrifying, more frequent, and more memorable.

'What do you see that frightens you so much?' Bridget asked her one night.

'All sorts, Mam ... monsters ... they come through my window.'

'Tell me about them.'

'Dark shapes mostly ... some covered in hair ... some have long fingers like ... I don't know really. They come for me ... get close to my face ... and then they ... well they just stop there staring.'

'Poor baby. You must be so frightened.'

'That's not all though. It's their eyes, Mam. They're so large ... much too big for their faces ... and they stick out ... they don't move like ours do.'

'Come here,' said Bridget. She held her daughter tightly trying not to cry. She did not know what to do for her, what to say, how to help her.

The day had been beautiful with hot constant sun, no wind, the sky a rich blue from horizon to horizon. The night was balmy, the sort of night when covers were thrown back, when the body searched for cool places to rest. Bridget must have eventually fallen into a deep slumber, for it was Ailill who heard the shouts first, but as always did nothing about it. When Bridget failed to react, he pushed her out of bed, her body hitting the floor with a bump and waking her with a start.

'Go see to the bairn,' he said, his head hanging

over the edge, his face far too close to hers.

'My James wouldn't have made a noise like that.'

Bridget wanted for all the world to say something to hurt him but she'd lost the will to fight him now.

Siobhan was yelling for them to go away when Bridget reached her, but was still asleep. She woke her gently while wiping away the tears. When Siobhan had calmed, Bridget went to make her a milky drink, returning to find her daughter standing at the window, her body sideways on as though she could only allow herself to peek through, the fear of her monsters still inside. Bridget put an arm across Siobhan's shoulder gently bringing her body round to face the window full on. The night was magically clear, a full moon casting shadows across the fields and lighting up the roadway so that even the stones were visible.

'Look at the moon Siobhan. It's beautiful.'

'I can see a face, Mam.'

'It's the man in the moon,' Bridget said laughing.

'What's he doing there?'

'Oh, well now. Perhaps he keeps watch over us when the sun goes down and darkness comes.'

'Is it Paddy Youngen?'

'No dear girl. Paddy's down here with us, isn't he? Maybe the man in the moon's waiting for someone who needs rescuing.'

'Will he rescue us then?'

'Perhaps … one day. Who knows? Now, drink your milk before it gets cold and try to sleep some more. Remember, the man in the moon's watching over us,' said Bridget, tucking her daughter up and straightening the covers at the end of the bed. 'Sleep tight,' she said, blowing a kiss.

CHAPTER 18

A Blossoming Talent

Siobhan had shown promise with drawing since she was young, Bridget encouraging her to observe things and represent what she could see but Bridget had only bought the cheapest paper and pencils. On their next visit to town, Siobhan was allowed to choose decent quality paper and drawing equipment, Bridget using some of her savings to cover the extra cost. They bought two pads of paper, a range of pencils that made different sorts of marks, some charcoal, and a few colouring pencils. Bridget was hoping Siobhan might be persuaded to catch her monsters on the paper, maybe confront them so they might leave her alone. She was disappointed to see no sign of them. What she did see, amazed her.

Siobhan began sketching her surroundings,

fishing boats in the harbour, men in their typical workwear, the day's catch spread out on the harbour wall. She walked in the fields, capturing birds and other creatures she found there, up the road towards Ballywalter to the quaint cottages with their beautifully coloured gardens. Sometimes she would come home with a rough outline of a scene and complete it at the kitchen table. On other days, she would sketch the lines and shapes of tiny elements of plants or walls.

Bridget, though not in the least artistic herself, could see that her daughter was quite gifted and showed Paddy some of her finished work.

'These are wonderful,' he said, 'very impressive Bridget. Has she shown them to anyone else?'

'I don't think so. Who does she know to show them to?'

Paddy sat on the stones silently studying the pictures then said,

'Look at these fishermen, they're all here. There's my Pa and Peter,' he said pointing them out. 'And these fish, they're almost real! Where's Siobhan now? Does she know you're showing them to me?'

'She's away up the beach … look. And yes, she does know. That's why she's wandered off. She's embarrassed. She thinks they're no good and you'll laugh at them.'

Paddy jumped up, raced across the stones,

calling Siobhan's name, all the while slipping and tripping in his haste to reach her. Bridget watched. She saw him put his arm across Siobhan's shoulders and turn to face her. Her daughter's mouth had become an enormous smile by the time they arrived back.

'Mam! Paddy Youngen likes them.'

'I know dear. I told you he would.'

'I like them so much I have an idea.'

Paddy hoped his father and the other fishermen were still on their boats, or at least round the harbour somewhere and was relieved to see he had not missed them.

'Pa! Peter! Come and see these.'

'What've you got lad?' Paddy Olden, asked.

Paddy spread some of the pictures out on the wall but said nothing, anxious for their thoughts. They took a while looking backwards and forwards and then smile at each other.

'Where did you get them?' asked Peter.

'They're Siobhan's work. You know, Bridget's daughter.'

'Well, I must say they're darn good,' his father said. 'This's me, isn't it?'

'Yes. And that's you Peter,' Paddy said, pointing to another picture.

'I know that! Just didn't want to say in case it wasn't.'

'What do you think?' asked Paddy.

'I don't know about you Peter, but I'm taken with them. Like to have this one up in the boat.'

'Me too young Paddy. What does she want for them?' Peter asked.

'You'd buy them?'

'Would I,' said Peter, and Paddy's father agreed, so Paddy showed them those of the landed fish.

'Oh my,' said his father. 'These are amazing. You could put them on the wall at the fishmongers.'

'I was thinking that myself. Shall I find out if she'll sell?'

Being still early enough, Paddy Youngen knocked on Bridget's door and went inside.

'Pa, Peter and me ... we'd like to buy some of these pictures.'

'You would? I'll get her ... see what she thinks.'

Siobhan sat at the table beaming with pride while listening to Paddy tell of the reactions to her sketches.

'I want to put some of the fish in the shop and Pa and Peter wants those of themselves.' For a minute, there was silence, until Bridget said,

'What do you think Siobhan?'

'I don't know. I'd never thought they were good enough for others to see ... and I don't think they're worth paying for.'

'But they are,' said Paddy. 'That's the point. If people like them, they'll pay for them.'

'But I'm not an artist. I sketch because I love it ... it takes me somewhere ... here in my head ... somewhere I feel happy,' she said. 'I won't sell them Paddy Youngen. It would embarrass me, but I will give them, and maybe if others see them, they'll want me to do some for them. Then I'll sell them.'

'She's got an old head on young shoulders, Bridget.'

At the door, Paddy mouthed, 'I love you Bridget,' and forgetting herself, flushed as she was with Siobhan's good fortune, mouthed it back to him. Siobhan was looking through the pictures that were left as Bridget enfolded her, kissed her cheek and told her how proud she was.

'I know I can do better Mam. I think I'm learning all the time.'

'There's no rush. Experiment a bit ... see what the pencils and colours can do. Now, take them upstairs before your father gets home.'

CHAPTER 19

The Find

A week later, Paddy knocked on their door again with a box under his arm, beautifully wrapped with ribbons and bows.

'Come on in,' said Bridget.

'I've got something for Siobhan. Is she here?'

'Siobhan,' Bridget called. 'Paddy's here to see you.'

Siobhan came downstairs at such a pace the noise of her shoes on the wooden treads echoed.

'Hello,' she said, quite breathless.

'Pa and me ... and Peter have bought you a little gift in exchange for the sketches,' he said, handing her the box.

'I'm certain you didn't tie those bows and ribbons yourself,' Bridget said, smiling at Paddy.

'Thank you,' said Siobhan, 'But I didn't expect anything. It's so pretty ... it seems a shame to spoil it,' she said, laughing.

'Go on … open it,' he said.

She untied the bows and ribbons carefully, thinking she could use them in her hair. The paper came away less thoughtfully, thrown to the floor in her eagerness to know what the box held. Her face lit up, Bridget thinking it actually shone with joy. Inside there were artist materials; pads of superior quality paper, pencils, a complete set of colours, a box of paints, rubbers, brushes, and right at the bottom, Siobhan found a small tabletop easel. She sat back on the chair dumbfounded, her voice completely forsaking her. Her body trembled as she looked at Paddy, and a tear appeared in the corner of her eye.

'Are you alright?' he asked. 'Do you not like them?'

'Paddy Youngen,' she said, 'I love it all, but I don't deserve it.'

'Yes, you do, young lady,' he said, taking her small hand in his. 'You have a talent Siobhan, and talents need to be looked after. We wanted to say thank you and help you create more, isn't that right Mam?'

'You're a lucky girl,' said Bridget, 'because Paddy's right. You have a way with the sketching. Later today, we'll go and find Peter and Paddy Olden, and you can thank them too.'

At the age of fifteen, Paddy suggested Siobhan

work for him at the fishmongers in Ballywalter.

'It'll be good for you to get out of the house during the day, and you'll be able to buy more art materials with what you earn,' said Bridget. 'If you like I'll come with you tomorrow when you go to see what you've to do.'

'That would be good Mam. I'm already nervous about it … I've got no education … I'm not clever …'

'What are you saying! That I haven't taught you well!'

'No Mam,' she said as they laughed at themselves, 'but I'm afraid of getting things wrong.'

'We all get things wrong Siobhan. Nobody has all the knowledge or all the answers. We learn when we make mistakes. We learn to avoid them as well as remember what we should have done, or said, or even not said.'

Bridget told Ailill about their daughter's new work, but he showed little interest apart from saying she should watch that Paddy with her daughter. Bridget almost said she trusted Paddy far more than him, but managed to hold her tongue and went back to her book. At first, Bridget missed Siobhan dreadfully. They had never been apart so the house felt empty, forlorn, and sometimes she felt quite lost in it.

Spring was in its infancy and Bridget decided to give everywhere a good clean. In Siobhan's room, she took the linen for washing and moved the bed to clean underneath. She thought it would make a change to reposition the furniture and she would know that every corner was fresh. Completing one half quicker than expected, Bridget took the linen downstairs and prepared lunch.

Already weary from heavy lifting, she took the time to read another Chapter of her novel as she ate. Refreshed, Bridget looked at the wardrobe. It was going to be heavier to move than the bed and chests and she did not want to empty it first, so having cleaned the front and the sides, she began pulling it away from the wall. Behind lay a mass of cobwebs, and a few spiders darting here and there. She flapped at them with her cloth, before moving the wardrobe further out

Leaning against the wall, beneath the dust and grime, Bridget found an old sketch pad. She cleaned it off thinking it must have fallen there and been forgotten but when she turned the cover, the image exposed caused her to gasp. Sitting on the bed she turned the pages gingerly, revealing monster after monster on each one. Some were covered in waves of curly fur which, were it not for their faces, might have been cuddly. Others were almost skeletal, the rest somewhere between the two.

What they all had in common were enormous eyes, far too large for their heads, eyes which bulged and stared from the paper almost three-dimensional, terrifying eyes with no lids. Each of them was behind Siobhan's bedroom window, the glass swelling as if molten where their fiery claws sought to enter. They were all black apart from their eyes, which for each of them were two different colours. One brown and one blue. Bridget cried for her daughter as she reached the last picture. There it was. Siobhan's father monstrous behind the window.

Closing the pad Bridget held it tightly against her chest, willing its contents to leave the pages, to enter her and leave Siobhan forever. She could not know if, by drawing them, Siobhan had confronted her monsters, but knew she could not acknowledge having seen them. They were her daughter's secrets. She replaced the furniture where it had always been, returned the pad to its rightful place and closed the door.

Bridget knew as she descended the stairs, that those sketches would remain with her for as long as she lived.

CHAPTER 20

Provocation

Bridget and Paddy walked miles along the coast no matter what the weather, and because it was so isolated, rarely met another soul. Sometimes Paddy would brush his fingers against Bridget's hand once or twice almost holding it. She remained steadfast however in her view that while she was a married woman, she could not respond. It did not stop her mind from imagining the kiss, his soft flesh, the feel of him against her. It did not stop the longing in her chest, the fluttering of her stomach, or the trembling of her body, when she was with him. She knew she was being unfaithful to Ailill inside, which was almost as bad as laying with Paddy.

'Have you noticed a change in Siobhan of late?' Bridget asked.

'Not really. I don't see her so often now. She works hard, is always on time and she's good with the customers,' he said. 'The lad hasn't mentioned anything. Why?'

'Since she turned sixteen, she's become a little morose … you know … gone into her shell. She's mostly in her room now straight from work … and some mornings she's out before breakfast. She's not herself Paddy, and I'm rather worried about her.'

'Perhaps she's just growing up. Any signs of a young man?'

'Not that I know of.'

'My Mam always said I turned funny when I was that sort of age. Something about growth spurts and hormones.'

For reasons unknown to Bridget, though Ailill was quite drunk that evening, he did not go to the shed after dinner but sat by the fire in the chair she favoured. He was looking old these days, she thought. His head was back, and his eyes stared at the ceiling as though he were in some deep all-consuming thought process, his brow wrinkled in a frown. She would never know what it was, for he barely spoke to her now.

'Is there something amiss, Ailill?'

'Should there be?'

'Of course not, but you seem a little tense.'

Bridget went back to her book, almost finished now so she was eager to see how it ended. Being totally engrossed in the pages, she failed to hear

Ailill calling her name, until he shouted it.

'What?' she said.

'Can't you hear that? You're always with your head in a book. Go see to the bairn.'

Bridget ran upstairs hearing Siobhan cry, and found her lying on her back, sobbing.

'What's the matter my girl? You seem to be in tears a lot lately. Are you unwell?'

'No Mam. I'm fine. It's nothing. I'm so tired. I seem to be tired all the time … even in the mornings.'

'You work hard. Perhaps you should talk to Paddy about a couple of days off. We could go into Ballywalte like we used to.'

'If I see him tomorrow, I'll ask.'

'Good girl,' said Bridget, hugging her. 'Will you not do some sketching? That usually helps.'

'I'm alright Mam. I'll be fine now I've had a hug,' she said, smiling through her tears.

Downstairs, Bridget went to pick up her book from the seat but it was not there. She looked about thinking she must have left it elsewhere. As her head swept the room, she saw a thin, mean grin on Ailill's face and following his gaze to the fire, noticed the last scorched pages of her book light up.

'What've you done?' she shouted, trying to save something, but it was futile. She turned to him, rage building from the pit of her stomach. 'That's not mine. It belongs to the library you foolish man,' and she pummelled him on the chest.

It was possibly the worst thing she could have done, for in that moment Ailill saw his father bending over him, threatening him, punching him. He threw her off; kicked her while she lay on the floor. Bridget curled herself into a tight ball, yelling as loudly as she could.

'You're nothing but a monster Ailill ... a bully ... you don't care about anyone ... I hate you; I hate you; I hate you.'

She heard him move across the room, slam the door, and walk across the stony path. For a long time, she was unable to move. Every part of her hurt, every nerve jangled, and her head ached, so that she had to force herself to relax enough to unwind.

CHAPTER 21

Town Gossip

The force of him coming through the cottage door made Bridget jump, quickening her heart even more.

'Where is it then?' he said. No hello. Nothing but cold demand, the tone of his usual drunken state. She fetched his dinner, the plate hot from being over long in the oven and set it on the table. He already had his knife and fork in his hands, standing sentinel, his large fists on the table full of expectation. She watched him study the dried-up meat and vegetables, the congealed gravy that had left brown marks round the rim and the anger fermented in her belly. Bile rose in her throat which she had to force away.

'What's this?'

'Your dinner Ailill. We had ours long ago.'

'This is what a man gets after a hard day's

work?' He was not shouting, more like loud unbelievability. He looked at her, the first time he had really turned her way. 'What's the sour look for?'

She was unable to speak to begin with, knowing what would follow her words, what always happened in these situations. She wanted to prolong it, to keep it at bay, hoping that this time she would be strong enough to tell him the truth and not take the cowards way out as she so often did. This time it was different.

'I know,' she said, softly.

'You know what?'

'I know everything,' she said, getting up from the chair. 'I know what you've been doing. Ballywalter is full of the talk ... two young girls carrying Ailill Blair's children. How could you? How could you bring us so low?' The look on his face was like a festering boil, ready to erupt and she hated him even more then, this man she had loved so much. The softness and loving nature she knew when they were courting, was now turned bitter and violent. She blamed his father, with his never-ending badgering, and wondered if a part of him had just been waiting to be unleashed.

'So,' he said. 'Maybe there'll be a boy there somewhere!'

'You've become a monster,' Bridget shouted, moving towards him, shaking her fists as though to punch his smug face.

'You believe gossip over your own husband?' He shouted, in return. 'Cat got your tongue at last?' She was trembling now, and knew she had to speak the truth.

'Say it woman … you believe the gossip, don't you?'

'Yes,' a quiet voice now.

'What? Say it louder so I can hear.'

'Yes Ailill, I do.' She shouted. 'Yes. Yes. Yes, I believe it. I believe it all and that's the truth.'

He lunged at her, his plate spilling its contents as he picked it up and threw it. Bridget tried to duck, the still hot plate catching her forehead before it skittered away and broke on the kitchen floor. As she fell, she hit the back of her head, felt the thin skin open up. Then there was only the hard slamming of the cottage door. Siobhan was beside her in an instant.

'Mam. I'm sorry. I couldn't come down while he was here.'

'It's alright. Help me up and into the chair please and get something for the blood before it goes everywhere.'

There was less than she expected but she was not prepared to give him the satisfaction of knowing he had injured her. Siobhan brought through a cup of steaming sweet tea and said,

'What will we do Mam?'

'We'll leave in the morning. It's not safe here now. Pack as much as you can. I'll put my case in your room tonight and we'll go as soon as he leaves for work.'

'Stay in my bed tonight, Mam.'

'No. He'll be back at some time, probably with more drink in him. We mustn't give him any reason to suspect. I don't know what he's capable of anymore.' Her voice trailed off as she thought about the possibilities.

'Where will we go?'

'To your aunty, my sister Cora. She'll help us work something out. Come on now. Let's get started before it's too late.'

'What about Murphy, Mam? We can't leave him here.'

'We can't take him either, Siobhan. We must leave him. Be sure to bolt your door.'

'Mam ... what about Paddy?'

'Paddy will understand ... he'll be better off without us ... perhaps he'll find a good lass to marry and have a family with. Now, get yourself to bed and try to sleep well.'

'But Mam. Paddy loves you. It's not fair on him to leave without saying goodbye.'

'I know he does ... and I love him too ... but it's better this way. Go on now, shoo.'

Before going upstairs, Bridget found some food, just bread and butter with a cake she had made that morning and packed it away in paper bags. She gathered all the money she could find and her savings from the hidden tin. Thankfully, there was enough for their journey. She was sure Siobhan would have some left from her wages.

Bridget looked at the bed, at the bedspread she had made when they were first married. She'd been so proud of her handiwork. She looked at the furniture he had made ... he was good at woodwork. All these things they had painstakingly provided for a life together, once so good but now destroyed, her husband almost unrecognisable as the man who had said, *I do.* If she had any doubts as to her next course of action, the pain in her head, bruises on her body, the knowledge of his appalling, unforgivable deed, set her mind straight. She was still awake when he finally came home, so much worse now, he could only flop on the bed. She was thankful for that.

When Siobhan thought her mother safely in bed, hopefully asleep, she unbolted the bedroom door carefully, crept downstairs and threw on a coat. The latch on the front door squeaked, as always, but she did not think it was loud enough to wake her mother. In her hand she clutched the scrap of paper on which she had written her note to Paddy, and walked quickly down the short road to the harbour. She did not expect to find anyone there. They would all be out night fishing but she knew where she could leave the paper so that Paddy would find it and weighted it down with a large stone. Walking up the road, her heart beating fast, she prayed that it would still be there when they returned to harbour in the morning.

As soon as Ailill left for work the next day, Bridget said, 'Bring the pram round Siobhan. It'll save us having to carry.'

Filling it with as much as it would take, they laid their coats and winter hats and scarves on top.

'Will you push it down the road please while I make sure everything is as it should be.'

Siobhan said goodbye to Murphy and did as she was asked. Bridget knelt beside her faithful friend, stroked him, and held his head in her arms.

'I'm so sorry Murphy. We can't take you, but we love you and will think of you every day.'

Murphy cried, a high pitched mewl breaking Bridget's heart, but she forced herself to stand and look back into the home she had shared with Ailill for nearly twenty years. Her head was awash with conflicting thoughts and feelings. She had been a young bride when she first came, expecting lasting love, hoping for children who might run about after each other, for Ailill and her to grow old together, for companionship and support. Her memories of those first years together would always seem sweet compared to the bitter taste left by the man her husband had become. She would lock all that inside now as she closed the door softly, tears for Murphy, for memories of pain, for loss, and for her daughter flowing freely. She ran to catch up with Siobhan and took the pram, now battered and weather beaten from lack of use and care, and without looking back they headed for Ballywalter.

PART 2

**Credenhill, Herefordshire
Rhys Jones**

A Life Remembered

CHAPTER 22

Nineteen Ninety-Six
Rhys Jones Aged 46

Not an Ordinary Problem

Rhys Jones had a problem. The truth was that his life had been beset with problems from an early age. Rhys never felt he belonged, sensed that he was different somehow from the rest of his family. He was shorter to start with. Not short for a man, about average height, but everyone else was on the tall side. He was blonde with blue eyes, where they were more a mousy colour and had brown eyes. Apart from these physical differences, Rhys didn't have the same temperament as his brother and sister. He felt constantly misunderstood, almost as though his inner workings were faulty somehow.

Rhys had never really known who he was. Well, that's not strictly true. He knew he was

Rhys Jones, but it's that he was not sure who Rhys Jones was. Someone, or something else walked with him and it had always been like that, though he did not fully recognise it until he was in his early teens. It didn't have a name when he was growing up. It was never an imaginary friend, like some children have, where a place must be set at the table. A place that stays empty for all but the child. An absent friend they talk to and play with. One who almost becomes part of the family until he's no longer needed. This had never been like that. He wished it had been, for life might have been a whole lot easier.

Rhys would hear an awful squawking in his head, and when it was there, he would do things. Usually they would be nasty, or at least negative things. He might screw up the drawing he was doing for no reason or knock down the tower Beth was building so she'd run crying to his mother. But it had never felt like he was doing it, almost as if in that moment he wasn't in control of his body.

His current problem was not one of those everyday things like the gas boiler breaking down, or the fridge failing to work. This one was terrifying, life-changing and it consumed his every waking hour. He couldn't sleep, and yet craved sleep just to be free from it. He had an uncontrollable urge to yell, to scream, to kick out at something, to feel pain so that his mind had something else to focus on.

It all started when Rhys put black polish on his new tan shoes, though he would come to recognise that this was simply the catalyst, the last straw so to speak. What happened was so catastrophic his mind snapped, like a dead twig underfoot. In that one instant his brain scrambled, became mush, so he didn't know where he was, who he was, or what he was doing. Everything became dark. Inside and out. He couldn't remember what happened directly after that. In fact, his mind became a complete blank … nothing there … just a frightening darkness. He didn't know how many days passed, or remember being found by his brother Al.

Rhys made a cup of coffee. Perhaps drinking coffee didn't help, but it was his drink of choice. He was in the big armchair in what used to be his daughter's bedroom, his favourite room in the house. No longer a bedroom, but his comfort space. The window had a view over the garden, where he was able to see the sun set and watch the birds if he was not in that place that sees nothing but darkness.

The rest of the room was Spartan save for a bookcase and a coffee table to rest a lamp on. A recently purchased table sat by the window to work at, low enough for him to continue using the armchair, and on it was a notebook and pen. It had been like that for about two weeks, but all he had done so far was look at it.

Rhys didn't know where to begin, though he was acutely aware that begin he must, because it was the only way … the only way to fight the oppressive and devastating thing that had happened. He had to write it all down, the memories … good and bad … before life could continue. Maybe not as it had been … but at least out of the endless tunnel. He took a gulp of coffee … ugh … he must've left a grain on the rim, the taste bitter in his mouth … but it had at least taken him out of his lethargy.

Over the previous two weeks he had tried to remember the past, but it was so difficult. Memories didn't appear in sequence, and then when they did show themselves they were usually the sad, dark ones. He had to dig deep to find those that were happy. He must have been working on it, evidenced by the stuff written on scraps of paper littered about the table. Now it needed organising. He opened the book. A crisp clear page waited for the pen, and Rhys wondered for a moment what his first words should be. He flexed his fingers and, there. Done. He had done the most difficult bit. He had started.

CHAPTER 23

Rhys Jones - childhood

A Growing Awareness

It had been hot for the last few days, the air muggy. Last night Rhys had been woken, not by the raging storm, but by the noise of some dying howl as though a beast was breathing its last below the bedroom window. It took him a while to realise it wasn't in his head, as was so often the case, but the strong gale force wind funnelling in the small gap of the open window. Hard to believe it could create such a blood curdling sound.

Rhys was twenty, born in Dovecote Lane, Credenhill, his brother Alwin, who preferred to be called Al, already ten when he was born. His parents had tried all those years for another child, only for two to come along close together like waiting for a bus. Bethany, Beth, arrived just seventeen months after Rhys, so their Mum had her hands full. She'd even told him once, that with a new baby, she didn't have time to look after him as well, so said she was lucky that Rhys had been a good child and never cried much, that he occupied himself. What they didn't know was that Rhys had been intensely lonely. Beth was the girl they wanted ... spoilt beyond belief. Al sometimes played with him but as a teenager had his own friends. If he had to look after Rhys, he was a yoke round Al's neck. He mostly made it clear when his friends were at the house he wasn't happy to have Rhys about. So, Rhys had no choice but to occupy himself.

Rhys hid most of the time, his favourite place being in his father's shed. It was close to the house but if he managed to get inside without being seen he could hide in any number of places, like behind the deckchairs during the winter when they were stored in the corner. Summer hiding was more difficult but as he grew older, he'd move things about to make a sort of cave. A small stream ran along the bottom of the garden, fenced off of course for everyone's safety.

One day Rhys found a pair of cutters in the shed and cut a hole in the fence. He wasn't very old and on reflection, realised it was a miracle he hadn't injured himself. The wire was tough but he was determined and when the hole was large enough, he crawled through the gap. When he was taller he climbed over the fence. Sometimes he wandered aimlessly up and down the stream. Other times he would just sit on the bank under the trees that grew along it. Hours of his young life were spent this way, and he became an unhappy child without knowing it.

Rhys recognized that Al and Beth were treated differently to him. Beth was always believed even if she had been lying, so mostly when things went wrong it was his fault. Being constantly blamed for things he hadn't done, he came to accept he must have done them. It was easy from there to believe he was not a very nice person, that he wasn't worthy of his parents' love. He knew in his heart that his Mum and Dad loved him ... he simply didn't feel it. Angharad and Owen, Mum, and Dad, were good parents. They provided for their children. His mother never worked so was always there caring for the family, creating a lovely home. His father had retired from flying in the RAF after an accident left him with a pronounced limp and he was transferred to an administrative job. That was when the family moved from Wales to Credenhill, just outside Hereford. Al was born in Wales so he and his parents were Welsh. Beth and Rhys, were English.'

People often commented that Rhys was a placid child, like his father and it had even been said that he had an old head on young shoulders. Rhys didn't understand what that meant at the time.

He'd always tried to be a good person even with the thing inside him. He clearly remembers the first time he was horrible.

It was at junior school during an art lesson where they had to sketch out things on the paper as the teacher said them like, on the left of your paper there's a tree. That sort of thing. Rhys looked at what Lucy, the girl beside him was doing, and hers was so much better. Rhys wasn't making much progress in the art department. He had leaned over and scribbled across her work. Not just a bit, but heavy pencil scribbles from corner to corner. She'd burst into tears and made a screeching noise that pierced his ears. Mrs. Johnson, the art teacher and their religious education teacher, had squeezed her large overweight body between the desks, looked at Lucy's work and then at Rhys.'

'Rhys Jones, what have you done now?' she'd said, full of accusation. Rhys tried to tell her that he didn't know he'd done it, because it was as though the hand that held the pencil wasn't his ... it was some other hand he had no control over. He remembered being horrified to think he'd been so cruel. On top of that he'd committed Mrs. Johnson's cardinal sin ... one she reminded them of at every opportunity ... "you must have respect for everybody's work". That was the first time Rhys had been expelled from school ... for a week to learn how to have respect for others.

His mother was called of course, collecting

him from the office, dragging him outside across the playground and round the corner out of sight. She wouldn't listen to him either. Nobody would. Rhys was grounded for an entire week ... that meant no television, no football which he was really good at, playing for the school and local teams. It was painful, but not as painful as the growing awareness that there must be something terribly bad inside him. How else could he have done such a thing and not realise he was doing it?

Rhys didn't mind his own company when everything was going well ... when it wasn't, however, he needed people round him to stop him thinking. While he was alone for that week he did a lot of thinking in between trying to stop the black thing inside and it was during that week that Rhys gave the blackness a name. In the fields at the back of the house there were crows; lots of them, their nests built high in the treetops and Rhys had always been fascinated by them. He often wondered how they stayed put when the branches flexed wildly in intense winds. Sometimes the sky was filled with them squawking loudly as they flew in different directions; swerved to follow the leader; dived to chase off others during the mating season. They'd sit on roof tops and power lines in long rows, their blackness accentuated against pale blue spring skies. Close up they were enormous and when their feathers were ruffled they looked altogether like some threatening beast. It hadn't occurred to Rhys before that day that the noise they made was so like the sound in his head.

He named him Jack Daw. When he wasn't playing havoc with his head, Rhys thought about the sin he'd committed and how Mrs. Johnson had said they shouldn't take His name in vain. She said they should shout "chrysanthemum" if an expletive was needed, although she also said there were enough words in the English language without having to invent them. Rhys's mother grew chrysanthemums in the garden and Rhys loved them, so didn't see why they should be used as a swear word when he couldn't see Him, know who He was, and had no feelings for Him.

Rhys decided that day never to swear. It didn't last of course, but he'd never been one for using foul language and hated that some people used it extensively as though such words added meaning to their ideas. Another big decision made that week was about where Rhys thought he'd come from. His father had said he was born in England and therefore he was English, but Rhys thought differently. He believed that being born in England hadn't given him English blood, but having parents who were Welsh, going back generations his father had always said, meant he had one hundred percent quality Welsh blood running through his veins ... and that made him

Welsh.

Al had passed his eleven plus exam and gone to the gramma school in Hereford then straight to university. Beth and Rhys were both assessed for their secondary education, the Eleven Plus having been scrapped by then so they attended the local secondary modern; were laughed at and mocked by the grammar kids in their smart blazers with posh badges on their pockets.

The new school had been a whole different ball game for Rhys. He'd never had difficulty making friends, but keeping them was another matter, and he'd never understood whether it was him who pulled away, or if others saw something in him they didn't like. Only one person befriended him at school.

John was quite tall, so he almost looked down on Rhys and his hair was dark, as were his eyes. He was a quiet lad so they had that in common from the beginning and he had a gentle nature. John liked football too, and Rhys remembered being pleased when he got into the team. John was never judgmental. He wasn't constantly asking questions about why Rhys did things. It was as though John understood intuitively. They paired up together in the classroom and by the time they were in their second year had become close. John always supported Rhys when he got into scrapes.

As he grew, Rhys's mood began to change. It would go suddenly from calm to explosive ... and that's when he'd do things he didn't seem able to control, like the scribbling at junior school, but then it would change again so he was calm as if nothing had happened. His mother found she couldn't manage him and sought help from the GP, who announced that Rhys had Bipolar and prescribed tablets to take.

Rhys went to the library to find out about Bipolar. It said that people with Bipolar had extreme mood swings that could last for days or weeks and they were usually either emotionally high or depressed. He knew immediately that this didn't describe him. As far as Rhys was concerned, his emotions were pretty much on a level. He rarely felt low or high ... just sort of the same, like one of those sailing ships on calm waters ... neither tilting nor rolling ... not moving anywhere. His parents never knew, but he didn't take the tablets, and they never suspected, so that made him think he was right not to.

The squawking in his brain got worse as he got older. He had to work doubly hard at school because he never knew when Jack was going to stop him concentrating and one thing was certain. Rhys really wanted to succeed ... get the best GCE grades he could..

At the age of thirteen Rhys had the first physical

manifestation of Jack Daw. He'd taken a shower. It was a wonderful new top of the range piece of equipment a bathroom could have at that time and he'd rubbed the steam from the mirror afterwards. But it wasn't him looking back. He closed his eyes tight, such was the shock. As he opened them slowly and turned his head to face the mirror again, it was still there. The face was indiscernible, blurred by the moisture. What had stood out was the dark hair. Rhys was blonde, so the image in the mirror had instantly terrified him.

He stood there staring at it, afraid to look away but afraid to keep looking too. He raised a hand to clear the surface but there was no hand reflected ... and though the surface steam had cleared, the face was no more defined. Rhys's imagination worked overtime. He wanted to run downstairs ... to tell his mother what he'd seen ... but who would have believed him? There was nobody he could tell such things to when he had a reputation for telling tales ... for being wrong ... for doing things that embarrassed his family.

Rhys became increasingly reclusive during the following couple of years, sometimes seeing what he believed was Jack Daw, while also going for prolonged periods seeing only himself. He became more introverted at home than when he was with John, who had a knack of taking Rhys out of himself, not that John did anything in particular. Rhys thought it was just the way he was.

At home he was always having to be the perfect son or having to try anyway. He wasn't able to relax, or be himself, but then he didn't know what it meant to be himself. With John he never had to be anything other than who he was on the day. John accepted whatever Rhys presented and he knew he was extremely fortunate to have him.

Rhys came to accept Jack Daw as simply another side of himself, but perhaps he had no choice, no control over whatever it was so he had to learn to live with it. At the age of fifteen Rhys was forced to confront his situation with his parents. It was a Saturday morning. In the bathroom Rhys experienced something quite bizarre. He was floating, watching himself leaning over the bathtub washing his hair, watching as his blonde hair turned black, watching as his hair was rubbed dry and combed out, and with no notion of a change in his being, he was seeing the results of this work in the mirror. Rhys Jones had black hair.

CHAPTER 24

Family Times

Mrs. Owens went into a rare rage when she saw the black hair. Rhys could hardly have told her he didn't remember doing it ... that he'd watched himself from the ceiling. She would have called the men in white coats! His father said, it was no good crying over spilt milk and,though Rhys had never heard him say it before, he rather liked it. It became something he held on to ... told himself many times afterwards. It served him well.

Beth cried laughing. Al said he should have it cut short so it would grow out quicker, which is what Rhys did, but that only set him more part. The fashion in the sixties was for boys to grow their hair. All the new bands had long hair ... well, maybe not all of them, but certainly the rock bands had. To Rhys it felt as though the only people who had really short hair were older men and those in the armed forces. What he hadn't told his parents and couldn't have done, ... was that the whole thing had scared the crap out of him and he began to wonder if he was going mental. The idea of it was so scarry he decided to tell John.

Even though they were the same age, John had already developed an unusually adult take on life, from his parents, who Rhys knew to be lovely people. Being an only child may have had a bearing on John having become a model of them. If John had been shocked at what Rhys had done he hadn't shown it. He took Rhys to his bedroom and sat him down. Rhys was close to tears by the time John brought up a cup of tea. He was never able to remember those hours spent in John's room that Saturday, but he knew from his friend that he had told John everything ... about what had been going on inside him ... about Jack Daw ... about not being able to remember things happening ... about the face, or partial face, in the mirror. What Rhys did know about that day was that it was a defining moment. Perhaps because he'd shared it all and in so doing didn't feel the weight of it, or because he knew that from then on, he'd always be able to talk to John.

Rhys didn't know it at the time, but John had gone away and asked his aunty, who was a nurse, about what might be wrong with him and it was John, not doctors or psychiatrists who helped

Rhys cope. Instead of being frightened of Jack he began to accept him as part of his makeup and then found he could put him a box ... store him somewhere in his head ... go for hours or even days, without thinking of him.

Gradually Rhys stopped worrying about it. He still had those peculiar times when he heard the squawking and couldn't remember doing things, when he saw himself as though he were two different beings, but as time progressed, Rhys found he could laugh about it. He became calmer, more in control of life. His parents noticed the change and Beth said he must have acquired a new brain from somewhere. He managed to settle properly into schoolwork, determined to get those exams and by the time he was eighteen he'd passed six GCE's and two A Levels.

Al became deputy manager of a bank, the youngest person to hold the post, so their parents were full of pride. Beth left school when she was sixteen to take an apprenticeship in hairdressing. She'd had her hopes pinned for years on owning her own salon by the time she was thirty! Rhys had argued with his parents over going to university. All he ever wanted out of life was a job he could leave at the end of the day so he could go home to a family. It seemed the most important life experience one could have and how could he know if his mind would ever set Jack Daw free. Rhys thought the security of family life was something he could achieve. Al had never been interested in marriage or children and remained a confirmed bachelor. He even still lived at home with Mum and Dad.

It wasn't all bad though. Rhys's parents were sticklers for making sure they had a holiday every year. They were both born in Dolgellau so there were two sets of grandparents there, although the family never stayed with them. Instead, they hired the same little cottage each summer, equidistant between Dolgellau and Cadre Idris, this mountain being their favourite haunt.

The cottage was on the side of a hill, beside the main road to each place. Between the road and the cottage, trees deadened any road noise. From the door, if it was a clear day, the Pimple was visible, a mountain so named because on the very top was a small mound, looking exactly like a pimple. Al and Rhys used to look for it every morning. He loved it there. It was cosy, inviting, and though clean, it wasn't posh so the children didn't have to worry about making the sort of mess their mother would normally want to clean up every five minutes.

When Rhys had been young, he'd asked if he could have a dog. He wanted a pet to look after, to cuddle, and thought he wouldn't be as lonely. The answer was a firm no. His Mum and Dad weren't going to look after it when he got fed up. It wasn't long after that Beth decided she wanted a dog. The reaction was, admittedly, the same. However, Beth could never take no for an answer. She had whined … asked daily … made promises … until naturally, they gave in. They didn't go for anything expensive like a pedigree. They were keen to have a dog from a rescue place, so eventually Rusty arrived. He was a small cross breed, so they never really knew his content. White with reddish brown markings … hence his name. Beth was great at first. She took him out twice a day, fed him, brushed him and with help, made sure he was looked after at the vets. It didn't last.

The holiday cottage was open to pets, so Rusty always went with them, and as the garden was completely fenced in, he used to race up and down the hill, and round the garden, then sleep beside the wood fire when it was cold enough to need it. Unless the weather was particularly bad, they'd go out somewhere every day mostly to Cadre Idris, either to walk around it or up it as far as they could. When Rhys was old enough, Al would take him on his shoulders for some of the way or hold his hand to stop him falling off the loose stones.

It wasn't long before Rhys was nearly as good as Al, and they started trying to make it to the top. Most years they'd reach it at least once and then sit for ages looking around Wales at the fields laid out in rectangular shapes across the hills and mountains … the stone walls dividing them and keeping livestock off the roads ... the beautiful fluffy white and black sheep roaming everywhere. From their vantage point they'd experience the beauty of nature, Al teaching Rhys about flowers and trees.

Sometimes the weather changed while they were there. The sun might suddenly disappear, the sky darken with clouds that somehow fell below them so they were in the mist, unable to see much. The first time it happened Al became really anxious, not knowing what to do. They were a long way up; the tracks unstable; visibility poor, but Al held onto Rhys for the whole trek down and he'd never forgotten how safe he felt with his brother.

To Rhys, as a youngster, Al was already grown up ... twenty by the by the time he was first expelled from school, so they didn't begin to know each other until Rhys started working, when the years between them gradually diminished.

Rhys took a job as a conductor with a local bus company in Hereford, and though the shift work took a bit of getting used to, his body adapted after a while. It meant the whole family was granted free travel, and he could go anywhere in the country with his work pass. Working the buses was ok apart from the long hours standing and running up and down stairs.

From the beginning Rhys was paired with

Thomasina, Tom for short. They got on like a house on fire. She always made him laugh, her wit sardonic and dry. Their regular customers came in for many comments, some quite harsh ... but they were never meant unkindly. Tom gave them nicknames. Mr. Miserable was an old man with two walking sticks, who'd never allow Rhys to help him up the step from the kerb. Rhys had thought since that he probably wasn't miserable at all, just trying to remain as independent as possible. He wondered what happened to him.

Buses, especially when packed, always smelt. Tom kept a can of air freshener in the cab, and when the bus was empty, she would go round and spray all the seats. During hot weather they'd make sure all the windows were open ... but in winter the heaters drove the smelly air round and round. The worst days were when the fish market was open in Hereford. Passengers sat with their bags of smelly contents on their laps, the air becoming saturated with it. The two other difficult times were early morning and the end of school when most passengers were teenage children. They were nearly always rowdy, moved from seat to seat, and threw things at each other. Cleaning up after them was often a lengthy task.

And then there were the holiday seasons. Pushchairs vied with suitcases and bags for limited space in the luggage rack, and when that ran out, people put cases in the aisle making Rhys's job difficult. He often went home bruised and battered during those times. But as long as his money and ticket sales tallied at the end of the day, he was free. He didn't have to think of work again until the next shift.

John became a nurse, walked in his aunt's footsteps, his character well suited to caring for people. One of the avenues he trained in was mental health. Rhys never asked John but wondered if it was because of him. He was a paramedic now, often being called out as first responder to all types of grim situations. Rhys admired his friend, knowing he'd probably faint at the first sight of blood!

The two friends met up as often as possible, whenever their respective shifts allowed. They'd go down to the club they'd frequented as teenagers, or they'd meet at the football ground when Hereford were playing. They also spoke regularly on the phone, so Rhys remained supported by him.

CHAPTER 25

Nineteen Ninety-Six
Rhys Jones Aged 46

Props

It wasn't until the breakdown and Rhys's sessions with a therapist that he discovered the real nature of those early problems. He had a mild personality disorder, but since he'd managed to live with it there was no need, the therapist had said, for medication. Rhys was fine with that, not wanting to be reliant on more than he was already taking since the shoe incident.

Rhys was sitting at the table in his comfort room, a weak sun struggling to make an impression on the early spring day, clouds rolling past the window in a fresh breeze. He'd been attempting to revisit more of his past, but while he could remember the bad upsetting stuff, the happy memories eluded him as though they either weren't worth remembering, or the bad things had been so well etched on his mind that they'd overridden everything else. His marriage was a good example. He knew there should be tons of wonderful memories there, but the truth was he'd not been able to bring them to the surface. Rhys's wife, Catherine, had left him with so much hurt, it was possible that the experience wiped out everything else.

He found some old photo albums and sat in the kitchen with a drink, opened them on the table one by one until he found pictures of their wedding. As soon as he saw the one taken under the apple tree outside the church, another dam burst inside him ... watery images flooded across his eyes, and he thought how strange it was that something as simple as a photo could dislodge whatever stood in the way of memory? He remembered the day they met.

CHAPTER 26

Nineteen Seventy
Rhys Jones at age 20

The Girl of his Dreams

It was the end of the week, and Tom stopped the bus at the top of the road as usual and waved goodbye. Unusually, Rhys had been up late for the day's early shift so missed breakfast, and with only a chocolate bar for lunch the growls from his stomach had probably been audible half a mile away.

He thought of his mother's cooking as he walked down the road, and with it being so hot he took his uniform jacket off and slung it over his shoulder. He wondered what there would be for dinner, knowing it was most likely to be another salad, given the scorching heat, but almost certainly followed by one of her famous puddings. Perhaps a spotted dick with thick creamy custard, or a suet pudding covered in syrup. His mother was a good cook. There was always cake in the cupboard which Rhys and his brother would sneak pieces of when no-one was looking.

'Hi Mum. I'm home,' Rhys shouted, from the front door. His mother asked if he'd had a good day.

'Oh. You know. Busy, full up mostly ... bags and cases in the aisles, difficult to make sure everyone had a ticket. There's always someone who tries to get a free ride. We had an inspector on for one run so no freebies then! Tom was on good form. She makes me laugh and that makes the day go quicker. Where is everyone?'

'Al will be home shortly and Dad too. Beth's in her room getting ready for a night out with the girls. You going out tonight, Rhys?'

'Definitely. Got the weekend off. Looking forward to meeting up with the lads tonight and playing football tomorrow. Is my kit ready?'

'Of course. In your room with the rest of your clothes.'

'You're a star Mum,' he said, kissing her on the cheek before making his way to the bathroom hoping there was still enough hot water. Beth had grown into an opinionated teenager with no ears so as he climbed the stairs, he suspected that she'd have used as much hot water as she could just to spite them. Unsurprisingly the shower was almost cold, but then the weather was so hot, Rhys didn't have the energy to complain.

He found his clothes for the evening and packed the kit ready just in case a lie in could be had the following morning. Rhys had not long celebrated his twentieth birthday, and though he knew it to be strange, inside he felt more grown up as if the gap between being a teenager and being twenty was huge. He'd had a few girlfriends over the previous couple of years, but none of them interested him past the first few dates and he actually thought that being twenty would increase his chances! He checked himself in the mirror one last time noting he needed a haircut.

Rhys met John, and a few other lads they knew in the club.

'How're you doing?' said Paul.

'Good thanks. Is it me or is it crowded tonight? There's hardly any room to move, never mind dance.'

'Apparently there's a group in who're going to a stag do soon, according to Harry,' said John. 'What're you having?'

'Half of the usual please.'

'Half!' said Paul. 'You ill?'

'Football tomorrow. Need to keep my wits about me.'

It was overcrowded and noisy with the stag group. When they'd left, the club had seemed quite empty, but the music remained loud. The deep drumbeats resounded in his ears, and though there were only a few people on the dance floor, the room had continued to be dark and smoky.

Rhys enjoyed loud music, particularly the one by Led Zeppelin being played, but he went outside for some fresh air, leant against the door jamb and watched a group of girls clearly rather intoxicated, drinks in one hand, cigarettes in the other, smoke rising vertically in the still air. They were laughing loudly, shouting and swearing at each other, talking all at once so that he wondered how any of them could hear what the others were saying. He was fascinated by these unruly females, feeling himself smile despite their common behaviour. As he watched, he sensed a shift in the atmosphere.

Faces that were laughing became sour. One of the girls had begun to cry, flapping her arms about, though it seemed to him she had little control over where they were going. A heated exchange occurred between her and a much taller girl who had suddenly closed on her with a raised fist. The crying girl ducked and turned so avoiding the punch and ran fast in his direction. With her head down she hadn't realised she was about to collide with Rhys, so he was forced to step back to miss her but caught hold of her arm as she passed.

'Whoa! what was all that about?' Her face was

already puffy.

'Oh. You know … friends and enemies,' she said. 'Sorry I almost ran into you.'

'It's OK. Can I buy you a drink? My shoulders are broad if you want to talk.'

As they went inside, Rhys motioned to Paul and John, pointing to the girl at the same time and got two thumbs up in response. Her name was Catherine. They talked for a long time about everything and nothing and were still in the club long after both sets of friends had left. Eventually, she thanked him for the drink and the company then ran to catch the last bus to Hereford.

CHAPTER 27

Nineteen Seventy
Rhys Jones at age 20

Love Struck

Rhys didn't see Catherine for a while after that although he thought about her a great deal and looked out for her whenever he was in the club or travelling round Hereford. He couldn't say what it was about her that was so memorable. Even though they'd talked for ages, she hadn't given away much about herself, apart from to say that she had been born in Hereford and had no wish to live anywhere else. Rhys hadn't asked her about her friends, or what had happened for her to become upset. He thought if she wanted him to know she would have told him.

It was a few months later that Rhys bumped into her on the street in town. There was an awkwardness to begin with, neither of them knowing what to say, so it seemed like several minutes before they both spoke at once. The laughter that followed broke the spell.

'Would you like to go out one evening?' Rhys asked.

'It depends where.'

'Perhaps to the club, or the cinema … or for a meal?'

'Not the club,' she said, emphatically. 'Definitely not the club. A film or a meal would be nice though.'

A date was arranged and Rhys went back to work a happy man. They saw each other regularly after that first meal, Rhys becoming besotted with her, talking about her to anyone who listened and dreaming of her most nights. Early on, Catherine spoke about her friends, about some of the things they got up to together, things which Rhys would rather not have known about but over the months Catherine saw less and less of them. It was his friends they tended to mix with mostly.

Al taught Rhys to drive when he was eighteen, but affording a car had been out of the question so he hadn't taken the test. When his father bought a new car, a Ford Cortina, more modern than the Anglia, he'd given Rhys the old one.

'Whose is it Rhys?' she asked, when he pulled up beside her one day.

'Mine.'

'Really! You kept that quiet. How long have you had it?'

'A while now. Passed my test in the week. Kept it secret to surprise you. What do you think?'

'I love it. No more buses for me. I can be chauffeur driven now!' She said laughing.

'I'm not so sure about that. But it means we can go further afield. We can see places. Go at our own pace …'

'I love the colour too. I'll be able to spot this bright green anywhere.'

Rhys had wondered many times over the ensuing years, what might have happened had he stopped to listen to her more closely sometimes, or to some of the stories he'd begun to hear around Hereford. Her comment about being chauffeured wasn't the joke he'd taken it for but then he was blinded by all those emotions inside. The inevitable meeting of the parents had been quite stressful but had nevertheless proved successful. Catherine's parents seemed to take to Rhys straight away. Catherine was an only child and Rhys had thought they were glad she'd found someone at last. His parents said they liked her, but his mother hadn't done any of the gushing he expected. She was quiet after Catherine had gone, as though holding back her true thoughts. Rhys wasn't prepared to ask her … she'd say what was on her mind soon enough.

They'd been going out for some time when Rhys

began to have a nagging feeling which initially he fought against. At twenty-one, he was unsure as to whether he was still too young to commit himself, but no matter how much he tried, thoughts of Catherine wouldn't disappear. She was beautiful. Her auburn hair flowed in soft curls around her face, usually with a mind of their own. They settled on her shoulders, bobbed up and down as she moved and shone in red streaks in the sunlight. Her hair never looked uncombed or uncared for. Rhys thought she must pay regular visits to a hairdresser to be so manicured all the time.

Catherine was petite with small hands and feet, and her facial features were perfectly formed in miniature. In summer, her skin tanned to an olive brown, adding to her beauty. When Rhys put his arm round her waist, he was constantly surprised at the narrowness of it, being able to reach right round to her stomach. He wanted her. He wanted her so badly there were a few occasions when he almost gave in but always managed to hold out. It was no good. To have her he would need to marry her and he believed he wasn't able to live without her.

Rhys had become less and less bothered by Jack Daw. When he made an appearance John had always been there to help. The noise in Rhys's head was manageable, though forgetting things still happened, but there had never been a serious consequence of it. Over time he found a way to deal with it all. Rhys was athletic. He started running each day and it somehow stopped the squawking so he ran faster. It was as though whatever was in his head could be outrun. He began to find that he could leave him, or it, behind and be free of it for a few days, if he was lucky. He didn't really know if that was true, or simply an imagined outcome, but it kept him active and fit as well as happier. John joined him whenever he could; made it a joke, often asking, "has he gone yet?" The other strategy Rhys developed was playing music louder than the squawking. When his parents complained, he bought headphones and turned the sound up even louder. He began to realise he could outwit whatever was inside him.

There had never been a need to tell Catherine. Rhys supposed it was fortunate that nothing had ever happened when he was with her. Now that he wanted to marry her, he couldn't decide if she should know. He wondered if he'd be able to keep it from her. Would she run a mile if she knew about him; was he prepared to risk losing her; would it be morally wrong not to tell her? Those questions, and more, kept him awake at night for a long time, until he decided not to say anything.

Rhys asked Catherine to marry him over a gloriously expensive meal at an upmarket restaurant in Hereford, probably the most he'd ever lashed out for food. The weather had been wonderful, full sunshine against blue skies unlike the previous day, when it had mostly poured. That evening was balmy even though the sun had almost set, the lights in the restaurant beckoning people to enter. He hadn't done that soppy thing, going down on one knee, but she hadn't seemed to mind.

'I thought you'd never ask,' she said dryly, just a hint of a smile turning the corners of her lips upward. 'Yes Rhys. I will … I will …. I will,' she said, fully smiling so that the light from above danced in her eyes and a small tear found its way to her nose.

Rhys watched as she opened the ring box and knew he'd made the right choice.

'It's beautiful Rhys. I don't know what to say … I'm not sure I deserve such an incredible ring.'

'Of course you do silly. Here give me your hand.'

The ring, a solitaire diamond in an oval shape, was set in platinum with three small diamonds on each shoulder. The magnificently cut stone had shone on her small hand. When she looked up more tears had gathered.

'It's more beautiful than I could ever have imagined. The fit's good too.

There had been times since when Rhys thought, *No, Catherine. I don't think you did deserve it,* but what's in the past had to stay there, didn't it?

CHAPTER 28

Nineteen Seventy-one
Rhys Jones aged 21

A Marriage Made
in Heaven?

They were married in April nineteen seventy-one only a few months later, at the church in the centre of Hereford. Being an only child, Catherine's father provided a wedding fit for a princess. The church overflowed with guests, the air hummed with excitement and children made a lot of noise as they are inclined to do, until the Bridal March was heard from the old organ. Rhys and Al turned at the same time, both shaking with a touch of nerves, to see Catherine walking towards them. She looked like some ethereal apparition gliding down the aisle in white, her closest friend Tilly as her maid of honour. Catherine's beauty caught in Rhys's throat, a tear appearing at the corner of his eye. Catherine's father handed her to Rhys with a wink.

They had saved as much as they could and both sets of parents gave them money, so they were able to afford a deposit on a small house close to Rhys's Mum and Dad. Catherine wasn't in favour of becoming a housewife like their mothers, insisting that she wanted to keep her job as a typist in a solicitor's office. But much to Rhys's surprise she became quite domesticated, and had little in the way of ambition, enjoying her work but not desirous of anything more. She had plenty of spirit and warmth though, which she poured into their house, turning it in no time at all into a cosy home to return to after a hard day's work.

They were round the corner from Rhys's childhood home. In fact, each house could be seen from the other and they used to laugh thinking that they could all spy on the other one! If you can imagine two sides of a field, with a row of houses built on each side and backing onto it, that was how it was. The stream Rhys had frequented as a child ran at the bottom of his parents' house, but at the side of theirs, so he always felt as though his heart was where it should be.

John married the same year, Rhys honoured to be his best man. John's wife Marion was a wonderful person ... a teacher. They both worked long hours, but still always had time for Rhys, even though over the years they'd brought up two of their own children.

Rhys and Catherine admitted that the first few months had been a little strange, getting to know each other properly not having figured in their thoughts prior to marriage, but they rarely had cross words. If they did, Rhys would be sure to turn it around so they always ended up laughing. There were lots of family holidays too, sometimes to cottages in Yorkshire, or caravans further south, as well as the continued annual cottage in Wales. Many of their evenings had been spent filling photograph albums.

It was two years into their marriage when Rhys arrived home one evening to find the dining room laid with the best crockery, a vase of flowers at its centre, and two candles burning at each end. Catherine was busy in the kitchen when he went through but she barred his way. He looked around, searched for a clue. Had he missed her birthday, their anniversary? He was sure he hadn't, but this was most unusual and unnerved him. Once showered Rhys had gone back to the living room, listened to Catherine hum a variety of tunes until the wine began to affect him on top of an empty stomach. Eventually, she had appeared with food. Not just the ordinary food though, the usual mid-week sausage and mash food. She placed all the ingredients of a big Sunday roast on the table, took his hand and held out the chair. Rhys raised his eyebrows not daring to ask in case he should have known. After the main meal Catherine placed a trifle on the table and handed him a spoon. It was his favourite. He and Al used to fight over it when they were younger.Rhys was becoming more nervous, wondering what was about to come.

'Have I forgotten a special occasion,' he asked, nervously.'

'Well, Rhys.' She left a long pause. 'I'm giving in my notice at the office,' she said.

'Why?' It came out with more surprise than he expected, but since he had no idea what was coming, he was at the very least concerned.

'You and me ... we're going to have a little addition to the family. I saw the doctor today and he confirmed it,' her eyes bright and beginning to fill with tears.

They planned the nursery, found a selection of names, bought the tiniest of white baby clothes which Catherine would take out and look at imagining her little one in them. In February the following year, after a textbook birth, Katie had been born. She looked every bit like her mother, the same colouring and so, so small Rhys could almost hold her with one hand.

Life had been perfect then. Rhys woke up each day and wondered how he deserved it. Catherine surpassed herself, took everything in her stride as though she'd been born for motherhood and by the time Rhys arrived from work, Katie would be bathed, fed and ready for him to spend time with her. On top of all Catherine had to do, there was always a meal waiting for him.

Everyone could see how much Catherine loved being a mum. She walked Katie in the park, showed her off to friends, and visited her parents. Katie became the centre of their home. Even those mundane chores seemed to have a greater purpose with Katie about. If she ever needed anything, she only had to go round the corner to Rhys's mother who often agreed to look after her granddaughter while Catherine went into Hereford. It seemed to Rhys that Catherine took full advantage of it knowing how much Angharad doted on Katie, although sometimes she took Katie with her, and he discovered that on these occasions Catherine's parents minded their daughter, and Catherine's father brought them home.

Rhys never asked what his wife did on those occasions, but his parents had wondered why they never went out together, though they'd never asked either. Catherine's visits to town always took place while Rhys was at work. There had been more than a few occasions when Catherine arrived home after him, the house left in a mess, no food prepared. It was not that he didn't trust her, but nevertheless he did begin to wonder what the attraction was in Hereford.

Rhys was curious so asked her about it one night. She simply shrugged the question off saying she'd been to see friends.

It was her friends Rhys was concerned about. Catherine always seemed different after these visits, less loving, and more argumentative and though he was OK with Tilly, Rhys was less pleased to think she was still seeing the other girls, those she'd been with on the night they met. He thought them uncouth and Catherine seemed to be influenced by them.

Katie was four years old when Richard arrived. Rhys was overjoyed, Catherine too but not in the same way. Rhys knew a new baby took a lot of time away from Katie. It seemed to him though that Catherine had forgotten they had a daughter. Everything was about Richard. He was all she ever spoke about. She'd fuss over him in a way she hadn't done with Katie. The time Rhys had shared with his little girl as a baby wasn't allowed with Richard, as though Catherine was trying to keep him all to herself. There was always a relatively good reason given, but Rhys began to feel as if Katie and him no longer mattered very much.

CHAPTER 29

Nineteen Ninety-Six
Rhys Jones Aged 46

Old Photos

For two weeks Rhys was unable to write anything. The flood of memories had given way to further tears ... almost to where he'd been a few months previously so that he was unable to even think, never mind write. Another session at the therapist confirmed what he had said right from the beginning ... that however difficult, Rhys must keep going ... keep reliving all those years of hurt ... the alternative would be not to move forward. After a run, a weak, black, no sugar coffee and a conversation with Al, Rhys returned to the safety of his room.

Katie had been on his mind. He couldn't talk about it. It was too raw, even though it had been such a long time ago or so it seemed. Her photo, the only adornment in what had been her bedroom, kept him company; it made him smile. He kissed her every day.

Rhys looked at another album, one that held some of their holiday pictures. He smiled as he turned the pages at each face that peered out, even though some of them were no longer alive. He stopped at one taken outside a caravan and wondered where it was. Rhys thought he should know but couldn't bring it to mind. Beth and Al were sitting on the step, with the door open. Rhys stood beside Beth and his mother and Al were there too. They were all laughing, probably at something his father had said ... always the joker. Caister, he thought it was ... and then he remembered. It was the time Mum burnt the sausages! He thought he was about twelve then. Every day, they went to the water, their caravan being right at the edge of the park with nothing between it and the sea. Even though Al was so much older he always joined them on holidays. They were a close-knit family in spite of what Rhys considered was his devilment, or perhaps because of it.

They were preparing for breakfast when the siren sounded for the Caister lifeboat and they all ran down to the station to watch the launch. It wasn't an everyday occurrence and would be something to tell those at home. It wasn't far to run, but even so, when they arrived there were crowds lining up at the slipway, people asking others what had happened but of course, nobody knew. The huge bright orange vessel hurtled down the slipway on its chains and entered the sea with an almighty splash soaking those who had got there first so they turned and tried to run back into the crowd. Beth laughed at them. Once it was out of sight, out to sea and round the cliff, they ambled back.

Wispy smoke issued from the caravan. Their dad had seen it first. Then their Mum had gasped with her hand over her mouth and run as fast as she could along the beach. When they got there, thicker smoke was rising from the frying pan, black sausages stuck to it. Rhys's father grabbed the pan flinging it into the small sink, and turned to his Mum. He shook when he admonished her for leaving them on. She said she was sure she'd turned the gas off. They all looked at Rhys ... nothing was said ... but he knew they thought he'd lit the gas afterwards, even though he fervently denied it. In years to come they laughed about it, but Rhys was convinced his parents thought it was his fault. He remembered it well.

It transpired that neither Katie, nor Rhys had mattered to Catherine and yet he hadn't seen the signs ... or maybe he had but simply couldn't register them as meaningful. The day it all came out Rhys received good news from work. He'd passed his inspectors exam and couldn't wait for the day to end to tell Catherine the news. Even the wet winter's day, unavoidable dirty puddles wetting the hems of his trousers, hadn't been able to dampen his mood. The promotion to Inspector on the Hereford buses would mean Catherine could stop looking for work and stay at home. Katie was nursery school age by then, but Richard still needed his mother.

CHAPTER 30

Nineteen Seventy-Nine
Rhys Jones aged 29

Neglect

As Rhys opened the front door, he noticed immediately the empty space where the pushchair lived even before he heard the sound of Katie crying. She was in the living room strapped into the playpen, which was far too small for her by then. Her little face was screwed up in abject terror, tears dripped from her closed eyes. Her mouth was like a great cavern from which came noises he'd never heard before. Rhys picked her up and held her tightly until she felt safe enough to relax her body.

'Where's Mummy?' he asked, cradling her head into his neck and feeling her tears soak his shirt, her snot over his skin. He walked with her through the house expecting to find Catherine somewhere but there was no Richard and no pushchair, so deep down he knew she wasn't there. There were plenty of unwashed dishes in the sink, the laundry basket was overflowing and toddler paraphernalia lay strewn across the floor, but no sign of life. Rhys made hot sweet tea for Katie, imagining scenarios as he worked that might have made Catherine leave their four-year-old daughter at home on her own. He called his parents and then her parents, but nobody knew where she was. Rhys called Catherine's friend, Tilly. It was the first time they'd spoken since the wedding, which made the conversation difficult but Catherine wasn't there, nor had she been there. Tilly said she would let him know if Catherine stopped by.

Panic began to rise, starting in Rhys's guts and continuing up into his chest. Surely the weather alone would stop her going out but he was not thinking rationally. Never mind the weather, what possible reason would she have to leave the house and not take her child. It was clearly planned, otherwise Katie wouldn't have been strapped into the playpen. Why did she not ask someone to babysit? How long should he wait before calling the police … the hospital? 'Where the hell are you, Catherine?' he yelled. 'What were you thinking of?' He settled Katie with toys and a sandwich, all the time feeling this volcanic anger in the pit of his stomach. As he moved about the room he caught his reflection, only it wasn't him. Jack Daw looked back ... the first time Rhys had seen him for years. He was in no mood for his shenanigans. He pointed a finger at the mirror. 'Don't you dare,' Rhys told him. 'Don't you dare appear now when I need to keep a clear head. Get back in your box!' He was angrier than he'd ever been and even while the situation was dire, Rhys actually took time to wonder if Jack was a representation of his anger.

About forty-five minutes after he'd arrived from work, the front door opened. Rhys walked slowly to the hall carrying Katie to see his beautiful Catherine smiling at him as she stored away the pushchair and took Richard out. Rhys was stunned.

'Where've you been?'

'I just had to pop to see Tilly for a minute. You know ... women's things,' she said, as though she had done nothing wrong. 'I wasn't long.'

'That's strange, because Tilly said she would call me if she saw you. She hasn't called me Catherine, so I'll ask again. Where have you been?'

'I told you. Tilly must have been distracted and forgotten.'

The first pangs of fear tightened Rhys's chest, beneath which more anger began to boil, such as he'd never known before. These days he was a passive man with infinite patience. He detested arguments, aggression and violence and would do anything to quell a storm brewing, to dampen difficult situations. At this moment though he was unsure if he could handle himself.

'You've been to see Tilly, but you didn't take Katie. Why not?'

'Well … it was raining, and she'd have to walk. I thought she'd be better staying here. I knew I wouldn't be long Rhys.'

'There's so much wrong with what you're saying Catherine. I've been home almost an hour now. That means you left our five-year-old daughter alone for more than an hour. What were you thinking of?'

'She's fine, aren't you Katie,' Catherine said, as she sauntered past into the kitchen. 'Oh. You've cleaned the kitchen. Thank you.'

He followed and stood there for a few minutes looking at her, wondering what planet she was on, how she could have thought of it never mind done it. Rhys put Katie on the floor, took Richard from Catherine and said,

'Sit down.'

'I can't. I've got dinner to cook.'

'Sit … down.' His voice sounded quite unlike him, having risen in pitch and volume. Strange to her too so that she sat with her hands laid flat on the table. The atmosphere in the small room was so strained now it was almost tangible. Rhys looked at Catherine, wondering what lay behind those perfect eyes.

'Please. The truth now.'

'I went to see a friend.'

'Who?'

'Someone you don't know.'

'OK … Why not take Katie?'

'I didn't want to take her.'

Rhys shouted the words back at her so that her smiling face changed as she admitted she was very much at fault by not keeping her daughter with her. Was she at last beginning to realise she wouldn't be able to pass this off as something and nothing?

'Did it occur to you at all that she could have come to all sorts of harm on her own?'

'But she didn't Rhys,' she said, and a snide selfish grin appeared where he thought there should have been shame. 'She's fine and I need to get dinner now,' she said, getting up.

Anger erupted through the fear in his stomach. He grabbed her arm, forcing her to sit down again.

'You're hurting me,' she yelled.

'We're getting this … whatever this is, out into the open before tonight's finished. Who's your friend?'

Catherine looked at him, into his eyes and said 'Robert.' She was playing, goading him, wanting to hurt him, to make him angry and Rhys realised she was truly enjoying this. There was no need to ask if she was having an affair … it was written all over her face. Rhys let her go, sat on the sofa and asked himself why, how, how could he not know … how long … so many questions, and Catherine calmly cooking dinner.

CHAPTER 31

Nineteen Ninety-Six
Rhys Jones Aged 46

Apple Blossom

A storm was brewing. Rhys watched the dark clouds drift by; the heat of the day having turned muggy. Summer storms had been prevalent, sunny skies giving way to a build-up of cloud by late afternoon. He had seen magnificent lightening, both fork and sheet, with an odd bolt that rushed to earth, all followed by loud thunderclaps. The crows danced about the sky, blown on the wind which gusted from the west. They were beautiful … sometimes hidden against the darkest of clouds, at others silhouetted against lighter ones. Their nests must have been clinging on for dear life. Rhys had a sudden vision of Catherine on their wedding day … pure in her white … not so pure he learned later. They married in apple blossom time, wonderful pink and white trees the backdrop to their photos. He used to sing that song to her...

I'll be with you in apple blossom time,
I'll be with you to change your name to mine,

It made her laugh ... she said he couldn't sing for toffee but it became one of their favourite songs. Rhys couldn't really remember when the nastiness began, but he did recall the first time his wife was violent towards him.

CHAPTER 32

Nineteen Seventy-Nine
Rhys Jones aged 29

Betrayal

Richard was about nine months old. Rhys arrived home from work, happy and pleased to see them ... asked Catherine if she'd had a good day. She had just made a pot of tea as he went to kiss her, the steam rising into his face. She picked up the pot, and without any hesitation threw the contents over him. Rhys was dumbfounded ... and she simply stood there as though nothing had happened. Thankfully his uniform was thick and took the heat so no harm was done ... none apart from the gulf that was clearly growing between them. The woman in front of him ... the woman he loved ... his wife ... who was she.

That was the start of what became daily physical

pain she inflicted on him. Little things often, more violent sometimes. Rhys was ashamed to admit that he was a battered husband.

They didn't talk about it for a long time … the affair … the change in Catherine … why she wanted to hurt him but one evening Catherine had punched him in the face, slammed the front door and left. He never found out why, and she hadn't commented on the superlative black bruise that blossomed behind his left eye. At work they thought it amusing … Rhys walked into a door, ha, ha.

The next day, he poured them both a glass of wine. The children were in bed so Rhys thought they might have a sensible conversation … try to sort out whatever was wrong with their marriage … with him. Catherine didn't, then or ever, say she was sorry. It was as though remorse was not in her makeup, never mind vocabulary. Rhys let her tell him, or how much of it she was willing to tell, at her own pace. Of course, he wanted to hear it all … not the details … but he wanted to know when, how and why. Most of all he wanted to be able to put things right, if it was him she was unhappy with.

She said she met him at the post office … so Rhys knew he must have seen him and immediately wondered if this man knew who he was, if he was laughing at him and his mind wandered a little though Catherine kept talking. Rhys came in when he heard her say she would wait for his window to be clear before banking her savings! She had deliberately made a play for him. Rhys wondered who this woman was opposite him, and whether she thought he really wanted to know this.

And then they met in the greengrocers one day and he stopped to talk to Katie; that he was really sweet; played with her! This man asked if she would like to go to the park with him, so he could push Katie on the swing. Rhys could feel a red mist rising, creeping up his legs which had suddenly gone cold ... reaching his neck ... misting his eyes.

He forced himself not to explode, believed that Catherine hadn't even noticed his slow deep breathing. When he managed to calm a bit, he stopped her ... asked her why she went with him ... after all she hardly knew him ... he could have been a pervert asking to play with their daughter. She looked at him and said that he'd excited her, that it had made her feel good ... someone else showing an interest in her.

Rhys asked her how long it was before the sex began and for a moment wondered if he could continue ... because she said about a month after the park. A month!! Rhys went to the kitchen for more wine, unsure if it was a wise move to have more but had it anyway. At the door, he stood and watched her, relaxed, her feet up on the seat, sipping her wine, all ladylike, as though what she'd told him meant nothing.

He wanted her to cry, to say she was sorry, to ask for his forgiveness, to tell him it would never happen again. He wanted to take her by the throat, shake some sense into her, remind her they had two young children who needed them, to tell her he needed her. He didn't though. He could never have hurt her physically. He could take it from her, yes, but not dish it out. She was too precious in spite of everything. Tears welled up in him instead, as he sat down, having half emptied the glass.

They sat there in their lovely home, almost strangers. But there was worse to come. He asked her if the affair had ended ... knowing it hadn't, because she'd just been to see him, hadn't she but a bit of him hoped that the visit was to end their relationship. Quite calmly, in almost a whisper she said, 'No. I can't,' and when he asked why not, she looked him in the eyes ... no remorse ... not even a sideways glance to let him know she felt something other than triumph. 'Because Richard is Robert's child,' she said

Because Richard is Robert's child ... If she'd stuck a knife through his heart, it would have hurt less, and in the silence that followed, Rhys felt his world spin.

Rhys made his way slowly to the club, wanting to be there, but not in the mood for the hustle and bustle, though he had agreed when John suggested it. His mind was awash with thoughts of how life was changing, had changed almost without him realising it. He followed the shout to see John holding a pint in the air and made his way to the quiet corner.

He took a long draught. The rain of the day had disappeared turning into a cold crisp winter evening, the welcome fire roaring close by and giving off so much heat he had to remove his coat and the hat he'd deliberately worn.

'Christ Almighty, Rhys. What's with the black eye and shaved head?' John said, with a smattering of bewilderment. The eye was better than it had been, not so purple or spread across the top of his cheek, but nevertheless he still looked as though he'd done a few rounds with Mohamed Ali. John peered at him like the paramedic he was, seeking damage.

'Accident or Catherine?'

'What do you think?'

'Like to know what you did to her to end up looking like that,' he said, pulling a face.

'I only need to be there these days.'

They sat for a while drinking. Rhys tried to relax, knowing that only after the second pint would he begin to achieve it. He was conscious that their friendship had changed too, John always there to support him but there was sadness that they'd lost those wonderfully comfortable times when being together meant sharing life in such a different way.

These days Rhys leant on John so much, he hardly got to talk about himself. After the second pint Rhys made the effort and asked how Marion and the children were. John said Marion was as stressed out as ever, the demands on teachers becoming greater each week. She had an interview for a deputy headship soon. That was stressing her even more. The children were good though.

Rhys listened, but didn't take much in. The words stressful and interview broke into his own thoughts and John asked what was going on, wanted to know if Jack was about. It all came out in a sort of rush then, about how his bubble burst after Richard was born. About the pot of boiling tea, how she'd been changing before, but it was gradual … so he hadn't really noticed it … then after Richard arrived, Rhys thought it was baby blues stuff and tiredness.

'What made you realise it was more?' John asked. Rhys went through it all, while his friend listened so patiently, right up to the revelation that could hardly be put into words. John thought it might be nothing more than a blip, but he told him it wasn't. Rhys spluttered the words, feeling sick as they floated on the air … Richard isn't mine.

He was so close to breaking; he couldn't look at John, who had slumped back into the chair and when Rhys managed to lift his head, John's face was as pale as his felt red. They drained their glasses. John asked how Rhys could be sure.

'Richard's blood is type O,' he said. 'Mine's AB and Catherine is A.'

Rhys hadn't needed to explain further; John knew that type O could only be from a parent with the same blood type. After a long silence, Rhys thanked John for listening, as he scraped his chair back. They shook hands, John pulled him into a tight hug and they made their way home.

CHAPTER 33

Nineteen Seventy-Nine
Rhys Jones aged 29

Shattering Glass

Rhys returned from the club to find the door locked. He shouted through the letter box, threw stones up at the bedroom window and called; tried the door again, which remained steadfastly locked, looked through the letter box a second time. If Catherine was at home, she was hiding herself and if she was out, where could she have gone at this time of night. Of course she's here, he thought. The door's locked from the inside. It was dark, the rain beginning to fall again; a light drizzle, the sort that soaks into clothes. He was tired. He went round to the back of the house.

On the lawn in the wet grass, he found his clothes, shoes, a case, all his personal things, and up at the top window, Catherine yelled at him like some tomcat screeching in the night; high pitched words slurring into themselves poured into his ears as though the bruises were not enough. He heard 'pack your bags' and stopped listening. It was no good even trying to talk to her now. He gathered up as much as he could, and went to his parents.

Rhys's mother was at the kitchen sink. It was close to their normal bedtime and his mother looked tired as he threw everything on the floor. She asked him what was wrong. Rhys apologised for the lateness; told her he needed their help, and said he'd explain later.

'Owen,' Mum called. 'Can you come?'

When his father appeared, already in his pyjamas, he quickly threw his coat on top and the three of them hurried back. Rhys picked up an old jumper he'd left in the garden, wrapped his right hand in it and punched the bottom corner of the glass pane in the back door. It took three blows to crack it and a fourth to break a hole large enough to gain entry. The sound of shattering glass echoed from the kitchen walls. Catherine appeared with the noise, staggering bleary-eyed and very drunk. Rhys asked his mother if she'd get the children and take them back to theirs for the night and said he and his father would come back in a bit and explain everything.

As his mother climbed the stairs, forcing Catherine to stay behind her, Catherine screamed abuse, reminding Rhys of that group of girls he'd first seen her with. Once Katie and Richard were safely away, Rhys cleared the glass from the floor, ignoring Catherine's shouts and fists in his back, while his father looked on aghast. He had no idea things had become so bad. He'd not seen his daughter-in-law behave like this. Once they'd boarded the panel in the door Rhys turned his attention to Catherine, now sobbing on the settee. Trying to keep calm and in control, he told her things would look better in the morning ... but didn't know who was he kidding. So tired and wrung out from alcohol, shouting, and crying, she had given in and allowed herself to be tucked up like a baby. Rhys locked the back door, and they walked home.

His parents listened while Rhys explained and by the time he'd finished, his mother was crying, his father was angry and Rhys let his head fall back against the chair. He asked if they'd mind keeping the children with them the next day, as he would take the day off and needed some space to work out a way forward. Catherine would have to sober up before he'd let her near Katie and Richard.

The following morning Rhys slid off the settee still fully clothed and aching from cramped sleep, took a long shower and went in to wake Catherine. He thought he might let her sleep, but the reality was that he had to know what last night was all about and he wanted her to be awake, whatever state she might be in. He pulled the covers back, shook her shoulders gently and called her, until she roused; told her to get up, while downstairs he cooked a full fried breakfast. It wasn't that he was hungry, more that he thought he should have a full stomach to face the day.

Rhys listened to her in the bathroom, vomiting loudly, not pleasant, but he was quite pleased she was suffering. He heard the shower running, pictured her naked, her beautiful hair flowing down her back. A pang of something squeezed his heart. He loved her despite all she did, but last night ... all his belongings thrown into the garden after being told about Richard made him realise life could not continue this way. When Catherine eventually appeared in the kitchen she was all dolled up, hair done and makeup on. She had the temerity to say she was going to work when he'd taken the day off to sort their marriage out.

Rhys could hardly believe her next words. She asked what there was to sort out; said she was going and didn't expect him to be there when she got home. Rhys laughed involuntarily at the absurdity of the idea, that she could believe it was her right to stay. He had been determined not to be angry, to try for an adult conversation but it was clearly not going to happen. When he asked her to stay and talk through the state of their marriage, she walked towards him slowly and deliberately, her face close to his, and without saying anything, landed an open-handed slap on his left cheek. It was so hard he reeled from the sting, bringing his own hand up to sooth it. When he turned to her again, she spat in his face and left.

CHAPTER 34

Nineteen Ninety-Six
Rhys Jones Aged 46

Jottings

It was evening, the sky darkening, the lamp lit. Rhys watched the last of the light fade into night; realised he hadn't eaten much at all and was hungry. Writing consumed most of his time, and remembering brought on a slight headache. As he threw together some food, his thoughts continued to invade every part of his body. He didn't know Catherine at all really ... and he thought that if he didn't know himself, how could he possibly have known who she was.

She'd told him she'd tried to be the woman he wanted her to be, but in the row that ensued after that night, Rhys learned more about the person she'd been before they met, her promiscuous behaviour so not a virgin.

Her love of night life and those friends with their coarse language. Rhys thought she should be given some credit for trying but didn't feel magnanimous. The only good thing to come from their marriage was Katie.

It had been months since Rhys last wrote anything. Revisiting that part of his life had been profoundly painful. The problem was that once it came to mind it was like it'd happened only yesterday. He had to get it down on paper before he became overtaken by it and couldn't focus. He'd forgotten how exacting writing was, it was so many years since he had to write an essay, never mind anything of this nature.

His comfort room had become more like a hiding place, dragging him back to that darkness. He didn't want to go there again. The positive aspect was that he recognised it … knew it for what it was … a dangerous place to go and that proved that he was in recovery. He made a conscious decision to close the book, books now, shut the door and do something physical. To add to the difficulties, Jack had begun to appear; a clear indication that running was necessary.

For a long time Rhys had neglected the people he loved too, staying shut up in that room all those hours, not to mention the housework and garden. John, Beth, and Al had always kept in touch by phone, but it was never the same as seeing them. The football season was just beginning. He arranged to go to a match with Al and loved it. He realised how much he missed seeing a ball being kicked from one end of a pitch to the other! Every morning, he ran as far as he could with a shorter run at night, as long as the weather permitted, and not long after he'd closed the door of Katie's room, all three of them came to dinner. It was an amazing evening. Drink, good food and lots of banter. None of them asked what he'd been doing. They knew instinctively that he needed that space to sort himself out.

Winter was harsh. Evergreen trees were bowed low with the weight of snow, which had fallen day after day for the last month. Deciduous trees looked as though someone had been round with white paint, forgetting to do all sides. It didn't matter that nothing had been done in the garden; everybody's looked the same under snow, glistening in the weak winter sun. The stream was frozen. Birds skated on it, slipped left and right as they landed; tried to find water to drink. Rhys watched a man walk along its banks with a metal rod breaking the ice for them. There were some wonderfully thoughtful people in this world. Football pitches were frozen hard, too dangerous to play on so there hadn't been any matches for the last couple of weeks. Even walking the pavements proved too much for many, especially older people who, it was reported, had broken bones from their falls.

It reminded Rhys of that first visit to the therapist, when he had introduced himself as Dr. Peter Raven. The medication he'd been taking for a few months by then, had helped enormously, but not enough for Rhys's dark mind to see the humour in his name. He had laughed about it many times since! On the table lay all the jottings gathered in the last few weeks. Scraps of paper torn from here and there to catch thoughts that might otherwise fly away if he'd taken the time to look for proper paper. It was time to sort them out and record them again.

Rhys wasn't proud of what he did ... but nonetheless he did it even though his already breaking heart was close to snapping. He still loved her. While she slapped him and spat in his face, he loved her ... while he emptied her wardrobe ... collected her personal things from the bathroom ... gathered her make up, hairbrushes and little trinkets from the dressing table, he still loved her.

There was a time when he'd have forgiven her anything and still would, if it had been just an affair. After all nobody's perfect. He must have contributed somehow to her need for the company of another man. But to have his child, and more ... to let him think all those months Richard was his. Rhys couldn't live with that. He couldn't forgive her for not talking to him about what she'd done … doubts she might have had over Richard's parentage … her obvious lack of feeling. And for months afterwards he berated himself for being such a poor husband … for not being able to keep his wife happy, and perhaps most of all, for not realising that the changes he was seeing in her were a real threat to them as a family.

CHAPTER 35

Nineteen Seventy-Nine
Rhys Jones aged 29

No Going Back

Rhys heard the sounds of the locksmith working on the front and back doors. He'd called the company first thing and they'd kindly agreed to do the job straight away. When it was finished, Rhys went to his mother to see the children and hugged them both; it wasn't poor little Richard's fault that Rhys was about to let him go. His mother said they'd both been as good as gold ... what grandmother wouldn't say that whatever had occurred. Rhys could see that his father was still tired from the night before when he came through, stretching and yawning. The first thing he said was that if Rhys needed their help, they needed to know exactly what was going on.

Well ... there was no easy way to say

everything, so Rhys told it as it had happened. All the sordid details of life over the previous months and years. They were visibly shocked, though they knew that things had not been right, but what they were hearing about their daughter-in-law now, outraged them. His father said, as gently as he could, that things like this are never one-sided and he wondered what Rhys may have done to cause the change in Catherine's behaviour. Rhys told them that if he knew he would tell them, but that she was his whole life. He loved her and didn't know why she'd done this. That was the moment Rhys gave in. He hadn't wanted his emotions to spew forth but they did. He cried like a small child in his mother's arms, his father leaving to be with Katie and Richard. He couldn't watch his son's meltdown.

'What do you intend to do?' His father asked.

Rhys explained that Catherine expected him to be gone by the time she got home.

'Surely, she's worth fighting for,' his mother said, and it did Rhys good to say how he felt out loud … for someone else to hear … to tell him if he was being unreasonable.

'If she wants to end the marriage,' Rhys said, 'I won't stand in her way, but I'm not leaving our home for another man to move in.'

It was dark when Catherine tried her key in the front door. Rhys heard it rattling as though she thought it wasn't in the lock correctly and waited a minute before opening it. She looked tired; not surprising given the amount of alcohol she'd consumed the night before. She said she hadn't expected him to be there. Rhys let that hang in the air, not moving from the foot of the stairs, three cases beside his feet, Richard in his arms.

She ignored them. Rhys was sure she'd not even noticed the cases, the pushchair out and ready to take Richard. She marched past them to the kitchen where she searched for her stash of wine and when she couldn't find it yelled,

'What've you done with it?' Rhys pointed to a box by the back door full of empty wine bottles.

'You bastard,' she yelled, only just managing to stop herself hitting him when she saw Richard's face crumple. Rhys told her they were done; marriage over; it wasn't worth saving.

His hope had been that during the day she might have thought about it all, perhaps even found a little remorse and that she would come back ready to put things right. But Rhys had suddenly come to know her better than ever before.

'Take Richard, the cases and anything else you need, and leave.'

She started crying then; asked where she would go; who would she turn to and then it occurred to her that Katie wasn't in the house.

'I'm not leaving without Katie,' she said, and refused to leave, pummelled with her fists on his back, and suddenly there were no more tears.

Rhys's father appeared round the corner of the living room door which Catherine found hysterical, shouting about him needing backup. Something about not being able to manage a poor little woman on his own. Had it not been so tragic, Rhys might have laughed.

His father went to the front door while Rhys put Richard comfortably in his pushchair. The image of his tiny face looking up at him, a windy smile playing on his lips, would be something Rhys would never forget. He kissed his forehead, said a silent farewell, and pushed him outside, his father already having moved the cases and bags. When Rhys turned round, he was pushing Catherine out of the house. With the door locked it was done. There could be no going back. Father and son sat on the bottom stair listening to Catherine bang on the door, shouting and yelling abuse. Heaven knows what the neighbours must have thought. Nobody ever commented; perhaps it's not so uncommon.

With Katie tucked up in her own bed, teary from not seeing her Mum, Rhys looked through the rest of Catherine's things, cleared everything into a large box, taped it up and left it in the hall for the morning. He sat on their bed, wondered how he'd get through the next few days, and let his body relax enough for the emotion to flood through. It was already late when the phone rang. Rhys felt inclined to leave it, didn't want to wake Katie. He knew who it would be at that hour. He listened to the angry voice of Catherine's father, ranting and raving about how he'd hurt his daughter, how she was devastated her marriage was over, how Rhys hadn't allowed her to take Katie. On and on, the voice rose in volume so that he had to hold the phone away from his ears.

Finally, when there was a break in the tirade, Rhys managed to suggest that whatever Catherine had told him, it was unlikely to be the truth, at which point her father accused Rhys of slurring his daughter's character. He almost laughed. He almost slammed the phone down. He almost left it on the table, walked away, so that her father could continue his rant to thin air. He didn't though. It had to be done before bed. He didn't want anything left till morning. Rhys told Catherine's father about her affair, that Richard wasn't his baby, that he should discuss this with his daughter before shouting at him, and afterwards there was silence on the other end. Rhys waited patiently until a quieter voice altogether said that he would be talking to his daughter.

In bed, Rhys could smell his wife on the sheets and the pillows, which he cried into with abandonment. The following day the bedding was removed. He didn't want to be reminded of this woman who was not who he thought she was.

CHAPTER 36

Nineteen Ninety-Six
Rhys Jones Aged 46

Anniversary

During the first few months Rhys missed his wife but looking after Katie and a vastly different lifestyle to organise, he was always busy. The new role as an Inspector meant he continued to work shifts and take advantage of overtime. His family were amazingly supportive, not just with Katie, but with making sure he had company, and didn't dwell on things. They became closer during that time. He had always been close to Beth because they'd grown up together, but he found a new and amazing friend in his brother. Al helped him sort out loads of money problems, the bank, the mortgage, and though Rhys waited the mandatory two years before filing for divorce, it was still a painful experience, especially when Catherine sought custody of Katie. Al had been his rock.

With his parent's help, Rhys managed to negotiate the uncertain path of raising a child on his own, not always easy, and often frowned upon, but nonetheless, very satisfying. Beth had come to the rescue with the onset of adolescence. She was amazing, having Katie to stay so she could talk to her about periods, boyfriends, and pregnancy.

Beth owned her own hair salon by then, giving her time to take Katie shopping for clothes and girly things Rhys knew little about. Katie loved her aunt, their relationship more than aunt and niece. Beth had become a mother figure for her, Catherine flatly refusing to have anything to do with her.

Rhys often saw Catherine out and about in Hereford. Sometimes she'd have Richard with her, the child growing up. Catherine's mother walked with her on occasion and over the last few years she was seen with a man. Robert maybe, somebody else she'd met perhaps. At first Rhys wanted to tell this man about Catherine, about how she'd put on a persona to lure him, for that's how he saw it. He wished he could warn whoever he was of impending change, Catherine's true character biding time until she had what she wanted and then wanted more.

It was all so long ago, and yet sitting there writing about it, it might as well have been yesterday. Some things in life become so imprinted in the mind, they're impossible to erase. Lately Rhys had been thinking about love; not for himself. He would never remarry. He lost faith in himself a long time ago. More importantly perhaps, he didn't feel he could trust women. There must be so many wonderful women out there but what do they hide, he wondered. Rhys didn't think he could ever give himself to someone so completely now. He began to question his perception of love; what he meant when he said those three words; what any of us meant when we said, I love you. How could it be that he still loved Catherine but wasn't able to live with her? Surely love should be able to surmount anything. Rhys accepted that there were many different types of love, all of them valid in their own right, but had come to the conclusion that there was only one abiding love; one that was unconditional, that endured whatever life threw at it; one that was unquestionably powerful until one's breath ran out. That had to be the love a parent had for a child.

Rhys was there when Katie was born, his excitement tempered by Catherine's pain. It seemed to him in that moment life was full of paradoxes. The miracle of birth versus the pain of enabling it. He wanted to take her pain to allow her the luxury of knowing this wonder as he did. He watched as Katie's head emerged, the fingers of his left-hand cracking under Catherine's hold. He saw their baby's screwed up little face as the rest of her body slithered onto the bed and asked himself how something like this tiny new life could be so beautiful amidst all the gore of blood, and mucus.

From that single moment, his life changed, his heart grew tenfold. His future would always be centred on his family. He felt the same when Richard was born, but he'd never been his, and though he felt love for him, it had stayed in the past; remained with him at just a few months old. If Rhys believed in God or anything spiritual, he'd pray that Richard knew who his father was.

Rhys was unsure how his day would go. It was an anniversary; one which gave him no pleasure, but one that he could not avoid, and would never be able to. He had dreaded having to write about it, putting it off, always thinking of something else that needed doing but it must be faced; he needed to do it to get his life back on track. As if that wasn't enough, the weather had chosen the day to match his mood. Water droplets ran down the window, joined up and streamed towards the sill. There was no wind, so it came from the sky in perpendicular lines, fine and almost feathery. Everything was grey out there. Rhys put the lamp on to cheer the room and braced himself, picked up the pen and started on a blank page.

CHAPTER 37

Nineteen Ninety-Two
Rhys Jones aged 42

A Bright Full Moon

Rhys waved Katie and his mother and father off to wherever they were going. They had refused to tell him where it was, not wanting him to let it slip. The surprise outing was for Katie's birthday, although it was several months past it, so they could take advantage of better weather. As Rhys closed the front door, he pondered on how Katie had become a teenager. Thirteen! She was a beautiful young girl, her auburn hair kept short while she was a child, but then grown longer and curlier, and he saw Catherine in her every day.

At the end of his shift, the sky dark, and studded with stars, a full moon cast shadows in the garden, where he sat with a snack. It smiled down at him. He remembered the night when they'd all stayed up to watch the first man step onto it. All those years ago. He remembered too, the night he held Katie in his arms, she'd have been about six then, when she'd had a nightmare, and it was warm and balmy in the garden. He'd shown her the bright full moon, the man living in it, and it had made her laugh, her giggling reaching out into the night while she pointed a tiny hand towards the sky.

Katie was staying with Mum and Dad that night, as they would be home late, which gave Rhys time to enjoy the silence, a half pint and to read more of the paper. He didn't hear the phone at first, its ring not reaching the garden. It was Al, asking if they'd arrived home and were at his. He said they weren't but maybe were stuck in traffic or something. It was already quite late. Al was worried; it wasn't like Dad, he said, not letting them know, and Rhys had to agree. He suggested waiting another half hour, and to call again if they weren't home.

Rhys hadn't been back in the chair more than a few minutes after Al's call, when there was loud insistent banging on the front door. On the step were two policemen. They held their helmets in their hands, as they sat on the sofa, twisting them in unison, as if it was the prelude to some dance. One of them was short, about Rhys's height, but broader in the shoulders. He had black hair in the typical cut of his vocation. He was young, perhaps not very experienced. His colleague was quite the opposite, tall and stick thin, considerably older. It was him who looked at Rhys with compassionate eyes and said there'd been an accident.

Rhys could hear Beth sobbing before he'd closed the front door of their parents' home. She was crying onto Al's shoulder. He wrapped his arms around them both. People were moving about in the kitchen. He could hear water running, a rattle of cups and whispered conversation as though far off in the distance. He couldn't grasp the situation, his thoughts like a highway of night traffic, zipping along the road so fast he was unable to hold onto a single one. A policeman came through with a tray of sweet tea and a plate of biscuits, which he made them eat for the shock, and then they all left, leaving details of how to contact them.

Alone in the family home, that only yesterday had buzzed with activity, the only sound now, the whirr of electricity in the background, none of them knew what to do. Beth wandered about aimlessly, touched things, hugged things and was generally unaware of her brothers. Rhys felt he was drowning, the well so deep he might not survive. It was as though someone had flicked a switch. Their parents, and his beautiful young daughter caught in a nightmare event he believed they would never recover from.

CHAPTER 38

Nineteen Ninety-Two
Rhys Jones aged 42

Procession of Coffins

It was a long time before they knew the truth of it … that their father had suffered a massive and unexplained heart attack. He'd never had any heart problems before so how could he know that driving would be unsafe? The police told them that they would all have died instantaneously … and whether true or not, it's what they wanted to believe. Afterwards, once the shock had worn off there was so much to do that none of them had really grieved properly, and it was just a month later, that they gathered at the local church where their parents and Rhys's little girl were buried.

Al and Rhys each held onto one of Beth's

hands, their heads turning to watch the slow procession of three coffins make their way up the central aisle. The small church in Credenhill was overflowing with family and friends. Katie's school had allowed her classmates the day off to attend. Some were with parents, others in groups on their own. As he swept the congregation, Rhys felt an overwhelming sense of pride that Katie had been such a popular girl, a pride swiftly replaced by grief as her coffin passed them. Around the graves they could only weep as their family were lowered slowly into the ground, the sound of earth hitting wood barely audible. People began to move away until only they remained to say those final farewells.

The house in Dovecote Lane was, by contrast, almost merry, another of life's paradoxes. Relatives and friends, not having seen each other for years, catching up, the bustle of refilling glasses and refuelling stomachs uppermost in their minds. It was good to keep busy. They chatted to people they, or at least Rhys had, not known until that day, relations never met and some form of family clarity occurred as little pieces of jigsaw fell into place. Everyone seemed to have a camera. Everyone wanted to record this huge, unexpected gathering. Groups were formed one after another, until most people would eventually appear in several pictures. In years to come, albums would be taken out, and they would relive the day with comments about how young so and so was then, or she was beautiful even as a youngster, or those poor children, losing their whole family like that.

When all the guests had departed, and the resulting mess considered, it was decided to leave everything until the morning. Beth promised to arrive early. They sat with full glasses, Beth, and Al with their arms round Rhys's shoulders. They toasted their parents and Katie.

CHAPTER 39

Nineteen Ninety-Four
Rhys Jones aged 44

Old Toys and Furniture

To be at home after all that was intolerable. Even though John visited regularly, Beth and Al rang every day and Rhys worked plenty of overtime to keep him occupied, the house had become nothing more than bricks and mortar. The life had gone out of it. Returning to an empty place, sapped his energy as though Katie had left some residual part of herself within its walls, pulling him towards her. Rhys often sat in her bedroom knowing he ought to do something with it but unable to fathom what it should be. In the end Beth helped. Together they went through Katie's things, sorted what might be useful for her cousins or her friends, and Rhys wanted Beth to have something in memory of her niece.

All Katie's photographs, her schoolwork, and certificates, were kept with a few other bits and pieces he knew she had treasured. Beth chose something for Al to keep should he want it, and the rest was either given or thrown away.

Rhys didn't know how he felt once it was done. In a sense it was like a betrayal, as though he'd banished Katie, like she had no place there. Another part of him knew that life must move on, that he couldn't live as if nothing had changed, and that Katie would always be with him even if her earthly things were not.

'Decorate the room.' Beth had told him. 'Katie's in all our hearts, Rhys. You don't need this room as a shrine to her. Get Al over to help.'

Rhys took her advice, but it wasn't without its own pain. He made it into the room he now wrote in, sat in, looked out of the window from, and generally lived his life in. It had become a cherished space, one in which he retired to after dinner, a place where he could watch life go by, people walking their dogs, lovers strolling arm in arm, and children playing football. It's the only part of the house where Katie had a presence. Somehow her spirit lingered. Sometimes Rhys used to think she wanted to send a message, but of course he didn't believe in such things. Still, it pleased him to feel her there whether it was in his head or otherwise.

When it came to the family home the task seemed considerably easier. For a start time had elapsed, the grieving process had taken its natural course, and they worked together. None of them were financially stretched, so it had been agreed that Al would stay in the home for as long as he wanted, and it was a further two years before he made the decision to move into something smaller. The house in Dovecote Lane was put on the market.

The process of clearing the old home had become a necessity, and they decided to begin at the very top, the loft, and work their way down. Al said it made sense ... you know, let the dirt fall, and clean everything up later. There was little room to stand in the loft, never mind take all three of them, the entire space being cluttered with cases, boxes, files ... you name it, it was up there.

Old pieces of furniture. Chairs, a table, standard lamps, kitchen equipment, all vied for space. There was even an old rocking horse on the far side, just visible by the top of its head and mane, and when Rhys had found a way to it, he remembered the horse being downstairs when they were young. He recalled rocking Beth backwards and forwards on it, even though he had not been much bigger than her. Behind the horse, almost thrown rather than stacked, were a load of childrens' toys, as if their parents hadn't been able to throw them away. Rhys called Beth and Al over to see an old tricycle, a push-a-long dog and a doll's pram.

'Look what they've kept all these years,' he said, in disbelief.

'I always wondered where that had gone,' Beth said. 'I looked for it when I was pregnant and they said nothing about it being in the loft.'

Everything they touched was covered in a film of dust, cobwebs flowing from one item to another, and they fell from the beams to mingle together on almost all the available space. Beth was not amused. Al and Rhys brushed them aside to see the treasures unmasked. It was as though that corner of the loft had been a memorial to their childhoods, stored away and then forgotten.

They took those down first, Rhys standing at the bottom of the ladders to accept what Al squeezed through the hatch, while Beth trundled up and downstairs putting them in the conservatory for later inspection. It was late in the evening by the time they'd finished, but at least it was done, and they stood together surveying the clutter that now engulfed the downstairs rooms. They decided to continue the next morning.

Rhys hadn't been home long, maybe an hour, when the phone rang. Al said he'd been cleaning some of the filth and found a number of boxes with their names written on. By the time he had finished searching, he'd discovered seven boxes for each of them, named and numbered.

'Typical Mum,' he said. 'She might have been a hoarder, but she was an organised one.'

Over the next few days, they sorted all that could be discarded, filling a skip hired for the purpose. There was little disagreement, most things being old-fashioned and not worthy of modern homes. Beth decided she would like to have two old chairs reupholstered and use them herself. She remembered them from her childhood, knew them to be comfortable, and thought she would feel close to their parents when she sat in them.

CHAPTER 40

Nineteen Ninety-Six
Rhys Jones Aged 46

The Loft Find

Winter of 1996 rolled over into spring, unwilling to release its hold on the land. Snow in April, frosts in May, the sun playing hide and seek with ominous clouds that burst forth soaking already waterlogged ground. Rhys couldn't remember a year like it for such prolonged cold weather and yet the plants Catherine had tended all those years ago were stronger than ever, spreading their colour across the garden in defiance.

There was plenty of warmth in the sun, as might be expected for the time of year, but the constant north wind was bitter, and Rhys was still wearing jumpers. He smiled, looking down at the fairisle one his mother had knitted

... smiled at the thought of her watching Val Doonican on television, losing herself in his voice, and attempting to recreate some of his famous jumpers.

For some reason Rhys couldn't fathom, his thoughts had taken him to some other, philosophical place the other day. Perhaps he'd been thinking about Katie, or his parents, but anyhow it occurred to him that the human brain was a remarkable organ. Beyond what it does every minute of every day its resilience was quite awesome. It could deal with the deepest of grief, the fear of a disappearing future, the feeling that life can't get any worse, and yet it bounced back. It even tricked us into believing we could laugh ... have fun ... be ordinary. The medication he'd been on since the shoe episode had played a part in that, but he thought that was the point really. When he had wanted to stop taking it, his doctor had said that if he'd broken a leg, he wouldn't refuse to have it plastered ... wouldn't be ashamed of it ... so, his mind was broken ... it's nothing to be ashamed of ... it's not working properly ... think of the medication as the mind's plaster ... OK.

Rhys had made the decision to move into something smaller, rather like Al had. It hadn't been easy, but then when was it ever going to be and he believed it was time to move on. He'd taken a week's holiday to sort the house out hoping that the sale would go through quickly.

The last thing he wanted was a long-protracted exchange and all the hassle that would involve. Climbing the steps into the loft and flicking the light switch was like being in his parent's loft again. His was much the same, full of this and that, life's forgotten dreams, childhood toys, and those boxes, the ones he'd taken from Dovecote Lane and not thought of since. He took them to the living room, set them out in order wanting to rip them open, but not being quite ready for the secrets he thought they might hold, so made lunch and stared at them as he ate.

Rhys assumed they contained his childhood. Be good to work backwards, he thought. In the first four, his school days spilled out across the floor, reports, certificates, football memorabilia. Each contained a portion of his life aged from five to eighteen. There were photographs of sports days which, when put side by side, evidenced his physical growth and there were exercise books showing educational progress. Rhys was fascinated by the intimate history discovered; sat for hours reading. He looked at teachers' names, at the unauthorised doodles he'd made in margins, and at essay marks with comments. Rhys had every intention of discarding what was no longer needed but by the evening everything had been returned to the boxes, each one resealed and set aside. He clearly wasn't ready to throw away the past. He phoned Al and they spent the evening reminiscing and laughing about their respective attic finds. It was the best day they'd both had for a long time.

Early the following day, Rhys was ready to look through those last three boxes before going back to the loft. The day was brighter. The garden needed tidying first. It would not do for it to look a mess should prospective buyers be round. Before he realised it, almost three hours had passed. It had been therapeutic seeing the borders neat, the lawn cut and edged and the few pots he'd planted, rearranged. He'd even washed the table and chairs. It was by no means perfect, but then he was not a gardener.

In box number three, Rhys discovered a multicoloured array of toys; wooden trains, metal cars, a rather sad looking dog, its ears chewed, and its fur matted in places. He wondered why on earth his parents had kept it for so long, never mind thought it would be something Rhys would want in adulthood, but then he had an image of sitting up in bed in hospital, feeling very poorly, and his father visiting with a soft toy dog. It made him smile and setting the toy aside, he tipped up the box to release all the others. He decided not to keep the rest, amusingly only the dog having any real meaning. Everything else would be going to charity or the bin.

Box number two held toys as well, but toys

from earlier childhood, building blocks, alphabet letters, rattles and so forth. One of the rattles was silver, a longish handle with a ball at the top which was decorated with pierced work. When he shook it, the sound was a little tinny, and he wondered how old it was, for it appeared to be much older than the other things. Could it have been something handed down? Or perhaps a christening gift. Wherever it originated, he would hang on to it but most of the contents went the way of box three.

The last one was much smaller, almost not a box at all, more a deep manuscript sized container. Peering inside, Rhys saw something woolen spread across the top, neatly folded, once white but now yellow in places with age. A beautiful shawl revealed itself, an intricate pattern at its centre, it was knitted in fine thread with a wide equally intricate edging. It was like filigree, the sort of thing women knitted for new babies back in the day. Folding it carefully he laid it on the floor, and took out a handful of baby clothes, mostly white with some blue here and there; tiny jackets and cardigans, bonnets and mittens, charming booties, among sets of matching clothes. He assumed them to have been his. Then there was a little pair of sheepskin slippers, that tied with leather at the ankle, but he couldn't imagine how they would have looked.

Catherine had kept nothing like this of Katie's

baby days, and it made him realise how much his mother must have treasured them. Rhys was all fingers and thumbs trying to fold them neatly. In the end he gave up and simply laid them on the shawl.

Beneath all this, Rhys found a birth certificate folded in three which he assumed to be the original. He had only ever had a copy because his mother had told him his birth certificate had been lost, yet there it was. She must have known it to be in the box. Maybe it is possible to forget such a thing.

Laying this aside, he found a photograph with a slip of paper on top. It was of a new-born baby perhaps only a few days old, tightly wrapped in a blanket, or a shawl. The picture was old, out of focus, the colours faded, and it was difficult to make out any detail. The piece of paper was a fragment clearly torn from a larger sheet. Like the shawl, it had yellowed and browned with age. It bore some writing but that was illegible, perhaps water damaged or simply faded by time. Anyhow it was indecipherable.

When Rhys looked closely, this little scrap of paper was clearly the same piece of paper which had been pinned to the baby's blanket in the photograph. It still had the now rusty pin in it. He couldn't begin to think of how this was part of his life. Kneeling on the floor for most of the afternoon had begun to affect the circulation in his legs, so he stood gingerly, placed the picture and paper on the table, and put the kettle on. By the time coffee was made, a sandwich to go with it, and a piece of stale cake found in the tin, Rhys was at the dining room table by the back window.

It occurred to him that perhaps this child was one which didn't survive, maybe between Al and himself. He didn't bother looking further into the box, because he was intrigued as to why the photo should have been stored with his things.

He rang Al. Asked him if there'd been a baby born between the two of them, perhaps one that died, but Al wasn't aware of any other children. He thought if there had been they would all know about it. Rhys described what he had found, said it was a bit perplexing and told Al about the photo. Al said he couldn't begin to explain.

It had occurred to Rhys that he hadn't looked at the back of the picture and wondered if there was anything written there to give them a clue. Al held on while he looked. When he turned it over, Rhys felt a rush of something he couldn't easily identify. Returning to the phone, he told Al it was a photo of himself, that his name was written on the back, but couldn't understand what that bit of paper meant. Al had no idea either and offered to come over so that they could look at it together.

Al shut the back door. Rhys was making a pot

of coffee and laying out biscuits. Al carried the cups through and said he thought there must be some simple explanation for it, but Rhys wasn't convinced. It felt wrong, weird; the sort of discovery you don't want to make, and he was torn between wanting to find out about it and wishing he hadn't opened the box.

'Do you remember that TV game show, where contestants had to decide between the prizes they'd already won, and opening a box which could contain a fortune?' Rhys asked. 'Was it Hughie Green, or perhaps Michael Miles ...? I can't remember now.'

'Michael Miles,' Al said.

'Anyway, that's how all this feels to me. I opted to open the box ... to find something lovely ... but what I got was a day trip to Blackpool!' Rhys said. 'Al, do you remember me being born?'

'No. I was sent to stay with the Gramps in Wales. When I got home you were here.'

'What about Mum being pregnant?'

'Rhys ... I was only ten. In those days ten-year-old kids didn't even know what pregnant meant. I just did as I was told. I do remember Mum and Dad going away somewhere and then there you were ... a tiny bundle of arms and legs. They said you were my new baby brother. I didn't question it.'

Rhys was scared, looked in the box and found an envelope; withdrew it. It was quite thick and clearly old, but nothing was written on the outside to hint at its contents. He had a terrible, inexplicable feeling. Why would the photograph have this piece of paper pinned to the shawl? It was bizarre. Who pins paper to a baby? Somewhere deep inside, his guts had twisted; knotted like the worst of all stomach cramps, and he told Al he knew he had to open that envelope. It couldn't just be packed away again, but it was scaring him. Al put his hand on his brother's arm, and said he'd do it with him

CHAPTER 41

Nineteen Ninety-Six
Rhys Jones Aged 46

The Defining Moment

A weak smile played on his lips as Rhys opened the seal with the silver letter opener he'd been given by his parents as a fortieth birthday present. Tentatively, he pulled out the contents, comprising a sheaf of papers in a foolscap folder. As he opened the card cover, his stomach somersaulted. He rushed to the bathroom, just making it, hugged the toilet bowl when his knees buckled. Rhys was in that position for a while before he felt strong enough to stand. He cleaned up, washed his face, sprayed a bit of aftershave on himself and round the room, and ventured downstairs again, to find Al looking at it, his face pale.

'I didn't know what to think when you phoned

me,' Al said. 'Looking at this I'm not surprised you've been throwing up.'

Rhys thought it strange how some conversations seemed to be imprinted on the mind word for word, after years of not really thinking about them, while others much more important at the time disappear, like the autumn mist when the sun comes out. Rhys spoke softly, almost to himself rather than Al and tears welled into the corners of his eyes, over the edges, to make their way across his cheeks.

'I'm adopted. I'm not your brother. Beth's not my sister. Mum and Dad weren't my parents,' Rhys said, his heart constricting.

'How could they do this Al? How could they not have told me … us? How could they leave me to find out like this?'

Al drew him into an embrace, a rare hug.

'I don't know. Maybe we should look at these documents together,' Al said. 'You've had a shock … I reckon there'll be more to come.'

'Probably. I don't think I can go through these on my own.

'What about Beth?' Al asked. 'Do you think we should get her here as well? We've always done things together since Mum and Dad died. It's not late; still early evening, and I'm sure she'd want to be here.'

While Al made the call Rhys went out to the garden. The evening was still warm, daylight not having faded so the sun, a ball of fire, warmed his back as he gazed at the morning's gardening efforts. Rose scent filled the air, and drifted on the faint breeze, aromas of food, being cooked in surrounding homes found his nose. It reminded him that he hadn't eaten properly all day, and that his stomach was now completely empty. In the freezer he found some sausage rolls and ice cream, and put the oven on to heat, as Al appeared in the kitchen.

'Beth's on her way,' he said, and seeing the packet on the worktop added, 'my favourite snack. Have you had anything like a proper meal lately?'

'Not really, but the smell of food in the garden made me suddenly hungry. Can you get plates and bowls out? There's ice cream to follow.'

Beth arrived as the hot snack was being served. They saw her tear-stained face as she approached, hugged and kissed them both and then blew her nose.

'I don't know what to say. I've been thinking about it on the way over, and can't believe it,' she said, taking a chair at the table.

'I don't understand how Mum and Dad could do something like this.'

'We've waited for you so we can look at the paperwork together but first, what do you think of this?' Rhys said, passing the photograph and slip of paper.

'Oh my God! This poor little babe can't be you Rhys. There must be a mistake. I can't believe this is you; can't believe that Mum and Dad lived their lives pretending. Even worse, that they allowed you to grow up in ignorance.'

'Look, let's have this food. Al, will you open a bottle? I think I need to know everything tonight, so let's get started.'

Rhys was completely calm, as if the task was unrelated to him, like a work project or something. He had a quick flick through the documents, noting that there were letters, certificates, and more photographs. The top letter was from the Liverpool Foundling Society and dated April fourteenth Nineteen Fifty. He read it out loud.

"Dear Mr. and Mrs. Jones,

I write to confirm that the baby boy you will adopt, has arrived here at our institution, where he will be well looked after until you are able to collect him.

We find him to be a very calm child with a good appetite. He sleeps well, sometimes all night. Our staff are quite taken with him, but we know he will find a good home with you, so pray only for his safe keeping.

Please arrange a day for your travel and inform me of when to expect you.

Yours sincerely,
Sister Mary"

'It's true then,' said Beth, fresh tears dripping

from her chin.

The next letter was dated, twenty-eighth March nineteen fifty.

"Dear Mr. and Mrs. Jones,

Further to our previous conversation regarding your desire to adopt a child, I write to inform you that we have a foundling baby of about three weeks old, a boy in need of a stable home. The Board here have agreed that you would be suitable parents.

We know nothing about him, found as he was on the step of our main entrance, save that he was well wrapped against the cold, and had clearly been well looked after during his first few days. A photograph is included.

We are anxious to find a place for him while he is still able to bond with new parents. If you decide to go ahead, the child will be taken to our sister institution, in Liverpool, where the necessary documents will be organised for your signatures.

Please let me know as soon as possible, so that final arrangements can be made.

Yours sincerely,
Sister Monica"

Rhys held up his empty glass for more liquid courage and watched Al measure out full measures for them all. He sat back in the chair exhausted, yet still felt a strange calmness. Were those letters really about him? Was there some huge mistake here? Could it be some dark joke?

Evening had drawn in while they'd been reading, through the window a cloudless sky and a full moon were visible in the half-light. Everything seemed cloaked in a stillness, as though the world had stopped, as though Rhys was looking at himself from a far distant place reminding him of those days when Jack Daw accompanied him. This was unreal. Rhys jumped as Al's hand gripped his arm.

'You alright?'

'Yes. Come on, finish these sausage rolls, Beth?' Almost chirpy he was. Can shock do things like that? Beth took one and he saw the look she gave Al. A look that said, he's not alright, is he? Al shook his head. Beth stretched and yawned, shifting her position on the chair.

'You're tired, Beth,' said Al. 'Want to go home?'

'Difficult day at the salon. Had to fire a girl,' she said, with obvious sadness.

Beth explained that one of her girls had snipped a client's ear, not for the first time either. Quite rightly she said she couldn't afford to lose clients because the girl gossiped too much and didn't concentrate enough. There was a lull before Beth said, with some renewed vigour, 'Wait a minute. What were the dates on those letters, Rhys?'

'Er … fourteenth of April and er … twenty eighth of March.'

'And your birthday is…?'

'May second.' They looked at each other,

puzzlement furrowing their brows.

'It can't be you then,' Beth said.

'Who else would it be? Why would all this be in my box? Why would the photo have my name on the back?'

'What else is in the paperwork, Rhys?' Al asked.

Looking through again, Rhys found certificates. One showing the adoption and two birth certificates.

'Oh God. Look here.' He spread them out on the table so they could see.

The adoption certificate was quite straight forward, showing that a baby, but with no information regarding birth parents, was adopted on May second, Nineteen Fifty by Mr. and Mrs. Owen Jones. Their signatures appeared at the bottom, and the document was dated. Of the two birth certificates, one was completed with only the words "Foundling," but also stating a birth date, "about March fourth nineteen fifty". The other was a recognisable British Birth Certificate, exactly the same as the one in the box and the one Rhys had always known. The most remarkable aspect of each document was that any reference to place had been blacked out, apart from Liverpool.

'Rhys, what're you thinking?' Al asked.

'Hm … don't you think it's strange that all the headings have blacked out information; that only Liverpool has been left? Why would they have done that? For what purpose? And ... I think perhaps this birth certificate is fake. What do you think?' They both agreed.

'Do you think Mum and Dad would have had anything to do with faking it?' asked Beth, not wanting to, but nevertheless thinking the worst of her parents.

'Maybe it was just general practice then. A lot of mothers had their children taken from them, and unmarried mothers in those days weren't treated well,' Al said.

A heavy blanket of silence fell over the room, each of them having turned inside themselves; to their own thoughts; to this new knowledge of the parents they had loved and trusted; to what this discovery meant for them; to how they would move on. To whether or not anything had really changed. Beth rubbed her eyes, sore from the crying, stood and said, 'I think I must go home. I'm so tired. We'll talk more tomorrow, shall we?' They stood and gave her a hug.

'We'll be fine,' said Al. 'I'm staying tonight.'

'Thanks for being here,' Rhys said. 'It means a lot to me that I didn't have to do this on my own.'

With Beth gone, Al and Rhys relaxed on the sofa, their backsides aching from long hours spent on dining chairs. Rhys made coffee for himself and filled Al's glass again. Between them they finished the last of the sausage rolls. The silence was not particularly comfortable, neither really knowing how to start the next conversation. Al was a bit wired from the evening's revelations, and eventually turned to his brother and said,

'Whatever's happened here tonight Rhys, you are still our brother. Nothing has changed for me and Beth.'

Rhys started to say that he felt the same way but trailed off ... his sentence not quite formulated enough to express. Al waited a beat before asking,

'But?

'But it has changed Al. It's changed big time for me, hasn't it. I don't even know when I was born, never mind where. I don't understand why I feel so calm.'

'It's probably the shock ... your head not knowing how to react. Of course I don't know anything about these things but perhaps it needs digesting ... sinking in so your mind's able to sort out the jumble. Heaven knows I feel like that, so you must surely.'

'Perhaps I'll feel different in the morning. Thanks for staying. Do you want a shower first?

'No. Think you should while I'm up ... just in case.

Rhys slid between the sheets, crisp cotton so that whatever time of year, he received a cooling sensation. He lay on his back, snuggled his head into the pillow, and tried to steady what had become erratic breathing. He rarely had difficulty sleeping, but when he did, he knew how to relax the body, shut out any lingering thoughts. That night was different. He lay there for what felt like half an hour, willing his limbs to feel heavy, telling his brain to stop thinking but he was still wide awake despite the tiredness. He tried turning onto one side and curling into a ball. That did not work. His mind simply kept filling up; so many questions; so many outlandish hypotheses.

Rhys sat up, thrashed the pillows about a little, and leant against them. Al was right about his thoughts being jumbled. There seemed to be no rhyme nor reason for the way they flashed about. One second it was the mere fact of having been adopted, the next that his birthday was not his birthday at all. What was it all about? Rhys got out of bed and walked around the room. Finding no consolation he went through to Katie's room, sat in his favourite chair and looked out of the window. The moon had moved round sending shadows to various parts of the garden. It was soothing to watch it, that man up there, that amazing resemblance to a human face which had fascinated him from a young age. He thought of Katie and realised that she hadn't been related to the family either, his family, this family.

Rhys must have drifted into sleep, because the next morning he remembered dreaming of a wonderful holiday with his parents, when he and Al had raced as high up Cadre Idris as they could before collapsing on the soft grass between rocky outcrops. He was still in Katie's room, his body aching from lack of proper sleep and awkward positions. He stood, stretched the old limbs, and cleared the sleep from his eyes before taking a shower.

Rhys could hear Al downstairs in the kitchen, water running, the sound of crockery being stored away, and above the sounds, his nose detected the rich aroma of fried breakfast. It was half past eight by the time he sat at the table. Al presented an overfull plate of bacon, eggs, mushrooms, and fried bread, sat opposite and tucked into the fare. Rhys must have been staring at it because Al chided him, told him to get on with it, said he needed it to get him off to a good start!

Al had cleared away last night's dishes, so there was little for Rhys to do. Shame really as he needed something to keep him occupied.

'How are you feeling?'

'Had a sleepless night, so many questions. Think you're right about it not sinking in. Don't know how I'm feeling to be honest. But ... I have made a decision. I'm going to take the house off the market for a while; not sure I could cope with all that now.'

'I think that's a wise move. There's something I need to do at home. Do you mind if I go after breakfast? Beth and I are only a phone call away should you need us.'

'That's fine. I appreciate your help. I'll have a closer look at the paperwork later.'

CHAPTER 42

Nineteen Ninety-Six
Rhys Jones Aged 46

Shoe Polish

Alone in the house, Rhys wandered aimlessly from room to room, having no notion of how he felt, or what to do. He fidgeted with things, moved small objects from one place to another, wiped his fingers along the bookcase, and noted how much dust had accumulated. Sunshine from the previous day had turned to rain, multicoloured clouds blew from the East and flower heads, which only the day before had stood to attention, now bowed as though giving thanks for their long-awaited drink.

Al had put the documents back into the box on the small coffee table. Rhys wondered if he really needed to look at them again. They would surely not tell a different story just because it was a different day, and after all, he knew only too well what they said. There was no need for confirmation to see it all in print again. Yesterday morning he'd been brother to Al and Beth. Today he wasn't. Then who was he? Who was he really? It wasn't the first time he'd asked himself the question, but it was the first time he realised he seriously didn't know who he was. Rhys had to know. For forty-six years he'd believed himself to be Rhys Jones. He'd been a son to parents who suddenly were not his parents. He couldn't fathom it. He was a bundle of conflicting feelings and yet was unable to give them words.

Without thinking about it, Rhys removed all the furniture from the dining room, hoovered the large carpet that filled all but a small edge, emptied the hoover, and did it again. He prepared a bucket of soapy water and scrubbed. Colours gradually returned to those he'd known when he'd first purchased it. When it was done, he turned the carpet through a semi-circle, retrieved the furniture, and restored the room. It had taken most of the day.

With so little sleep the effects of both the physical work and the mental anguish caught up with him. The exercise had not had any calming effect, his body and mind still jittery. Rhys made a pot of coffee; the answer to so many tricky situations, sat at the table and looked at the box. No, he decided. He didn't want to look at it unless he really needed to, but he had to know. In procrastinating he was simply putting off the inevitable, yet part of him said that it still might just go away, that life would be normal again tomorrow, that he would wake up having had a nightmare.

When the sun began to appear through what had been continuous cloud, Rhys went for a walk. It promised to be a fine evening, but where he went, he couldn't have said by the time he reached home. He only knew he'd been out for an hour, probably aimlessly walking the streets, across the fields at the back, perhaps into areas of the village he rarely visited. Then he remembered he hadn't contacted the estate agent and left a note on the kitchen worktop to do first thing in the morning.

That night Rhys managed a good few hours of rest. On Saturday his body felt better. He called the estate agent as soon as they opened. At least one positive thing accomplished. The week's holiday had achieved nothing, and he still didn't really understand how he was feeling, but he had to consider work on Monday morning. Not quite knowing what to do first he decided to clean his shoes. He collected them all, laid them out on newspaper in the kitchen, and fetched the box from the cupboard beneath the sink. It was the routine, something his father had always done; start with the black, they take longer to shine than the others. Two pairs had been completed when there was a knock on the front door. It was John. Back in the kitchen, Rhys put the kettle on while John found an empty chair to sit on.

'Can't believe you're doing something so mundane,' he said. 'How are you?'

'It's good to see you.' It was all Rhys could think to say.

'Al told me,' he said.

'I'm pleased he did because I wouldn't have known how to tell you.'

Rhys put coffee on the table, sat opposite his friend and said, 'I don't know where I am to be truthful; don't know why I'm doing this.' He pointed to the shoes.

'I think you're still in shock. Do you fancy a beer, or maybe a bite to eat?'

'Honestly, John, I don't feel very sociable today. Think I'll stay here and mooch about.'

'Well ... I'm thinking of you. You know where I am if you need anything.'

'You've always been a good mate. You've been my only mate! I'll see you soon ... and thanks, John. I really do appreciate you.'

Rhys went back to the task, plastered the brush with polish, and smeared it over the next shoe. He looked in horror, aghast at the swathe of thick black polish covering his new tan shoe. In that instant, everything changed. Rhys's life imploded.

He fell to the floor, salty tears ran down his face, dripped on the tiles; a darkness so thick, he imagined being underground, buried deep in the earth. No light, no air to breathe. He knew his arms were wrapped round his head, perhaps instinctively protective of it, and he could feel himself rocking backwards and forwards. An unearthly sound filled the kitchen. A wail he didn't recognise at first as coming from his own body.

CHAPTER 43

Nineteen Ninety-Seven
Rhys Jones Aged 47

No Joy

After that, Rhys locked himself away from life ... away from Al and Beth ... away from John. Sometimes there would be knocks on the door, or the phone would ring. They went unanswered. He'd find notes posted through the letterbox. To begin with they remained unopened, but as time wore on, Rhys forced himself to look, only to find that the three people he loved most had been worried. Rhys chastened himself for this lack of thought for the very people he needed, and yet still did nothing about it. From the back window, he watched the seasons pass.

It would soon be the turn of the century, another millennium no less, his fiftieth year, but there was no joy in a new millennium when you didn't know who you were. There was no joy in being fifty when your family had so suddenly become ... not your family. There was simply no joy. The days passed by. How many he didn't know. Each seemed exactly like the last ... each one to be filled with something. Yet he did nothing. The days may have dragged, but it didn't feel that way. They came and went. Sometimes the curtains remained closed so that he wasn't sure if it was day or night. How often he ate ... he couldn't say. How often he washed and dressed ... he couldn't tell you. Rhys was totally lost ... a blithering blob of liquefied human being.

Simultaneous, insistent banging on both the front and back doors, flooded Rhys's mind. He tried to ignore it but when it didn't stop went to the front door. John and Al stood there, pizza boxes and cans of drink balanced on their arms. Without waiting for an invitation they walked to the kitchen. Al unlocked the back door for Beth, who was struggling with a large cake box, a bunch of flowers and her handbag. With her things deposited on the table she took him in her arms and hugged him tightly. To say that Rhys was bewildered would have been an understatement. He had no idea what the month was, let alone the date, but apparently, it was his birthday ... or the one he'd believed was his birthday.

'My God Rhys. You've no idea how frightened we've been.' Beth looked at him, her face grimacing at his lack of personal care. 'Right. Go upstairs ... take a shower ... and when you come down, we'll eat.' Rhys looked at her ... felt like a scolded child. 'Go. Go on. I'm not sitting at the table with you like that!'

Rhys could hear Beth crying as he went upstairs, and wondered why, until he reached the bathroom. His reflection in the mirror, shocked him. He was unrecognisable. His clothes were filthy, his hair unkempt and grimy so it stuck up at peculiar angles. It was the first time since it had happened that he realised how low he'd sunk. By the time he joined them, he not only felt much better in himself, but hardly recognised the dining room as being his.

Rhys hadn't quite regained his composure so that he didn't know how to react to this lovely thing they'd done. Al opened the beers and the mood changed from difficult stilted talk, designed to fill the space, to a lighter banter. Eventually John looked at Rhys, and said,

'I don't know what it's like being where you are, mate. Can't begin to imagine what you're going through but ... we've been talking ... a lot ... almost every day and we're going to work together to get you through this.'

'Perhaps we could get a DNA test done to start with,' Al said. 'The results would reveal the truth and if it were to be true ... well having a DNA test might help you find your birth parents.'

'It's only a suggestion, Rhys,' Beth said, quickly. 'If you don't want that ... well then that's ok.'

Rhys listened to them, watched them looking towards each other for approval and already felt physically better for having a full stomach. The beer, his first for a long time, surged through his head making it swim a little, but not so much that he couldn't feel the love flowing from them. He realised for the first time in months how his behaviour, uncontrollable though it was, had affected them all.

'I'm so sorry,' Rhys said, his head down. 'I'm really sorry you've had to put up with me.'

'Don't be stupid!' John said, a little cross now. 'None of us have had to put up with you. We love you ... all we want is to see you get better ... to be your old self again.'

John sat against the back of his chair and looked at Beth, who smiled. Rhys looked at Al, whose mouth was upturned in a huge grin and then they were all staring at him waiting for something to happen. There was something in their actions, in their demeanours, in the way they were talking that tugged at him in the dark place he'd inhabited for so long.

'Come to the salon tomorrow. I'll give that hair a good working over,' Beth said, raising her glass towards him.

Al called his name, questioningly. He hadn't realised that he was crying, that huge tears had rolled down his face.

'I've just realised,' he said, 'that I've felt something. For so long I've had no feelings,and if I had I couldn't name them ... but now ... I truly feel loved ... and it's so strange ...'

Al said, 'It makes no difference to us whether you're our blood brother or not, you are still our brother ... and we've told you that before ... and we'll keep telling you until you accept it. Now come and give us all a hug.'

The celebration of Rhys's birthday, was a major turning point, not drastic to begin with, more a growing awareness of what he needed to do to regain his life. The image of his gaunt face, cheeks so sunken the bones looked like some artificial makeup had been applied and the incredible weight loss might have been enough alone to shock him into action.

The clothes he'd been wearing for months went into the bin. He made himself breakfast with food that his family must have been stocking his cupboards with. Al went with him to buy new clothes, almost an entire wardrobe full.

CHAPTER 44

Nineteen Ninety-Eight
Rhys Jones Aged 48

A Whole Life a Lie

Rhys parked the car in the first available space, switched off the engine and sat for just a few minutes before getting out. Early morning clouds had dissipated leaving the sky a watery blue but the day was bitterly cold. Recent heavy snowfalls had begun to thaw, slush had gathered in puddles and gutters and ran down the hill, drains unable to cope. He pulled the thick winter coat round him, turned up the collar and thrust his hands into the pockets as he walked down the road.

Rhys looked like a vagabond, having allowed himself to retreat since his birthday, the impetus to retain a sense of dignity too difficult to maintain. The only sign to say otherwise was his highly polished shoes. His hair was dishevelled, a stubble of black growth surrounded his chin and cheeks, and under the coat he still wore an old tee shirt and an even older jumper with those loosely fitting grey jogging trousers. He didn't care what he looked like. He'd waited a long time for this; the intervening period having passed in bouts of highs and lows.

By the time Rhys found the place his shoes were soaked through, his mood heavier than when he'd woken. It was at the bottom of the hill, one of a row of houses, smart with three stories, nice frontage. Steps led to the door and on the wall beside it a plaque read, Dr. Michael Raven, Psychiatry, Psychology & Behavioural Therapy Clinic. Rhys hesitated. There were still five minutes before the appointment. Back on the pavement he walked up the hill a little way, turned and looked down. Was he ready for this? Did he really want to go in there? He was halfway between the clinic and the car. Did he go up or down? Back to the car meant more misery. Down to the clinic meant some help, at least. Inside he was screaming.

Dr. Raven shook Rhys's hand and pointed to a chair. It was hot, almost uncomfortably hot, but then he was wrapped up against the bitter cold. With all the domestic issues covered, Dr. Raven asked Rhys if he was happy with them. He said yes, but the truth was that he'd not taken anything in. That first conversation, if it could be called that, had been awkward ... unnatural ... full of meaningless 'ums and other little expressions people make when they're uncomfortable. He asked Rhys how he was, which Rhys thought was a stupid question but then he replied with an even more stupid answer.

'Fine ... I'm fine,' he said, quickly, his head down, looking at his knees and hands which had gripped each other, almost in a praying action.

Neither of them spoke so that an awkward silence filled the space. It was too quiet. Rhys wanted to fill it but didn't know what with.

'Can you lift your head? I'd like to see your face, Rhys.'

It wasn't at the doctor, but towards the corner of the room that Rhys looked, where there was a couch, and Rhys wondered how bad you had to be to be able to lie down. Though he tried, Rhys couldn't bring himself to look into the doctor's eyes. He couldn't look into anyone's eyes now, not like he used to be able to.

'How do you feel?' It was a simple question, but it hung in the air for a while. Rhys didn't have an answer, didn't know what to say.

'Take your time,' the doctor said.

Inside Rhys's head, the scream got louder, the buzz between his ears increased, yet when it came out, the word was so softly spoken, Dr. Raven asked him to repeat it.

'Nothing,' he told him. 'I feel nothing.'

There was a long pause, awkward and extremely painful, until he asked how long Rhys had felt this nothingness and when he thought about it, it seemed to be years.

'I can't remember a time when I did feel anything.'

Rhys sat in his chair in Katie's bedroom, his coat still wrapped round his shoulders and looked out of the window onto the frozen patches of grass, the unkempt borders, the lifeless trees. He wondered what had just happened. He wanted to remember things. He'd searched his mind for memories from before that day but could only see those new shoes, those lovely new tan shoes ... and the black polish he'd smeared over them.

That was when it happened, as though, in that fraction of a second, the sure and certain bubble he'd lived in, the calm and even-tempered man he knew himself to be, burst open, flinging minute fragments of his mind and body into eternity. His insides hurt, as if someone had shoved a clawed hand down his throat and pulled the very essence of who he was from his body, his heart, his soul, leaving only an empty vessel. He had become a monster, the image staring back at him from the mirror a fake. A whole life lived in a lie. He'd punched the mirror, watched as the face splintered with the cracks, unrecognisable as Rhys Jones. He'd left it hanging there, a reminder of what he'd become. A major emotional breakdown the doctor had said. He no longer cared about the shoes, knew the incident was only the catalyst but couldn't grasp the enormity of this emotional state, even though he understood its true cause.

What was left of the cold afternoon had faded into dusk, lights from houses and streetlamps ushered in the night. Rhys didn't move. He heard the voice of Dr. Raven, urging him to write down thoughts, not just memories, but any tiny scrap of what came to mind. Not today, he decided. Today had been enough for any sane man to manage. Rhys went to the kitchen where he sat with a cup of coffee and contemplated the last few years.

Several sessions into his therapy, while still unable to get passed the 'I'm fine' response, Rhys felt better in some respects. Spring was on its way, the days lengthened, the evenings stayed lighter, and the air turned to a very pleasant, no coat, warmth. Rhys believed his childhood had been largely unremarkable, the sort that must have been happy, no awful incidents that so often plagued people even into adulthood. He knew it had been a privileged time so tried to think of it as just that, without attempting to stir the mire in his brain. It was the chest thing he wasn't able to be rid of. The feeling that all his organs had become a coagulated blackness.

Thick, rock like, sitting in the centre of his chest, so that the heaviness of it weighed him down constantly. Even remembering the day he met Catherine, and the happy years they'd had before Richard was born, made no impression on this granite. He could only believe that he had, maybe in some distant past, been a profoundly horrible person, one now brought to the fore by that dreadful day.

However much longer it might take in therapy, Rhys began to understand that recovery would be down to nobody but himself, that only he could mend his broken mind, that it was his breakdown and ultimately, he had to work his way out of it.

Dr. Raven couldn't hide his surprise, nor his pleasure, in seeing the change in Rhys by the time several months had passed. Rhys's visits continued until the end of the following year before the doctor was satisfied that he would be able to manage in society so another set of seasons went by. He was increasingly able to appreciate them. Gradually life took on some meaning. The results of the DNA tests came back in November, not long before Dr. Raven, signed him off. Rhys admitted to being pleased that he was still having those sessions then, because the tests showed clearly that he was not related to either Al or Beth. Therapy had been an incredible support in coming to terms with such unquestionable evidence.

CHAPTER 45

Two Thousand
Rhys Jones Aged 50

Where to Begin

Rhys and Al had spent a fantastic Christmas at Beth's, which had a profound effect on Rhys ability to set about the daunting task of tracing his birth parents. He'd been retired from work on the grounds of ill health for a long time and though it had crossed his mind to find other employment he decided against it. There were no worries financially, what with the inheritance and the savings he'd managed to accrue. He put the house back on the market. There was nothing to worry about, save to keep himself healthy and sane.

Al retired at the end of the year, having turned sixty and they'd developed a plan. Some days they worked together ... other days separately but every day they spoke about what they had found ... or not found. Despite the age gap, their quite different characters, not to mention that they were no longer blood brothers, the task brought them closer than ever.

'I've found something,' said Al.

'Where ... show me.'

Al turned the computer screen which showed a birth certificate with Rhys's name and the information they expected to find, but looking closely, the words, 'Signature of Registrar,' had been crossed through. In the box beneath, 'Sister Mary, of The Liverpool Foundling Society,' had been written.

'Does this match the certificate you've got?' Asked Al. Rhys found it. It was a partial match.

'Your birth certificate must be a fake then.'

'How so?'

'Well ... look. Yours has a registrars signature and yet all the other information is the same.'

'Yes ... Ok, but where's this getting us, Al?'

'Not sure ... let's look at all the evidence sensibly.'

They rearranged the paperwork on the dining room table in order of when things must have happened.

'We know the names of this foundling society. Why don't we start with that?' Rhys said.

'Guess we should have done that to begin with!'

They searched Google but drew a blank. They

searched using other words, such as adoption agencies, but found nothing to move them forward.

'I suppose it was too much to ask,' Rhys said, a little downhearted. 'Those sorts of places would have disappeared years ago. Everything's done through social services these days.'

They paused while they each reflected on the task. It was getting late … they'd been researching for some hours, so were weary eyed from looking at the screen.

'How old do you think my birth parents might be?'

'Easily in their seventies … probably eighties … although, you'll be fifty-one this year. It's not likely that a woman in her thirties would have given away her child, unless the circumstances were really dire. What do you think?' Al said.

'Maybe they were young or unmarried … so perhaps they'd still be early seventies, or even younger.'

'I've got a suggestion. We could research for months and never find anything positive. What about trying something more direct … like a newspaper advert?' said Al.

'Mm … It wouldn't hurt to try. Of course, I know they might be dead but I'm praying that they aren't. I need to find them, Al.'

'Let's leave it here tonight, think about it again tomorrow. You want to phone Beth … let her know?'

'I tell you what. You phone her, see if she can come for fish and chips. I'll go and get them.'

Time may be a great healer, Rhys thought, but it can't wipe out the hurt or the suffering caused by secrets. It was some weeks after he'd posted adverts in newspapers around Liverpool. A simple statement along the lines of, man seeks birth parents, possibly in the Liverpool area. He deliberately didn't add a name but gave an address and telephone number.

Rhys was still emotional much of the time and seemed unable to manage without falling back into that quagmire, although now those episodes didn't last as long. The strategies Dr. Raven had given him worked as long as he was in a frame of mind to use them. By far the most difficult thing was his long-held understanding of being so different from everyone else.

He remembered his mother saying that his height and facial shape were a throwback to previous members of the family, and yet he'd never seen photographs of anyone else who looked anything like him. He'd asked about it at different times, each time receiving the same response and he trusted his parents so always let it go.

Now, those memories, those deep inner feelings of his difference haunted him ... proved that the questions had been valid. When he was in that mire, they caused him to hate his mother and father for their lack of truth, their lies, their cowardliness. In one of his darkest moments, when he thought he might be dragged right back he called John, tears flowing unchecked, and he was there.

'Don't get me wrong. I love my parents. They gave me a home, a good life but I hate them sometimes too. You remember the funeral wake? All those relatives we'd never met. I was so pleased to know our extended family. Now? I wonder how many of them knew I was adopted … how many of them kept the lie … if any of them could have told me then, when there was a chance,' Rhys said

He sniffed.

'Sorry mate … it's just that I can't talk to Al or Beth about this. It isn't their fault. They're not responsible for what our parents did or didn't do.'

'It's ok. Keep it coming. You'll feel better when it's out,' said John.

'I don't want to be in that place again … dark and lonely … insignificant … wanting to end it all but not having the courage. I felt I was imploding … might suddenly become nothing. Sometimes I willed it to happen. I don't know who I am, John. I don't know where I came from. I have no history. All those relatives … they're not mine … they're not my heritage. I want to find out who I am, because at the moment I'm a nobody.'

'Have you heard from anyone ... you know from the adverts?'

'No. Not a dicky bird.'

'Will you post them again? It might take a long time to be seen by anyone with an interest. And even then, if your parents are out there, they will have had different lives. They might be conflicted about getting in touch.'

'I know. I've thought about all that. I've been telling myself not to get my hopes up ... that my birth parents might not want to know me after all this time. My head swims with it all sometimes.'

'Do you think a holiday would be good for you right now?'

He heard what John had said but spoke without reference to the question.

'I'm not a bit like Al or Beth. Beth's got the salons ... Al had his vocation ... the only thing I ever wanted out of life was a family. Strange that, don't you think? I didn't even manage to keep the family I had. Catherine turned out to be someone else ... Katie isn't here anymore ...'

John went to the kitchen, listening to the agonising sobs, and came back with kitchen roll.

'Here. Blow your nose Rhys. You're dripping everywhere.'

John didn't have many pet hates, but a runny nose, sniffing and wiping on a sleeve, were things that almost made him gag. He waited while Rhys blew hard and long and took the offending paper to the bin.

'What about playing football again?'

'Too old for that, unless there's an old man's team,' Rhys said, managing a smile.

'Ok. There's always coaching or perhaps joining a team of youngsters. You'd be good at that. You've got the skills and the patience. They'd listen to you. You could even set up a new team.'

'I don't know John. Everything seems pointless. I thought of getting a dog ... maybe one that needed rehoming ... but then I'd have to walk it every day. Sometimes I don't want to do anything. It's enough work looking after myself.'

'I think that's a great idea. First it would give you something else to think about. Second it would make you go out and enjoy the fresh air and third, a dog would be such great company. I'd go walking with you at the weekends. The wife wouldn't mind at all. It'd get me out from under her feet.'

Rhys looked at him, saw him smiling, and knew he meant it.

'I'll think about it again.'

CHAPTER 46

Two Thousand and One
Rhys Jones Aged 51

Liverpool

Bonny ran towards him jumped up and wagged her tail so fast it was almost still. She'd come into his life not long after that last bout of depression. As a rescue, he didn't really know how old she was but they'd said possibly about eighteen months. People always admired her, asking about her breed. He'd never been sure though so described her as a Westie. He loved her dearly, spoilt her and let her lie on the sofa which Al and Beth thought was a mistake.

It was the first positive decision Rhys had made for years. John had been so right. Bonny gave his life purpose, the walks and cuddles, the undeniable love she afforded him, the sheer pleasure of having another living thing he could call his own, all steered him gradually towards a new perspective. He'd had an offer on the house, one that he thought would be acceptable, because the second important decision, had been to visit Liverpool.

Rhys resolved not to continue recording memories. It was time to focus on the here and now. The future would be whatever it turned out to be regardless of his past. The books full of it were stored in the bookcase, perhaps never to be reopened. It didn't matter. He was in a very different place and knew that with help he could continue forwards. Instead, he bought new books, intending to record events as they happened. It seemed he'd been bitten by the writing habit.

Bonny fetched her lead, as she always did when she thought it was time to go. These days Rhys was able to look outwards when walking, the bowed head and eyes to the ground something he'd actively fought to avoid. It was a bright day. The end of spring was warm, the air soaked in rich floral aromas, the ground dry after a few days of sun. When they got to the field at the back, Bonny was allowed off the lead to run about in her own world, meet other dogs and try to steal children's balls. Rhys stood and watched her, called her away from danger, or admonished her for ignoring her own ball in favour of others.

She was his lifeline. He could not imagine being

without her. She even made it possible for him to talk with other dog walkers, mostly regulars they got to know. There was the old man with an Alsatian, almost bigger than himself, who used to sit on one of the benches when walking became too much, his faithful companion waiting patiently by his side. Then there was the woman in her mid-fifties who walked about eight different breeds of dog for other people. It made him laugh inwardly when their leads became tangled, and she shouted at them to stay still. If he wasn't careful, Bonny would bounce up to dogs much bigger than herself wanting to play, only to discover that big dogs can floor her. She never seemed to mind though.

Rhys fed Bonny her favourite after-walk treat while the kettle boiled. He checked that all the paperwork was packed in the right bags for ease of access. He went through everything else he needed to do for his journey up to Liverpool. With the drink finished, Rhys prepared dinner for the evening. Al, Beth, and John would be arriving in a few hours, and he wanted the food to be well cooked. He was great at feeding others and had put a sumptuous looking joint of beef in the oven to cook slowly. He prepared the vegetables and found the cheat's answer to Yorkshire pudding. With the back door open and the dining room windows slightly ajar, there was a welcome breeze flowing through. Bonny joined him in the garden, and they were both soon asleep.

The hotel in Liverpool was one of those cheaper chain affairs … all clean and bright with no individual atmosphere, staff only interested in their next pay day. Breakfast was extra so Rhys had decided to find a café nearby where he thought the food might be more interesting. The hotel's only benefit was its location close to the centre, meaning he didn't need to use the car to get about. On Monday morning following a poor night's sleep, Rhys found the Liverpool Records office, climbed the stairs to the second floor and asked for Mrs. Broomfield. While he waited he sorted out his paperwork feeling nervous of this initial delve into his past.

Very soon a striking woman of medium height, Rhys thought to be in her late fifties, joined him. She wasn't beautiful but Rhys was struck by her dazzling smile and fiery eyes. For a minute he didn't respond to her outstretched hand.

'Mr. Jones,' she said.

'Oh. Please call me Rhys.'

'In that case, call me Brenda. There's a room we can use where we don't have to whisper,' she said, moving away.

Rhys scraped the chair on the floor and several heads turned towards him. This place was quieter than any library he'd known. He supposed there must be serious research going on so he crept out behind her. There was a little pause after they'd sat down. Brenda spread a number of documents on the table. It struck Rhys as a good sign.

'Thank you for your letter and copies of what you have,' she said. 'I've done as much research as possible given the meagre amount of information available. I'm not sure how far we can get but let's have a look.'

Rhys was a little mesmerised by her softness. He'd dated a few women since Catherine but never wanted anything to come of it. The truth was, he found it hard to trust women now. He wasn't bothered by living alone. Being in a relationship would have made all this more difficult. Brenda seemed to give off a warmth he found instantly drawn to in a way only Catherine had been capable of so when she asked him if he was okay, embarrassment flushed his face. He had to shake his head to snap out of what had become a stare! They spent about three hours going through everything. Brenda had discovered the same document Rhys already had, but also another, which showed the same photograph Rhys held in his hand.

'This is interesting,' she said, 'because it would imply that you were moved from another society to here in Liverpool, and that backs up the evidence of the two letters you found.'

'Why is the information blacked out?'

'It was common practice at the time, solely to prevent children and their birth parents from making contact. These days it seems cruel ... but attitudes were different in the forties and fifties.'

Brenda looked at him kindly.

'You've been fortunate that this document hasn't been fully blacked out. It's at least given you a place to begin.'

'What would it have been like for babies and children put up for adoption at that time?'

'Okay. I can give you a brief outline since I imagine your mind conjures up all sorts of horrors! There were several reasons for babies and children being given up for adoption. Often, it was because their parents already had too many mouths to feed, and they hoped someone else would look after them.'

'The truth was that too many of them spent their lives in children's homes and not all such homes were run with compassion. Children were often put to work and then abandoned a second time when they were judged old enough to fend for themselves. Many turned to unsavoury activities simply to stay alive. The lucky ones found good families, the less fortunate didn't, sometimes being shipped between the home and different families until they either made it or not.'

Brenda smiled as she spoke, giving the distinct impression that she'd either been adopted herself, or had specialised in the matter, because there was a kindliness in her voice.

'Unmarried mothers homes could be found in every town and city, right up to the early seventies. These mothers rarely saw their babies as they were taken away immediately and sent to places such as you had probably been in.'

'I was a foundling though,' Rhys said, before Brenda could continue. 'It says so in the letter.'

'Indeed. Foundling babies were usually, but not always, left by their birth mother, perhaps because they weren't married and grandmother was not in a position to manage bringing the child up. I think that this is the most plausible explanation for you. The bit of paper you have may have given a name, or perhaps a plea to look after you. You were well dressed and warm when you were found and you weren't left anywhere but the most suitable place to be cared for. You really were one of the luckiest of foundlings. From what you've told me you had a loving family with wonderful siblings and a good upbringing.'

'I've wondered so often what was written on that paper,' he said. 'Do you think it might have rained while I was waiting to be found? That that's why the writing has blurred?'

'Perhaps. If your birth mother is still alive, she would know. You said you'd advertised in newspapers without many responses. If you continue to do that it might be worth mentioning the paper.'

'You must have a lot of experience when it comes to these sorts of requests. What do you think my chances are?'

'Well. Let's look at the evidence we've got,' Brenda said, with that deep warming smile.

'It's clear that you were transferred from another institution ... both the letters and this second document I found prove as much. Where that institution was is almost impossible to speculate. But I have found something else, though it doesn't provide much more information.'

She slid a birth certificate across the table.

'I discovered this and almost dismissed it at first. However, knowing the certificate you have to be a fake, this one, while it doesn't state categorically, is very close to what we know. I can tell you that it is a genuine birth certificate. The fact that there are no parents named, is not unusual in the case of a foundling, but there is a registration date, of March fifth, nineteen fifty.'

'Other evidence points to you having been in at least more than one institution, and it would appear that you were about three months old when you were adopted. That's probably about the shortest length of time it would have taken for the process to be completed.'

'Why would my adoptive parents have had this fake certificate made up and given me a birth date in May?'

'Only they can tell you that Rhys. You've told

me that your appearance in the family was rather strange, so perhaps it was to hide the very fact of your adoption.'

'I'll never know now, will I.'

'There's another lead here too,' she said, moving away from the obvious angst in his voice.

'This certificate states that you, or this child, was registered in Portpatrick in the county of Wigtownshire, Scotland.'

'So, I'm Scottish!'

'Again, difficult to say Rhys. If you were born there, then yes. But you might easily have been moved there from a border town. There's another possibility. Portpatrick is close to Ireland. There's been a link between the two countries for centuries and other research I've done may indicate that convents in Ireland often sent babies needing to be adopted, to Portpatrick. So ... you could have been born in Scotland or Ireland.'

'The mystery thickens then. Do you think I stand a chance of ever finding my birth parents?'

'You stand as much chance as any foundling. It might take you a long time, but I do think this little scrap of paper is your greatest hope. I suggest your next move should be to research Scottish records. If that fails, there's a distinct possibility that Ireland was your birth country.'

Brenda stood, indicating that there was little

else she could say, offered Rhys copies of the new documents and took his hand. He could feel the warmth radiating from it. There was something about her that said she understood his predicament … something that was silently wishing him the best of luck … something that almost reduced him to tears.

Back at the hotel after a stop for coffee … not to his taste but he was immensely thirsty after all the talking, Rhys spread the paperwork on the bedroom table, took a shower and peered at it for a long time. By late afternoon he was hungry. He didn't know how he felt, either about the possibility of being Scottish, or even Irish, or the knowledge of his birthday being three months earlier. The fact was, Rhys didn't know how he felt about any of it. The more paperwork he looked at, the more confused he became but at the same time, a glimmer of hope shone in his eyes.

CHAPTER 47

Two Thousand and Five
Rhys Jones Aged 55

A Bold Decision

Rhys had begun to write again, despite having decided not to. Talking to Brenda had inspired further research, which in turn had resulted in more confusion and short bursts of depression.

It had been almost three years. He was no nearer the truth. Research in Scotland had proved fruitless. His advertisements went unanswered. He set about drafting more than adverts; short pieces about himself and his search over the years, and some had been printed in local newspapers, sadly with no results. Rhys contacted editors for the main dailies, even *The Times*, and found little interest save for *The Daily Express*. They interviewed him, deciding it was a human-interest story. It was given quite a large section on page two.

After that, letters began to arrive sporadically. Some were immensely sad; stories of babies left in waste bins or under park benches; the desperation almost tangible. Others were brief, simply stating that the writer thought they might be his mother or father. However, none of them held the information Rhys was seeking; that he had been left as a foundling; that a scrap of paper was pinned to his shawl. Rhys answered all the letters. Whoever they were from deserved to know that their hopes had not materialised.

The first of October dawned. Black, blanket, low hanging clouds prevented any vestige of sun, so it felt more like the early hours than mid-morning by the time Rhys sat with his notes again. Thoughts of his parents, Angharad and Owen had been rolling round his head for the last few days. He wondered what they would have made of his quest; whether they would have been pleased for him.

It had crossed his mind that they may have seen it as a betrayal. A betrayal of the love they had given; of all the times they had stood by him when he was in trouble. But then, hadn't they betrayed him in a way? Hadn't they deprived him of his birth right; brought him up to believe he was English but of Welsh decent, when all the time they'd known differently? And hadn't they let them all believe they were true siblings, when the stark fact was that they bore no blood relationship at all?

Rhys would not have wanted to hurt them. He loved them as any son would, without question, but he couldn't help thinking that by not bringing him up knowing the truth, they'd somehow forfeited their right to be upset. And then he wondered what might have happened if they hadn't been killed prematurely; if he'd died before them, never being any the wiser.

Would that have been better? Would preserving such a secret really have mattered? Rhys had come to the conclusion that it would. If his birth parents were out there; if they wanted to know him as much as he wanted to know them; then, yes it would have been a travesty not to have been able to search.

Rhys closed the book. He'd got that off his chest and felt so much better for it, and it didn't seem to matter what the weather was doing; he was less miserable. Even his body had a lightness to it. He took Bonny through the woods, met up with a few other walkers and by the time they reached home, they were ready for sleep.

It had been a while since Al and Rhys had spoken. Rhys called and suggested they go out for something to eat. Al was all for it. He said he could do with the company, and Rhys needed to talk through his most recent decision. They were finishing off a rather delicious cheesecake when Rhys said,

'I'm going to Ireland.' Al looked at him, clearly surprised, but only said,

'Oh. Want to tell me more?

'Mm ... decided to rent somewhere and try to find more information.'

'What's brought this on?'

Rhys remained silent for a while, aware that Al was looking at him, his face giving nothing away.

'You know I drew a blank when I researched in Scotland. I'm not English, or Welsh, or even Scottish. Therefor I must be Irish, Al.

PART 3

Northern Ireland

Hope

CHAPTER 48

Two Thousand and Six
Rhys Jones Aged 56

Donahagdee

The house wasn't far from Belfast to the northeast, a little place called Donahagdee, through a couple of small villages, but mostly open countryside. Rhys had chosen it from those on offer because it was completely opposite in nature to Credenhill. He needed a change, not only of location, but more a complete change of lifestyle. He had looked purposefully for houses in very rural districts with access to the sea and good walking areas. He was unsure as to why he wanted to be near the sea, except that it would be a new experience. For som reason he'd been drawn to it during his searches.

The property was rented for six months initially, with the landlord's promise that it could be extended. Situated outside the village of Crawfordsburn, it lay on its own, settled among the trees of a small wood which stretched behind and across the road for some way. There were no near neighbours but a short distance to the north, a few houses had been built in a horseshoe away from the road, though easily accessible. Rhys felt sure he'd be able to meet people and make friends and if it didn't happen, well, then he was quite happy to have Bonny for company. The drive to Belfast was only a matter of minutes, so shopping would probably be once a week or maybe even less if he really stocked up and then, of course, the house was close enough to the port to be able to make the journey home easily.

His first two weeks were dedicated to making sure that advertisements were posted in every newspaper local to Belfast and its surrounds. After that they walked for miles along the coast, through the woods, exploring the locality. Rhys found a new and unexpected calmness; a security he hadn't had for a long time. He enjoyed the seclusion, yet in no way felt isolated. Al and John made the journey to stay for a week in mid-June, Al bringing paperwork to sign for the sale of his house.

'This's a wonderful spot, Rhys,' said John. 'The wife and kids would love it here. I'm going to take loads of photos for them. Perhaps I could bring them for a holiday and stay close by so we could see each other.'

'You can stay here. There's plenty of room, and lots to do. It looks as though I'll be extending the rental for a while. Haven't seen anything I'd want to buy yet. I meant to say, I've got a viewing on Tuesday. You can come with me, if you like.'

'Definitely,' said Al. 'I want to know what you're getting yourself into!'

'Have a look at the details while I make coffee. It looks big, but I don't mind having the space if the location's right.'

Al and John studied the details from the estate agent, mumbling between themselves about its size; much too big for one person. And then its situation; on its own right down on the sea, the coast appearing to be extremely rugged, although a little sandy beach was also close. Rhys could hear what they were saying but kept quiet. When he came with drinks, Al said,

'It looks enormous and it's almost in the sea, Rhys. What's the appeal?'

'Ok. I don't understand why, but I've loved being here by the sea. I never realised how bracing it is, how it seems to cleanse me, especially if the wind is quite high. Sometimes we get home from hours of walking and I'm never really tired. I actually feel alive, rejuvenated.'

'It's a big place,' said John. 'What would you do with the space?'

'I don't know! But then, I haven't bought it yet.

You can tell me what you think.'

'I'm still a bit worried about you making any rash decisions, Rhys. Suppose this doesn't work out for you?'

'Look, I know how you feel about me coming here … and I do understand. But it's something I have to do. I've a good feeling about it … that I'll find them. It doesn't mean that I don't love you and Beth … or you John, but I have to try. Otherwise, I'm nobody.'

'But why don't you just keep renting here for as long as you can … perhaps give yourself a time limit. I don't know … maybe a year or eighteen months, and if you haven't made any progress then, come back to England. We miss you. We all do.'

'For what it's worth Rhys, I agree with Al. If you buy here, you're probably going to be stuck here, financially I mean.'

They were quiet for a bit then, Rhys thinking about the conversation. As if to fill the space, Bonny jumped onto Al's lap and licked his face. When Rhys looked at the time, he was amazed to see that hours had passed, and it was almost Bonny's dinner time.

'I'll feed her and then we can go to the cliff and have a bite to eat, if that suits.'

Rhys had been in Ireland for a couple of months when they went to view the property. It wasn't easy to find, many narrow roads with twists and turns bordered by tall hedges or walls, made it doubly difficult and it was in an area Rhys hadn't yet discovered, but John's excellent navigation got them there. Rhys was instantly disappointed with the house seen from the road. It looked in need of a good paint and clean but negotiating the tiny track leading to what was its front, they were all aghast at both the house and its position.

It stood on a rocky incline called Grey Point, in Helen's Bay. It was a back to front property, two levels on the road with three at the front facing the sea. There was nothing between it and the coastline. It was quite spectacular, two wings jutting out from a central addition, almost like a three-story porch. The windows were large with wonderful views of the Irish Sea. Steps led down to a lawn and a path which meandered its way to the water.

Inside, someone had worked hard. Everything had been renovated to a high standard.

There was no garden, just a concrete space with a wall and steps to the lawn,but that didn't bother Rhys. Bonny would love it. Rocks tumbled towards a small sandy beach, the house having direct access.

'I love it,' Rhys said. 'It's got everything I could possibly want. What do you think?'

Neither Al, nor John, answered at first. Rhys looked at them quizzically.

'You've got an opinion, surely?'

'It's beautiful,' said Al. 'But it's so large. Why would you need such a grand place? What on earth would you do with all those rooms?' he asked, waving his arms across the front of the house.

'John, what do you think?'

'Well … I sort of agree with Al on that point. You'd get lost in it.'

'But look at it … look at the view, the beach. It's a magnificent site. Once my house is sold, I could afford it outright … no mortgage etc. You could all come and stay together. Think of it as a holiday home … somewhere to escape.'

'There's something else I worry about, Rhys. Suppose you find your birth parents,and they live on the other side of the island; you might want to move again; you'd probably lose out financially,' said Al.

'Perhaps that's a risk I'm willing to take. Ok. I know you're only thinking of me. I've had a good look. Let's drive down the coast a bit and find lunch. I'd like to see what's around.'

Along the narrow coast road, after stopping twice to take photographs, they reached Bangor where there was a quaint harbour. The sun continued to warm the air and reflect from little boats jostling about with the movement of water. They were all hungry and thirsty for some cool beer, though Rhys had to forgo this as he was driving. There was little conversation while they ate, but he could see Al's thoughts as if they were written on his face.

'Come on. I fancy a night in front of the box. Dinner's in the slow cooker. Shall we get some beers in?' Rhys said, acutely aware that neither of them were saying anything.

'Sounds good to me,' John said, and Al agreed.

We bought the drink from the pub on the corner and made our way home. Uncomfortable with the silence Rhys said,

'I think I'll put an offer in on that place. Maybe a really cheeky one, like ten grand below the asking price. See what comes back.'

'Please don't, Rhys,' Al said, his voice almost pleading.

'Why not? You both liked it. I loved it.'

'Because for one, it's been a shock to realise your intention to stay here. And two, Beth and I want you to come back.'

John sat quietly on the back seat. Rhys knew he had his own views about him leaving England for good, but he stayed silent.

'I think that's unlikely,' he said, 'and I was hoping you'd be happy for me!'

'You're part of us. You're our brother. We miss you ...' Rhys cut him off,

But isn't that the problem? I'm not your brother. I'm nobody. Can't you understand my need to find out who I am?'

'On one level, yes. On another, we don't want to lose you. Can't you just find your birth parents and then come home?' It all came out in an anxious rush, Al hitting the dashboard as he finished. Rhys jumped at the sound, and the car veered towards the path before he managed to right the steering wheel.

'For God's sake, Al! Please, will you just get off my back!'

All that could be heard for the remainder of their journey, was the purr of the engine, and every so often bleeps from indicators. Rhys unlocked the front door, let John and Al inside and fussed Bonny.

'I'm taking a walk,' he said curtly. 'There's plenty of veg in the fridge if you wouldn't mind doing it, and see what's on the box later, if you like. Come on Bonny … get your lead.'

Rhys crossed the road and entered the woods by the narrow pathway, feeling the temperature drop by at least a couple of degrees. His insides were a mass of different emotions, but he couldn't name them. While Bonny scampered off, free of her tether, Rhys slowed down and tried to reduce his heartbeat. He was both disappointed at what he believed was Al's selfishness and upset that his brother was not even attempting to understand. And John had remained silent. Rhys wondered if he really shared Al's views.

There was another emotion sitting there too, although he was unsure of what it was.

Rhys hated uneasy atmospheres, shrank from arguments and conflict of any kind. They had a tendency to reduce him to cowardliness. Recognising and allowing feelings to the surface had never been easy but therapy had provided strategies to explore what they were. He dug deep to remember other occasions when he'd felt like that and thought of finding Katie at home on her own. It was anger, a rare experience, but that is what it was. Al was being unreasonable, and he was angry. Rhys let the feeling rise, looked towards the leafy canopy, and opened his mouth. 'Ahhhhhhhhhhhhhhh' He heard it ricochet between the trees; birds took flight and small mammals scuttled into the undergrowth. Bonny came racing towards him at the sound. Rhys picked her up and held her tightly against his aching chest, while she licked his face.

Rhys could sense the atmosphere that had leached from the car earlier, as soon as he opened the front door. It was obvious that John and Al had downed at least one more beer, but they had also cooked the vegetables, laid the table and were ready to dish up. Bonny rushed in for her cuddles and sat beside her water bowl, to indicate it was also her mealtime.

'Thanks for doing all this,' Rhys said, while preparing Bonny's dinner.

'Well. There was an ulterior motive,' Al told him, 'we're both starving.'

They ate, the silence thick like stodgy pudding, until Al said,

'I've never had a slow cooker. This chicken's cooked beautifully. I might get one.'

'I use it a lot now; cook enough for two or three meals … freeze it. Saves a lot of work, and as you say, tenderises the meat fantastically. Cheap cuts are amazing.'

Rhys smiled inwardly at the thought of such a mundane conversation when they were all clearly unwilling to broach anything that might cause further disquiet.

'Have you looked at what's on?' He said.

'I had a quick shifty through the paper,' John chimed in. 'Not much in the way of films, but … there is a football match on Sky.'

'Would you be up for that Al?'

'Definitely!'

A steady trickle of beer, and an exciting match, tempered the mood, and with too much drink in his system, John decided it was time to retire. Al followed shortly after, wishing Rhys goodnight, with a wave of his hand. Though he'd become less tense after the match, there was still a lingering sense of disgruntlement, and Rhys wasn't ready to lie down. He had another look at the details of the house, trying to imagine himself living there, but in the end, had to admit that they were right. It was too large, and it was time for bed. He was close to dropping off when there was a knock on the door.

'You still awake, Rhys? He opened the door, dressed in his usual t-shirt and underpants to see Al's face peep round the corner.

'What's wrong, Al?'

'You remember Dad and his unresolved issue? Well, we've got unresolved issues. Can I come in a minute?'

'Sure,'

'Rhys, I'm sorry for badgering you ... for saying stupid things. I do appreciate your situation. It's just that I'm afraid for you.'

'Afraid of what?'

'That you might be hurt again; that things won't happen the way you want them to ... and ... that we'll not see you again.'

'For God's sake, Al. I'm a big bloke. I've been through what was probably the worst time in my life. I think I'll manage whatever comes next. And what's all this about not seeing me again? Do you honestly believe I could live the rest of my life without you and Beth in it? Don't you know me better than that?' He paused, not quite sure if this was the time for his next question. 'You and John had words while I was out, didn't you?'

'Not really ... but he did give me some good advice, and it's sunk in.'

'Good. John's my closest mate. He talks a lot of sense. Ready for bed now?'

'I am, but I don't think I'll aim for an early morning.'

'I've got to go into Belfast tomorrow, so if I'm not here, you and John can do what you want. I shouldn't be too long, perhaps home for lunch. Goodnight. Sleep well, and don't worry.'

'Has the postman been?' Rhys yelled as he went through the hall. He caught Bonny flying towards him. 'Hello little one. Have they looked after you?'

'Not yet,' came a voice from somewhere upstairs. 'We're getting ready for a walk … fancied the cliffs … you coming?'

John appeared at the top of the stairs, his coat over his arm. The weather had changed from the gorgeous sunshine of yesterday, to being rather humid, and cloudy, though the clouds were high, so the threat of rain was minimal, but there would likely be a chill wind off the sea.

'We were going to take Bonny. Thought we might have lunch in that lovely place you took us to on our first day,' he said.

'I'm up for that.'

'I'll drive if you like … give you a break and you can have a beer,' Al said as he joined them.

'You must be joking Al! I bet you're still over the limit after what you put away last night. Only needs one awkward copper, and you're done for.'

Bonny jumped straight into the car and onto John's lap, where she settled and instantly fell asleep.

'I'll put her in the cage if you like John.'

'No. She's fine. She can keep my leg warm.'

The weather began to cheer up as they drove further south, and by the time they arrived, a weak sun appeared, making the need to sit outside with Bonny quite comfortable.

'What'll you have?' Asked Al. 'It must be my turn by now.'

While they waited, John and Rhys took in the scenery, the cliff edge blooming with wild summer flowers. There were other people sitting around at the café and on the grass opposite; picnics spread out on blankets, with children running up and down; dangerous Rhys thought, so close to the cliff.

'How was Belfast?' Al asked when he returned with napkin wrapped cutlery.

'Got a lot done thanks. Put in that cheeky offer on the house at Grey Point.' Rhys waited for the expected response, but there were only raised eyebrows. 'Arranged two more months on this place to give me more time to look ... and posted some more ads, this time with the address here ... placed them all over the north. Cost a bomb but it'll be worth it if the right people see it.'

'I can't believe you actually had the nerve to make that offer,' said John. 'Who in their right mind would accept something so low?'

'Depends how desperate they are, I suppose.' Rhys didn't let on that he was confident the offer would be turned down, much less that he agreed with them. As the afternoon lengthened, the clouds began to disappear. They walked south along the cliffs, until they realised there was the return walk to do, but it was an amazingly refreshing few hours, which counteracted the tensions of the day before.

Three days later, Rhys waved goodbye to his brother and friend, wishing them a safe journey home. It had been a lovely week, one that made him realise he did miss the company of people, even though he was usually content with his own. Rhys turned to the post, which had built up on the hall table, and dealt with the important stuff over coffee. The end of June was hot and windless at the house, walks mostly taken in the shade of the woods. The onset of July brought weather more akin to autumn, and lasted well into the month, before any sign of summer returned.

CHAPTER 49

Two Thousand and Seven
Rhys Jones Aged 57

Millisle

Having only one more month of the house secured, Rhys began to look in earnest for somewhere to live, focusing mostly on the eastern coast, partly because he had come to love it, but more because it was close to Belfast, so there would be less travel to the port for getting to England. He investigated the entire coastline to the tip of the peninsular, coming across many small towns and villages he thought he could be happy in. Some were quaint, with old buildings, market squares, around which huddled independent shops, those huge supermarkets he hated so much, nowhere to be seen. Larger towns like Portavogie, had wonderful sandy beaches, facilities for holiday makers, and atmospheres to lighten any downheartedness.

There were still times when he became discouraged, especially when he had to extend the rent for a further few months, which was beginning to eat into the money from the Credenhill house, money which he desperately needed to purchase outright in Ireland. The postman brought letters from home, but nothing to help him believe his birth parents were out there, waiting for him.

Rhys and Bonny walked miles, and while they were out, he tried to recall everything therapy had taught him; about remaining positive; enjoying each day as it came, and staying busy to keep the mind on track, but he really began to feel the loneliness and tried to persuade Beth to come and stay, even though he knew she couldn't leave the salon at its busiest time of year.

As winter drew in, Rhys became acutely aware of this isolation, the easterly wind howling across open spaces, rattling the windows, and sighing in the overhead wires. He thought a lot about the past; tried to think only of the good times, but the shock of finding that box in the loft would not let his mind rest, although there were occasions when it could be subdued. Rhys began to wonder if he had made the right decision to live in Ireland; if perhaps he could have been satisfied with this persona of Rhys Jones, but deep down he knew, and would always know, that he was not that man; that he had come from somewhere completely different.

Rhys Jones was the man he thought he'd been. Now, he knew he was someone else, and yet he had no notion of who that man was. He was some man in the ether; someone with no name; no character or substance. Rhys began to sleep longer, go to bed earlier, watch more television, and generally slide into something he did not immediately recognise. It was a phone call from Al that jerked him out of another descending mire.

'No. I'm fine,' Rhys said, in answer to Al.

'No really. There's nothing to be concerned about, Al. I've been a bit low, is all.'

Rhys listened as Al began to remind him of how he had been during his breakdown and kept listening when his brother said he would come over. That he would not let him go there again.

'That would be lovely, Al. I'd really like the company ... you know, someone to share things with ... what about Christmas? Can you come for a long stay?'

It was agreed. Al would take the first available ferry. Rhys wept, realising how much he loved Al; how the need to find his birth parents had taken such a massive part of him, and how he had now lost some of the fire which had kept him going.

The day after the telephone conversation, Rhys made sure he was up early ready to clean the house for Al. It needed doing. He had been so lax over the previous week or so, nothing at all had been cleaned. It took some hours before he was satisfied. Rhys was hoovering when the post arrived, so he didn't realise for a while that there was something on the mat. Only one envelope from the estate agent. Over coffee and biscuits, and a treat for Bonny, he opened it to find details of a small cottage not far south of Donaghadee, and still close enough to Belfast. It was called Millisle and was right on the coast. The cottage, part of a short terrace, was a single story, sitting right on the pavement. Painted white, it had window boxes at each of the three front windows, splashing colour onto the road.

Rhys liked the look of it, albeit the other end of the scale to the house at Grey Point, but then that was never going to be suitable. This looked cosy, and interior plans showed a considerably larger cottage than the front concealed, the rooms going way back towards the cliff. It was situated on a main road, and while there was Bonny to consider, he could see from the photographs that the land at the rear was extensive. Bonny would never need to go out through the front door, and he could put a gate there to stop her bolting. The most interesting information was that this was a vacant possession. There would be no chain. It should take no time at all for the process to be completed. Rhys called the agent and made an appointment to view it the following morning.

Al was due to arrive in a couple of days, so there was plenty of time to shop, cook and view.

'Good morning, Mr. Jones,' the estate agent said, shaking his hand. 'I'm Robert. Shall we go in?' Robert unlocked the door and pushed it open, a musty smell greeting them.

'How long has it been vacant?'

'Well. A while now, I'm afraid. It sold some way back, but then everything fell through, so it's been on the market for a couple of years. It belonged to an elderly gentleman, who sadly died. I think his children have given up hope with it.'

'That accounts for the smell then. But if it's been vacant all that time, who does the flower boxes?'

'The neighbours take it in turn. They wanted it to look lived in.'

Inside, becoming used to the mustiness, Rhys could easily see the potential throughout the property. It would need some care and attention, but then he had all the time in the world and could see it as a long-term project to keep his idle hands busy while he waited for the next part of life to begin. He'd seen enough.

'I'm interested. I'm a cash buyer and I'd want things to move swiftly, because at the moment I'm renting further up the coast. My brother will be here the day after tomorrow and I'd like him to see it. In the meantime, I'll make an offer for you to take back to the vendors.'

'OK.' Robert sounded quite shocked, as though he was very used to showing this property with no positive results. 'What would that be then?'

The offer was three thousand pounds below the asking price, which to be fair, was not high, but with the amount of work that needed doing every penny counted. Robert smiled, perhaps realising a sale, perhaps thinking Rhys would have a shock coming to him. After all Robert knew the vendors, but as he locked the front door, he said,

'I'll get back to you later today, Mr. Jones. The vendors have asked for some feedback as soon as possible, and I don't think they'll waste time over it.'

Rhys stood on the road in front of the cottage. Looked at it for a while; imagined how it could be and felt a tremendous sense of satisfaction. Before going home, he walked along the road and cut through to the cliff, to have a longer look at the rear, and realised a surge of happiness.

A leaden sky with low hanging dark clouds, so that Rhys felt almost able to reach out and catch them. What had become of Summer he couldn't imagine as he watched for Al's arrival through the window. Bonny, tired from their long morning walk, the fine early drizzle having soaked her fur, lay stretched out fast asleep in her bed. The house felt empty, the lack of noise creating a stillness which unnerved him. More house details had arrived in the post, and though he flicked through them he paid little attention. The sound of Al's car outside changed the shape of Rhys's face from the long downhearted pose he'd been wearing to the biggest smiley grin Al had ever seen. Never had Rhys been so pleased to see his brother.

'Hi Al, good journey? Rhys hugged him hard as Al tried to extricate himself from the car.

'There's a welcome. Weather could have been better for the crossing, but it was ok. It's good to see you Rhys.'

'Likewise. Let's get all this inside and you can relax a bit.'

They spent a couple of hours just catching up on all the news, eating and drinking coffee, as the minutes ticked past. It was as though an inexplicable warmth had arrived with Al, and it filled all the space, which had become too big, too cold, and too bereft of joy.

'I've found a cottage ... put an offer in and it's been accepted. We've an appointment to see it tomorrow.'

'That's great. Got the details?'

While he was looking at them, Rhys located the small town on the map, so Al could see where they would be going.

'A bit different from that other place,' Al said with a wide grin.

Rhys smiled back at him. 'I think you'll like

it ... It's so good to have you here, Al. I hadn't realised how low I'd become. Perhaps the isolation's getting to me. It was great at first. Exactly what I needed ... you know, to clear my head and all the rubbish circulating inside. Now, unless I'm busy ... well, time can stand still. The days are so long, and it's like I'm rattling round in here, wondering how it's all going to turn out. Sometimes, I don't see anyone, never mind talk to people. I have to go into Belfast for that! In a way, it's been a good experience for me though. I might have gone to Grey Point, and that would have been the same. At least I realise I need people round me, otherwise life is day after day of loneliness.'

'Blimey, Rhys. Sublime and ridiculous come to mind,' Al said, laughing, as we approached the track leading to the rear of the cottage. 'It's so small.'

'Wait till you see inside.'

The outside did look quite small, but entering by the back door, revealed how large the extension was. It had been built some years ago, so work was needed even there, but it was large enough to house three bedrooms, the initial building only having one. The effects of its long vacancy were everywhere. Peeling, seventies style, wallpaper hung away from the surfaces. Dust and debris had been long caught between the walls and skirting boards, and there were even the remains of old wrappers in one corner of the kitchen. That was a large room, possibly two small spaces knocked into one, and seemingly a long time ago, evidenced by the period type of fittings.

'I can imagine the owners being so proud of their modern appliances,' Rhys said, as they wandered round. Strangely, the original fireplace had been retained in the kitchen, and he'd already decided to replace it with a big log burner and new hearth.

'I love this main room,' Al said. 'It must have been two knocked into one like the kitchen. It's really light and airy ... well it will be when the mustiness has disappeared.'

'The kitchen and bathroom are most in need of renovation. I've saved three thousand on the asking price, so I'm hoping that will cover the cost of both rooms with all the new fittings. Everywhere else will be fine for a while with a good clean and coat of paint. What are you doing Al?'

'Oh. Sorry. Looking for Miss Haversham behind the cobwebs. I'm sure she's here somewhere,' and as he said it, an extremely large spider crawled out of the corner, raced across the floor and disappeared into a crack in the wall. It made them both laugh.

'I might get a firm in to do a proper clean once I've gutted the place. It should only take a day I imagine, and I'll be able to start sooner.'

'Good idea. Save your energy for the best bits.

Shall we measure up?'

Before leaving, they strolled round to the front. The white cottage walls were looking sad, but generally bright, set between two adjacent properties which were painted in blue and pink.

'We're being watched,' said Al. 'The curtains are twitching to your right. Your neighbour's keeping an eye on us!'

'Perhaps I'll introduce us then.' I knocked on the door, the heavy cast iron knocker echoing on the other side. Nothing happened at first, and then the sound of a key turning, and chains being unlatched. The door opened only as much as to reveal part of an old lady.

'Hello. My name's Rhys Jones. I'm going to be your new neighbour. The gap widened a little, but not enough to see her clearly.

'And I'm Mrs. Fitzpatrick.'

'Pleased to meet you,' Rhys said.

'Who's he? You're not one of those gay couples, are you? She said grumpily.

'Heavens no. This is my brother Al.'

'You don't look like brothers … I'm not in favour of all that same sex stuff. Goes against His teaching.'

'It'll just be me and my little dog, Bonny, Mrs. Fitzpatrick, once everything's settled.'

'Not one of those little yappy dogs is it? Can't abide them.'

'She's a little white Westie. She doesn't bark

SUE ROBERTSON DANELLS

much, and I think you'll love her', Rhys said.

The smile on Al's face broadened as he took in this conversation and unable to stop himself laughing disappeared round the corner.

'I'm having some work done so there may be a bit of banging over the next few weeks. I hope it doesn't disturb you too much. It's been good to meet you', Rhys said holding out his hand. Mrs. Fitzpatrick took it gingerly without saying another word, and the door closed almost before he'd withdrawn it. As Rhys turned, he saw her face at the nets again ... maybe she needed to make sure he was leaving.

'An extremely positive first encounter', Al said as Rhys arrived at the car. 'I think you'll get on well with her.'

'Do my best!'

CHAPTER 50

Two Thousand and Seven
Rhys Jones Aged 57

A New Friend

Rhys thought about Mrs. Fitzpatrick and smiled as he thought of their first meeting. She seemed such a tiny woman peeking out behind the door … almost pixie like, but her size was no measure of her ability to voice her opinions to complete strangers. He wondered if they were hers alone, or perhaps those of her religion, or even if they were indicators of the villagers at large. Perhaps she was so forthright because he was not Irish … or so she thought.

Mrs. Fitzpatrick, with her fierce, dragon like exterior, was in fact more akin to a *Werthers* sweet … those hard ones which, as you suck them, reveal the softest and creamiest of centres. Once Rhys had moved in, and the place was

SUE ROBERTSON DANELLS

habitable, he asked her round to meet Bonnie, thinking that the poor woman had put up with God knows what noise from builders and the dog, to last her a lifetime. They'd spoken many times to acknowledge each other and pass the time of day, but Rhys wanted to build the sort of neighbourly relationship that had come easily with the family on the other side. Rhys shopped for some cream cakes and had several hot and cold beverages to offer, but he was still, nervous of the woman he'd first met ... expecting criticism and perhaps even religious bantering. When the front doorbell sounded, Rhys shut Bonny in the living room, and showed Mrs. Fitzpatrick into the kitchen, where it was warm and cosy. Without waiting, she sat herself in the comfy chair and looked around.

'My,' she exclaimed, 'you've been busy, Ryes. Where's Bonny then? Aren't you going to show me round the place?' He hardly had time to put the kettle on. Whatever sort of person she was, Mrs. Fitzpatrick was not backward in coming forward. He offered her a drink and placed the cakes on the table, telling her to help herself, before letting Bonny out of the main room. Naturally, she rushed in to see who the visitor was, and even though Bonny had only met her briefly, she made an enormous fuss of the old lady, trying to get onto her lap.

'I'm sorry Mrs. Fitzpatrick,' Rhys said in his most apologetic voice, 'she's rather fond of visitors.'

'But you're a beauty, to be sure you are, Bonny,' she exclaimed in her thick Irish accent. It's funny but when he first came to live in Ireland, the accent had taken him ages to fathom, and he thought he'd managed it. This old lady's accent was the broadest he'd ever heard, and he still often had to ask her to repeat herself. 'I'll talk slowly for you Ryes. You obviously have no ear for the tongue! And please call me Mary. Mrs. Fitzpatrick is such a mouthful, don't you think?'

'Thank you Mary. When you've finished your tea and cake, I'll give you the tour.'

She ate quickly, as though Rhys might change his mind and take the plate away. Rhys wondered how well Mary ate ... managed her shopping and such like. He'd not seen her going out with bags, but then he was not one for watching through the curtains! Mary was impressed with the renovations but still added that her friends would have found them too modern. As I let her out, she pulled a sour face and said she was sorry the window boxes had gone.

'All these years I've planted them up and now you've got rid of them!'

'I'm going to have the front of the house painted,' Rhys told her. 'And I'm not much of a gardener, to be honest.'

'Mm. Well now, my house needs some paint as well. To be sure it does,' she said, her sourness turning to a bright smile. There was a pause, while Rhys tried his best not to laugh and she just kept smiling.

'OK. What if I paint your house when I do mine? It's going to be white again, if that's alright with you. And in exchange, I'll replace the boxes, and you can continue to plant them up for me. How does that sound?'

'Grand Ryes. It sounds grand.'

'Done then,' he said as he offered her his hand. She was certainly some woman.

They each kept to the bargain, and after some months with frequent conversations and cups of tea, their cottages were sparkling in the sunlight, spring flowers blooming against the windows, and Mary and Rhys came to know more about each other. Rhys liked her. He liked the way she refused to be anything other than herself. She had enormous confidence, a bubbly ... yes, underneath it all ... a bubbly caring nature, and a wonderfully dry sense of humour. Very quickly, Mary stopped trying to convert him to her beliefs. She didn't like Rhys having no faith, but then again, accepted that this was his choice. Gradually Rhys began to reveal parts of his life to her, until one day he told her why he'd moved to Ireland.

'So! You'll be Irish then! All this time you've had me think you're English, and you're as Irish as me,' she said.

'I am.'

'Well, I knew it. I wouldn't have liked you so much if you'd been English!'

CHAPTER 51

Two Thousand and Eight
Rhys Jones Aged 58

Letter

A single letter arrived, postmarked London, the address handwritten, which Rhys thought strange as anything official would have been printed. Several days of blistering hot, uninterrupted sun had begun to shrivel the pot plants out the back ... yes! Thanks to Mary Rhys had become a bit of a gardener, well perhaps not quite a gardener, but a planter of pots. Against the wall he grew tomatoes and in between, a range of brightly coloured flowering shrubs, though he could never remember their names. It's about all he could do to remember to water them every day in this weather! With coffee in hand and Bonny lying full stretched upside down on her blanket, Rhys opened the letter, not quite managing to catch the newspaper cuttings which floated serenely across the yard.

They were his adverts ... many of them from different papers. While he'd never given up hope, he had begun to wonder if his birth parents were now deceased. The letter ... well just a note really ... simply said, 'To Rhys,' and went on to say,

'I have eventually found the courage to seek the owner of all these adverts, in hopes of finding my son. He was born in nineteen fifty. If this is not you, forgive my intrusion. If it is, or you think it might be, please do write to the address above.

In hope,

SB'

Rhys read it. Read it again, and then for good measure, read it a few more times. He didn't want to believe that after everything, he might actually be a step closer to locating his parents. The date was what he'd been hoping for, all other communications having failed to provide any legitimate evidence. Rhys sorted through the cuttings. Whoever had written the letter had been collecting almost from the start.

Was he, she ... were they ... afraid to make contact ... of being let down ... fearful of what their son would be like? He understood that.

How many times had Al told him his birth parents might be miserable, or nasty people, poverty struck, looking for something they could claim? How many times had he tried to persuade Rhys to give all this up because he might end up disappointed at least, or opening a can of worms? He'd lost count.

Rhys didn't know how much time passed, until he suddenly felt the full force of the sun on his body and hadn't noticed that Bonny had taken herself inside to find some shade. A long cool beer from the fridge helped to settle a strange mix of elation and fear. Was this it? The moment he'd longed for; a moment he almost began to believe would never come. He didn't say anything about the letter. That's not to say that he didn't want to. Part of him was bursting to shout it to the heavens, to call Al and Beth, for somehow, he knew … and was afraid … of what he wasn't sure, but it was definitely there in the pit of his stomach. Could it be that this small rectangular envelope represented the end of something, or the beginning of a completely unknown, uncontrollable destiny? Whatever it was, Rhys sat on it for a week; left it propped up against the kitchen tiles; looked at it many times every day, but didn't pick it up, and he wondered if the way he was feeling, was the way SB had been feeling while collecting the adverts and not acting on them.

Eventually Rhys knocked on Mary's door. As

soon as she saw it was him, the door opened, and she let him through. Perhaps she recognised something in his expression, because she fussed about, almost pushing him into a chair and bringing in coffee.

'Well, Rhys. What is it?'

'Mary. You know I've been searching for my parents ... well I think I might have found them.' Without realising it, his eyes had filled, and tears had begun to flow.

'That's good, isn't it?' Mary said, her face a picture of puzzlement. 'So, what are the tears for?'

Rhys couldn't help laughing then. The sheer joy of what lay ahead, and Mary's down-to-earth attitude made him feel stupid.

'If this is it, Rhys, I'm truly pleased for you, so I am. You're a good man and you deserve to find out who you really are.'

They sat in a comfortable silence enjoying coffee, and biscuits until Rhys thought he'd taken up enough of her time. Back in the cottage, he phoned Al and Beth, then watched a little television to take his mind somewhere else, before walking Bonny along the shore, where a cooler breeze freshened the air.

The following day Rhys wrote to SB. Not a long letter but enough to say that he'd like to meet. He suggested London, thinking he should travel. He didn't know how old he or she was, or of any physical difficulties that may be problematic. As he let go of the envelope through the post-box, a nervous tremble filled him, hope and a little fear mingling. The next few days would probably be long and anxious. Rhys called Al. He was pleased by the news and thought perhaps a couple of nights in a cottage would be good for them both.

Rhys travelled to England leaving a key with Mary. She was always happy to look after the house, to look after him. He'd sent a letter to SB to say where he would be, and it wasn't long before something arrived. They opened it together ... gingerly ... Al telling Rhys to get on with it. Again, it was not a lengthy letter. A few lines to say that SB would be staying in Hereford the week after next, at the Castle House Hotel, as he, or she, had business in the area, and would like to meet there for coffee or maybe a meal. Rhys couldn't help wondering why this person was only giving initials, but Al, in his usual common-sense way, suggested it might be because, should it not work out, he or she could remain more anonymous, and Rhys supposed it made sense to a degree. He replied immediately offering a couple of days that he hoped were suitable, and to his surprise a further letter, by return of post, identified one of them.

How is it possible to focus the brain when something you've searched for, hoped for, for so long seemed now to be imminent, Rhys thought. He filled the time with mundane tasks, many of which didn't actually need doing, and some of which he did twice simply because his hands needed to be busy. Reading was out of the question. Watching TV during the evenings helped, but even walking Bonny left his mind free to wander. Would this person be his mother or father?

He or she must be in their mid-seventies at best, so what sort of business would bring them to Hereford? Was he born in London? And then there were all those emotional questions. Would they like each other? How would he cope if they discovered they're not related? The most disconcerting question Rhys kept returning to was why had it taken so long to contact him if the adverts had attracted his/her attention. He could only speculate how much of it was anxiety, but then when he considered how fearful he was, it didn't seem unreasonable.

Beth gave him a good haircut, all smiles at the news as she deftly wielded the scissors. They hadn't seen much of her lately, her business growing rapidly over the last couple of years, so that she had recently opened another salon across town. None of them would have guessed years ago, when she was the annoying teenager who could think of nobody but herself, how business like she would become, and her success had all been down to hard work. She had employed a manager at the original salon and planned to do the same for this new one once it was established, so she could spend her time between the two. Of course, her children were adults now, both with good careers. She didn't have to worry about them. Al and Rhys were proud of her.

CHAPTER 52

Two Thousand and Eight
Rhys Jones Aged 58

Butterflies

Summer sun had continued into September, which felt more like July than the beginning of Autumn. Rhys dressed casually for the occasion, and leaving Bonny with Al, drove into Hereford. He purposefully arrived early to feel more relaxed and spend a few minutes making sure he was presentable. This was it ... the moment he'd waited for; a moment which might provide answers; a pivotal moment with the ability to change his life. Butterflies flittered across his stomach; nerve endings tingled as he walked towards the hotel, passed by, turned and walked back.

Rhys went through the large, glazed door into a lobby, richly decorated in warm colours.

Passing into the main reception area he stood and looked around. It seemed as though this hotel was full of business groups, the noise of their meetings subdued but also animated. Some couples sat at smaller tables with their newspapers or books, evidence of lunch waiting to be cleared. The décor was tasteful, plush, and welcoming. It was clearly not a cheap hotel. Rhys managed to catch the folder tucked under his arm before its contents spilled onto the floor. He was a little mesmerised and lacked concentration. There were only three single men within sight, but none of them looked up as if expecting a visitor, so he wondered if he was either too early ... or the unthinkable had happened ... SB had decided against meeting him.

Rhys approached the bar needing a drink to calm his nerves, when he heard his name called softly, questioningly, and turning towards the sound there she was, walking towards him. Rhys could feel his knees begin to buckle and shuddered as an image of Jack Daw flashed across his mind.

She was quite short with what must have once been dark hair, but was now peppered with flecks of grey, cropped into her face and neck. She was smiling broadly as they came together ... her face beautiful in spite of some evidence of aging.

'Rhys,' she said again. 'Please come and sit down. I've a table in the corner away from the humdrum, and because I wanted to watch you come in ... a little naughty of me but to be frank, I've been rather nervous.'

'You're not Scottish,' he said in response, sounding rather astonished.

'No. What made you think I would be?'

'Oh. Nothing really. Take no notice.'

'Look. Let's order something to drink and eat if you like, and then we'll start again,' she said laughing.

Rhys showed her the photograph without saying anything about it ... turned it to face her and slid it across the table. He knew that if this woman was his mother, she would instantly recognise it, but he wasn't prepared for the reaction. After all, it wasn't positive proof that they were related. SB picked it up immediately, hugged it to her chest, and though her eyes watered there was no faltering in her voice when she said,

'You're my son, Rhys. This piece of paper ... I pinned it to the shawl. It had the name I gave you written on it. I called you Seamus, after my uncle.'

She took Rhys's hand, holding it in a tight squeeze, and he watched as tears flowed gently across her face. Somewhat stunned, he appeared to have lost all knowledge of how to communicate. The questions he'd wanted answered for so many years became a jumble of indistinct words ... where to begin? With some unexpected clarity it came to him that this woman hadn't told him her name, and if she was his mother, he was definitely not going to refer to her as SB. Although it felt cold, even to him when she was crying, he asked,

'What does SB stand for?' This made her laugh. It was genuine, involuntary, and it lit up her whole face. 'Siobhan Blair,' she said.

They spent the rest of the afternoon talking about themselves, and although there was so much to know, they only spoke of those aspects that were less difficult. Rhys was pleased afterwards that he hadn't been able to voice those problematic questions for which he truly needed answers, because she said she'd like to see where he lived. They arranged for a visit as soon as Rhys returned to Ireland.

Back at Al's house there was a wonderful aroma of hot food. Rhys slumped onto the settee. Al fetched a glass of wine, his patience so endearing that it made Rhys smile to see him standing there saying nothing, showing no signs of questioning on his face.

'We're both sure we're related ... she's my mother Al.'

'Oh, my God. Come here for a hug. I was getting worried ... thought it had all gone wrong, and you'd slunk off somewhere to lick your wounds. I'll finish dinner and afterwards, I want to know every single detail of your day. Shall I call Beth and tell her the good news, or do you want to?'

'Err, … You do it. I might cry.'

It's strange that these days Al and Rhys were so comfortable in each other's lives that they could behave in both homes as if they were their own. The meal Al cooked was delicious, at first being devoured with little in the way of conversation, until he said,

'Beth cried when I phoned her. But I'll tell you what I told her,' he said, pointing his knife towards Rhys in a fashion unlike him, 'that it's early days and there's no proof yet that this woman is your mother.'

'Ahh. You say that, but look at this,' Rhys said as he found the picture and photograph from his folder. 'Siobhan's an artist. Before she abandoned me, she drew me and look.' he slid them across to Al, watching as utter surprise crossed his face.

'Wow. That's uncanny Rhys. Even though the photographs faded, and let's be honest, isn't the best, they're definitely the same baby. I can see why you believe her.'

'I've given her a copy of my DNA results. She's going to take a test. Then we'll know for sure,' Rhys said between the last mouthfuls of dinner.

'OK. That's good. Tell me what you know then.'

'Right! To start with she's not English, Welsh, or Scottish! She's Irish. She started painting when her mother bought her materials; that was after she began to have nightmares … she thinks she was about ten at the time. It sounds as though her early life was rather difficult. Her father hardly ever spoke to her and never called her by name. Can you imagine it, Al? I can't. Anyway, when she was seventeen, her and her mother left home.'

'What prompted that?'

'I don't know. There's a lifetime of events to discover for both of us, and it's not going to happen all at once. What I do know is that Siobhan went to art college in Belfast and became well known, selling regularly, and taking commissions, mainly portraits. Her landscape work is what she focusses on though, and she shows a number of pieces in galleries across the UK.'

'Does she live in London now?'

'Some of the time. She has a house in Ireland, her main home, and a flat in London which she uses whenever the need arises.'

'What did you tell her about yourself?'

'Much more than she told me. More or less everything really ... you know the main events. She asked me why I hadn't searched for my birth parents until now ... rather shocked, she was, to hear that I knew nothing about being adopted until our parents died. She cried when I told her I'd had a daughter ... showed her a photo of Katie. I think Siobhan's tears were more for the fact that she would never see her granddaughter.'

While they cleared up, Rhys told Al about Siobhan's visit to Ireland soon. As usual, Al tried to pull him back from moving too swiftly, but Rhys assured him that she'd asked to visit his home, and that he wanted her to meet Al and Beth. Rhys asked Al if he and Beth would stay with him in Ireland for a week.

Al's such a worrier … sometimes Rhys believed he still saw him as the little brother, instead of the man he'd become, so he needed reassurance that Rhys was prepared for whatever might happen in the future … that if Siobhan wasn't to be his birth mother, he was prepared to take it on the chin and keep looking.

CHAPTER 53

**Two Thousand and Nine
Rhys Jones Aged 59**

The Shawl

Rhys had warned Siobhan about Bonny's exuberance, so she wasn't surprised when he opened the door to see the dog racing round her feet, through the hall, and circumnavigating the settee. As calm returned, Bonny jumped onto Siobhan's lap, settling down to sleep.

'What a welcome,' she said, stroking Bonny down the full length of her body. 'She must be really good company for you, Rhys.'

'She is. She turned my life around … wouldn't be without her now. What would you like to drink? I've got all the usual stuff, as well as something cold if you'd prefer.'

'I'm fine with coffee, thanks. Strong with two sugars please.'

Upending Bonny, Siobhan followed him into the kitchen and sat at the table while he fussed about with drinks and sorted out cake.

'It's a lovely cottage you have. Would it be rude of me to ask to see round it? I'll be able to picture you here when I've gone.'

'Be my guest. It's small so it won't take you long!'

'It's so cosy,' she said only a moment later. 'A bit like my house here ... an older building. The London flat is modern ... not really to my taste but it suffices for the short time I spend there. I use it as a base for traveling round the mainland.'

Rhys had prepared some of those awkward questions on paper, memorising them as best he could, given the way his brain jumped from one thing to another when he was anxious. Siobhan was silent so he took the opportunity to ask the most pressing of them.

'Why? Why did you abandon me, Siobhan? Did you ever try to find me?'

Well. OK, two questions that seemed to come out together, as if chained to each other. As he spoke, he looked directly at her ... saw her bowed head slowly rise to meet his gaze.

'Rhys, it felt less like abandoning you ... rather more like an attempt to give you the sort of life I knew I couldn't. I was only seventeen when you were born, you see.'

'What about my father? Were you married?

Does he know what happened?'

Rhys took a deep breath. He was becoming emotional. Inevitable perhaps, but not good for sensible conversation.

'I wasn't married. I've never married. Your pa's dead, Rhys, and even if he wasn't, I'd not want you to meet him.'

'But why?'

'There's so much heartache in both our pasts,' and as she said this, she moved towards him on the settee, held his hand and her eyebrows furrowed with the tears that welled. 'This is going to be difficult to hear, but if you're determined to know ... well, it's not my place to keep it from you now that we've found each other. You have to be strong though, Rhys. You have to promise me that you won't regret this ... that however you come to feel about me, you'll remember that I've aways loved you ... always hoped that you'd search and find me ... I was only sixteen when I became pregnant...'

Rhys gasped before interrupting her to say, 'No wonder you gave me away!'

'Oh, no. That wasn't it at all. My mammy didn't want me to. She was willing to help me bring you up ... but I couldn't let you stay ... there was too much at stake.'

She fell silent, fiddling with the now empty mug between her hands. Rhys took it from her gently and made them both another one. He kicked himself for allowing emotions to push Siobhan into a space she was clearly uncomfortable with at this early stage in their relationship, but what was done was done, so he returned to the living room to try and redeem the situation. She was looking out at the back garden, hands in pockets, perhaps wondering how she might move on.

'I'm sorry Siobhan,' Rhys said, before she could say anything. 'There was no intention of hurting you, or to force you to tell me about what must have been a truly difficult event in your life.'

'It's OK, Rhys. I vowed a long time ago that if I ever were to meet you, I would be totally honest … there would be no secrets … but perhaps I assumed we'd know each other better by the time I needed to tell them.'

She gave a shallow laugh … as though nerves had got the better of her. Rhys motioned for her to sit down, handed her the coffee. And then thought it might be safer to ask about her parents, his grandparents.

'My parents had a very unhappy marriage … and … er … well Mam decided it would be better if we just left.'

'What happened after that?'

'We went to stay with mammy's sister, Aunt Cora and her husband Seamus. I didn't know I was pregnant when we left. You're named after my uncle Seamus,' she added with a smile. 'They helped us to get settled in a new home, but you were born at Aunt Cora's before that. You were so beautiful, Rhys. Your hair black ... and those tiny fingers and toes ... I've never forgotten the way it felt when I held you in my arms ... when you fed ...'

Rhys left the space for her. It was obvious she was remembering everything about that time. That his birth had never left her. Eventually, she said,

'I took you to a convent in Belfast ... left you on the steps early one morning ... that shawl you were wrapped in was the one Aunt Cora made for me when I was born.'

Siobhan was wistful now, her pain clearly as great as his, but he didn't interrupt her ... he would let her do this in her own time. 'It broke my heart.'

'I have the shawl. Would you like to see it?'

'Really! I can't believe it ... yes please.' When he gave it to her, she held it to her face, even before looking at it, as though there would be no doubt that this was the right one. She breathed in deeply and then spread it out on her lap, inspecting it ... feeling it ... studying each of the small patterns within it.

Rhys didn't know how long they sat in silence, their own thoughts and feelings taking over, but it wasn't in any way an awkward silence. On the contrary, it felt as though they'd known each other longer. Long enough for empathy and understanding to be shared emotions. Rhys wasn't sure where to go from there though … he wanted to know about his father and what had happened to her father … how she and her mother managed to repair their lives, but so conscious was he of her concentration, he couldn't bring himself to break the spell. Eventually, she looked up at him, and said,

'You know, Rhys, if I had any doubts about who you are, this shawl banishes them all. Mammy would have been thrilled to see it … to see you … to see us reunited.'

'Did your mother recover and enjoy the rest of her life?'

'Ah. She did. You remember I told you about Paddy Youngen? I left a note for him when we went. After we'd found a home of our own, I asked my grandpappy to go and find him … to tell him where we were. To mam's surprise, Paddy turned up one day with Murphy, who he'd rescued from the house, and they ended up marrying! Paddy and Mam that is!'

'So, your Mum divorced? That can't have been easy in those days.'

'She didn't need to, Rhys. About three months after we left, my pa was found dead. It was judged that he'd arrived home in a drunken stupor, fallen against the corner of the kitchen table and bled to death. It was a couple of weeks before they found him. Mam and I think it was no accident … there must have been plenty of angry fathers in the town willing to put an end to him, but there was never any investigation, so it was recorded as accidental death.'

'From what you've already told me; my grandfather was a pretty unpleasant man.'

'He was ... but you know what ... today's society would have recognised that he was unstable both emotionally and mentally. He'd have had help and maybe mammy would have been spared.'

At that moment, perhaps appropriately, the doorbell sounded. Bonny, who had been curled up sound asleep most of the afternoon, jumped off the settee and ran to the door, barking loudly enough to wake the dead. Al and Beth had been out most of the day, but now appeared at the living room door, all smiles and full of expectation as they greeted them.

'Al. Beth. This is Siobhan. She's my mother.' As he spoke those words, he felt the tightness of his face relax and knew he was grinning like a Cheshire cat. The three of them met at the centre of the room, Siobhan hugged each of them in turn.

'I'm so pleased to meet you,' she said.

'And we're pleased to meet you too,' said Beth, but without a pause, Al jumped in, saying,

'Before we go any further, I want to get this off my chest. The three of us may not be blood related,' he said 'but Rhys will always be our brother and woe betide anyone who gets in the way of that!'

Rhys was crestfallen ... looked at Al who simply shrugged his shoulders and held his arms out in a 'so what' fashion. Siobhan laughed.

'Well now that's done,' she said, 'you can rest assured that I will never come between my son and his brother and sister. After all, haven't you looked after him for me all these years?'

Rhys left them chatting and went to get Mary. Mary had played such an important role in his recent life, and he wanted her to share the joy ... to meet his mother. By the time she'd been introduced to Siobhan, there was an incredible sense of merriment ... celebration.

It was late in the day by the time Rhys found himself alone to gather his thoughts. Siobhan had to return to London the following day but had asked him to stay with her there in a week's time. She was happy for Bonny to go too, so they made arrangements, and parted with hugs and kisses ... and still so much more to find out.

CHAPTER 54

Two Thousand and Nine
Rhys Jones Aged 59

Questions, Questions

Rhys slept well considering the hectic nature of the previous day, waking in a kind of euphoria. A long walk was needed so Bonny played on the sand at the back of the house while he walked, jogged, and ran after her. They were out for about two hours, by which time his thoughts had turned once again towards all the confusion of information discovered and questions still unanswered. After lunch he sat down with pen and paper in an effort to make sense of it. He started with two columns, one for what he knew and the other for what he still needed to know, but that didn't work, so he resorted to two separate sheets of A4 and began with what he now knew.

All that stuff about his father didn't make any sense. Rhys began to feel that old confusion which so often generated the image of Jack. He couldn't go there again ... not today, when all he wanted was to clarify this new knowledge and come to terms with it. Coffee, as always, seemed to be the answer. A break in the thinking process, maybe take Bonny out again. Spend some time on the phone with Al; get the washing up to date; anything really! In the end he went for a run which cleared his head and arrived home ready to tackle the questions that he knew would continue to plague him until they were on paper.

Rhys wrote without thinking and on reading it back, recognised the inherent feeling he'd always had, that somehow he was apart from his family whoever they were ... unable to understand where he belonged ... tied to it only by circumstance. He might be Rhys Jones, but he was someone else too ... someone who has never been granted the opportunity to develop and grow up in his own country, with his birth parents. Was he ungrateful? Did he feel sorry for himself? Was he digging another mire to bury himself in? Why was he finding it so difficult to accept what he knew ... to enjoy a relationship with his birth mother without having to know every last detail? Rhys came to the conclusion after much soul searching, that because of the way he'd always been, knowing half of his parentage wasn't enough. Somehow, he was convinced that his natural parents influence was deep inside him. Beneath this shell that was Rhys Jones, lay the real man, Seamus Blair.

On Friday two cards arrived in the post. One was from Beth, a congratulations card in which she wrote about how happy they all were that he'd found Siobhan. The other was from Siobhan. The picture was one of her paintings ... a rather beautiful landscape. It said very little other than how pleased she was to have met him but included was her address and a map of how to find her.

By the following Wednesday Rhys was back with Al, in England. He met John that evening for a pint, but John seemed rather subdued and when Rhys asked, he said that Marion was suffering from stress at work ... a few teachers were off sick, and she was having to manage two classes at a time for some of each day. He was worried that she might be the next one to be signed off. Rhys was sorry to hear that. Marion had always been a confident person, and he imagined she'd cope well with the stresses of her vocation. It seems that we all have our breaking points. Rhys wanted to talk to John about his situation ... the way his mind had been affected again by recent thoughts, but it was his turn now for the supportive role, so they drank, and drank some more while chewing the cud, eventually parting with a decision to get tickets for a football match when Rhys returned from London.

The next day Rhys spent many hours searching Google for information about Siobhan Blair, wanting to know as much about her as possible before his visit and found quite a lot regarding her art works; where they were displayed, including quality photographs some of which he downloaded and printed out, against all copyright, but she was his mother and he didn't care. There was hardly anything personal about her apart from where she was born and grew up, where she studied and how she progressed to producing contract portrait work. There was a short quote from her on one site in which she had spoken of the portrait work as being her bread and butter, while her passion was painting landscapes. It seems that she worked in both watercolours and graphite, which produces mostly black and white images. Rhys was reminded of the picture of him she'd drawn when he was born. He had a sense of her as a very private person.

Google had a lot of information on Ballywalter too with maps, as well as numerous reports about its hotels, summer holidays and such like. Photographs showed its small harbour, narrow town streets, and one or two of its most prominent features. It looked like a pleasant place from the information available, and it wasn't far south of where Rhys lived. Ballyhalbert was a smaller place, being on the coast south of Ballywalter, but for some reason, he didn't have the same interest in finding out about it. Silly really, as that was where he was born. Perhaps it was because he only spent his first couple of nights there!

CHAPTER 55

Two Thousand and Ten
Rhys Jones Aged 60

London

With Bonny under his arm, Rhys knocked on the door of Siobhan's flat. The area was not at all as he'd imagined. When she had said she had a modern flat, one of these high-rise blocks came to mind, impersonal and forbidding. But this was an extremely pleasant part of London, the flats more like apartments in large houses, with gardens and parks nearby. Siobhan welcomed him with a hug and a kiss on his cheek. Rhys flushed … felt the heat rising … and turned rather more quickly than intended so that she flinched slightly.

'Have I done something wrong? She asked.

'No. No. Not at all,' he said. 'Well, to be honest, I've been rather nervous of staying here because

... well ... we've only just met ... you know ... we don't know each other ... I'm being stupid I think.'

'It's natural for us to have reservations, Rhys. We wouldn't be human if we didn't, and I'm sorry if my greeting was too familiar for you,' she added with a smile. 'Come on. Put poor Bonny down to have a sniff! I'll take your things to the bedroom, and we'll have a drink of something.'

Rhys looked around the space, which was modern, and wondered why she hadn't thought to change it for something she preferred. Bonny had run off to explore. He felt suddenly awkward ... out of place ... nerves gathered below the pit of his stomach. He'd been so self-assured in his own world ... perhaps that's an exaggeration since his mind had begun to slip back to somewhere unpleasant. It was more that he knew what he wanted; had the confidence to keep searching for answers. In this new place with a woman who was still a stranger, there was a sudden feeling of walls collapsing. His contemplation was interrupted by a feeble barking in the hall. Siobhan had a full-length mirror on the wall and Bonny was staring at herself, moving towards the other dog with little growls and barks, but not so brave as to go right to it. Rhys picked her up and laughed. Siobhan joined him, and that tiny act from a small dog seemed to resolve any awkwardness.

On the wall of Siobhan's living room, surrounded by a large frame, there were numerous portraits, of different sizes but all in the same medium Rhys now knew to be graphite. Each one was beautifully and individually framed, signed SB on the bottom right corner, and somehow, Rhys knew that these were not contracted portraits. Siobhan saw him move towards them as she re-entered the room, and said,

'They're only copies. The originals are at home. They're your family, Rhys ... the first portraits I did, so not my best work but it's like having them with me.'

'But they're amazing, Siobhan. Who are they?'

'This is my mammy ... your grandmammy, and this is her mammy,' she said, pointing to two of the largest images set at each side of the montage. 'And this is my grandpappy, so your great grandpappy.'

Rhys searched their faces trying to find any likeness to himself. 'Who's this? She's a very beautiful woman.'

'Ah. This lady was my aunt Cora, and she was beautiful, quite unlike Mammy, who had a rather plain face, although her beauty lay inside. You can see the likeness between Aunt Cora and grandmammy. Mammy took after her pa. This is my uncle Seamus, and this is Paddy Youngen! Of course, Murphy is here,' she said pointing, 'and you'll recognise this little man in the centre.'

'I do.' This was his family, He gazed from one to another. These were the people whose genes he'd inherited. They were inside him ... an intrinsic part of him, unlike those of the Jones ancestors. It's weird. A whole new set of people he wanted to know about. And then he noticed another picture at the top, ... an older man ... his father? 'Who's this?' he said pointing it out. 'Is it my father?'

'No, Rhys. Your father isn't among these portraits. This is Paddy Olden! He looked out for mammy and me when I was young, and of course when mammy and Paddy Youngen fell for each other, he encouraged it.'

'Why 'olden' and 'youngen?''

'That's something that stuck from long ago. Mammy and Pa used to use the terms when they were talking of the fishermen ... you know ... to distinguish between them. In my innocence, I always thought that these were their surnames. I've never called them anything else ... in fact I didn't know their surname until mammy married Paddy Youngen.'

'So, what was it?'

'Finnegan. The Paddies Finnegan!' she said laughing. 'I shall always call them youngen and olden though.'

There was an ease between them after that, as though those people were in the room too ... and Rhys wondered if their influence was yet to be severed ... it reminded him of how

Katie's presence lingered long after her death. But surely, he was being soft ... soft in the head maybe!

Siobhan showed Rhys round some galleries during his stay. He'd never been particularly interested in art, was useless at it in school and pleased when he didn't have to continue with it, but as they walked round the first one, he found some that appealed without really knowing why. They looked at a few of the great masters which, although Rhys had seen them on the internet and television, in the flesh so to speak he found magnificent. Brush strokes, light and shade, infinitesimal details were only apparent on those originals. He wanted to see some of Siobhan's work, so they went to a smaller gallery on the outskirts of the city. On the wall at the back of an alcove, six of her landscapes were exhibited, and Rhys discovered the feeling of being drawn into them ... that he could actually see himself in them. They were fantastic ... his mother was extremely talented. None of them were named; only her initials were present, but she said that each one had a title printed on the reverse.

'Where are these places?' Rhys asked.

'Two of them are Ballywalter. This one is the harbour, one of my favourite places. I spent a lot of time there as a child, meeting the Paddies, waiting for their boat to return, or playing on the beach across the road. When I first had drawing materials, it was their fish I drew, and Paddy said they were so good he put them up on the walls of his fish shop … rather embarrassing now I think about it. This one here is a row of cottages along the Ballywalter road, at the main town approach. Our house was at the top of harbour Road, almost the last dwelling in Ballywalter and a long way from the town, but mammy and me would walk there as often as we could, and these cottages became a landmark for us … she'd laugh and say, almost there Siobhan, and I'd know that my little legs wouldn't have too much further to go before we stopped to rest. I grew to love this row … painted it several times, but I think this is my favourite.'

'You told me that the portraits were what you mostly did as an income, but surely these landscapes sell as well?'

'Oh, they do, but an artist never knows when something will sell, or how many in any given time period, so I see them as extra income. I still have a waiting list for portraits, so I know I'll be able to earn consistently over the next year, possibly.'

She said it nonchalantly, as if it wasn't an achievement to be in such a position, but Rhys was pretty stunned. Imagine Rhys Jones having such an amazing mother, as he was beginning to realise Siobhan was.

By the time they'd spent several days together,

it had become clear that their personalities were not far apart. Like himself, Siobhan had a calm nature ... not even Bonny peeing on the living room carpet the second day Rhys was there, produced anything like displeasure. They laughed at things that happened on the streets and shared a similar sense of humour. Siobhan loved Bonny and made a huge fuss of her whenever she could, which naturally went down well with him, but Rhys wanted to know what made her who she was ... because they'd not even talked about mundane things ... their preferences for food and such like, never mind all those questions he hadn't dared broach in case they shattered the equilibrium. Rhys was musing on all this the night before he left and must have been away in his own little world, because Siobhan suddenly broke into it.

'Rhys?' She said. He turned towards her, seeing the frown, and wondered what had caused it. 'You've been miles away ... what's on your mind?'

'Sorry. I was thinking about how well we've got on together ... but also how little we've discovered of each other. I don't even know what your favourite food is!'

'Irish stew with dumplings,' she said without a pause. 'What's yours?'

'Ah! Now that you've asked me, I'm not sure. A good old-fashioned roast would come fairly close to the top of the list, I think. And then fish and chips.'

'My. You're so English!'

'You can talk, with your Irish stew!' Once they'd stopped laughing at each other, Rhys asked her why it had taken so long for her to contact him, since she'd clearly cut out so many of his adverts.

'Try to see it from my point of view, Rhys. I gave you away. I had no idea what had become of you; where you'd been brought up, although in my innocence, I assumed it would be in Ireland somewhere. I couldn't begin to imagine the sort of person you'd grown into Whether you'd lived in children's homes; were angry perhaps and maybe moved into inappropriate circles. I lacked the courage, not just to seek you out, but to know what you'd become. I lacked the courage to believe it would be in your best interests for us to be reunited. Can you understand?'

'Of course. I went through all the same sort of thought processes. Al was intent on me forgetting the search. He didn't understand my need to find you. He believed I'd be better off as I was. But how could I be, Siobhan?' he asked as he got up and walked to the portraits. Rhys turned to her and said,

'I'm only Rhys Jones on the outside. Everything that matters is linked to these people … to you. The fabric of my being has never been Rhys. It's always been Seamus, so how could I not want to find you? I'm so pleased that you found that courage.'

He sat back beside her, and took both her hands in his, looked her in the eyes and told her,

'I know you're my mother, and I believe there's already a bond between us that will increase as we move forward.' It was only as he untangled their hands that he noticed how Siobhan's fingers had begun to twist, and that different sized nodules at various joints were causing slight deformation. She saw him looking and smiled as she said that arthritis was hereditary... so watch out Rhys!

'What makes you angry?' he asked.

'Injustice ... inequality ... oh, yes. This rapidly increasing nanny state!'

'You certainly know your own mind. I'm sure I couldn't answer such a question without having to think about it,' he said, quite suddenly aware of a wave of tiredness, and that he still had to take Bonny out.

Stifling a yawn, Rhys stretched, fetched the lead, and left Siobhan making coffee while he walked down the still busy road. He was ready to go home even though in this short space of time it felt right being with Siobhan, but home is special, so he wasn't sorry that this was his last night. There was a lot from the week to take back and internalise, never mind Al's, Beth's, and John's natural desire to want to know every detail. That list of questions had remained in the folder. Rhys had resisted the desire to know everything now, realising, perhaps a little late, that Siobhan would tell him when she was ready.

CHAPTER 56

Two Thousand and Ten
Rhys Jones Aged 60

Who is Rhys Jones?

Rhys set off early in order to try and avoid rush hour traffic through London, not realising that in the city rush hour came early too. Joining the motorway, it seemed he would not get far quickly and added to the huge lorries going north, rain began to fall. Tiny drops on the windscreen at first giving way to windswept downpours so the wipers couldn't keep up, and the overhead gantries flashed speed restrictions and warnings of queues. The car swayed as the gusts increased, his hands tight on the wheel, so when the phone rang in its cradle, he was loathe to answer it. Al, came up on the screen at the same time Bonny began to cry, pulling on her harness.

With Bonny walked round the car park, relieving herself almost as soon as she jumped out, Rhys sat with a cappuccino in the passenger seat and rang Al. He did his usual big brother spiel about the weather conditions, which according to the forecast were going to get worse before they got better and even berated Rhys for not having stayed another night for the storms to abate. Telling him that there had been no storm in London and asking him to make sure the kettle was on, Rhys resumed the journey.

Travel continued to be slow, but thankfully traffic never came to a standstill. The wipers gave a gritty screech occasionally which was good, because their regular action lulled him into a weariness that if he was not careful would end in disaster. Before long, Rhys's mind wandered to Siobhan. On the passenger seat an envelope contained copies of the portraits of his family and pondering on them he tried to imagine what Al and Beth would think of them ... these people who, though he'd never met them, played such an important role in his life.

But they didn't did they? His life had been Rhys Jones. Rhys Jones is as much the product of Angharad, Owen, Al, Beth and even John, as this new family is to any inherited aspects in him. They're the family from whom he'd developed personal qualities. They're the people who made him Rhys Jones. It didn't matter how many times he tried to organise thoughts around those issues; he always came back to the same thing. To everyone he'd ever known or met, he was Rhys Jones, and yet this other him had always been present ... had always been inside ... had always had a bearing on the mind and body of Rhys Jones. Hadn't he known it from an early age?

Somehow with all the stormy weather continuing, and his mind less than it should have been on the driving, he arrived at Als. Bonny ran round as if she'd been away for months, sniffing all her favourite corners and playing with her fleecy blanket which he'd forgotten to take with him. Al was, as is usual when he'd been away, in the kitchen cooking. Rhys knew he took him for granted and chided himself for not having recognised it before.

'Tell me about your stay,' Al said as they made themselves comfortable, the fire throwing out more heat than he'd felt since leaving Siobhan's flat. He put his legs onto a stool and let the warmth filter through.

'I'm not sure where to begin,' he said.

'OK. What did you do?'

Rhys told Al all about the visits to art galleries and how he'd begun to see the magic in original art works. He was at pains to emphasise the talent he'd seen in his mother's work and suggested that they should go and see some of what was displayed locally.

'I can't say my first impressions of London

were favourable … too much traffic, and far too claustrophobic with all the tall buildings etc. But … the upside is that you can buy anything and everything … and eat such a variety of cuisine, such as you'd never find here. It really was an education! Wouldn't want to stay there too long though.'

'It sounds as if you had a good time, and you seem to have got on well.'

'We did. Siobhan's a placid person. I suppose I get that from her …. she's confident, knows her own mind, unlike me! She gave me these,' he said and reached for the folder, selecting the drawing of his grandmother.

'All these are her work and she has them displayed in her flat. The originals are kept at her home in Ireland. This is Siobhan's mother, so my grandmother. Her name was Bridget. She's dead now, as are all these people, so I'll never meet them.' He handed the pictures to Al and watched as he studied them.

'I know I've only seen Siobhan for a short while, but from what I remember, I can't see a particular likeness between her and Bridget,' Al said.'

'I said the same thing. She tells me she took after her father more … but she doesn't have a drawing of him.'

'Why not?'

'Because according to her, he wasn't a particularly pleasant man, to the extent that she prefers not to be reminded of him. This lady is Siobhan's grandmother, so my great grandmother, and there's little likeness between her and Bridget. Apparently, Bridget took after her father, who's here.'

Rhys continued to present the family pictures with explanations of who was who, Al wanting to know as much information as possible. He thought the artwork stunning, and asked what Rhys would do with them.

'I haven't decided yet. This is the montage Siobhan has in her flat,' he told Al and showed him the photograph.

'Is that you in the centre? He asked, pointing to it.

'It is,' Rhys said proudly, then scrolled through some of the other photos and stopped at the one of the harbour.

'That's beautiful. Where is it?'

'It's the little harbour in Ballywalter ... that's where Siobhan was born and still lives.'

'I thought you said she'd moved ... that you were born in Ballyhalbert ... or something like that.'

'That's true. But when Bridget and Paddy Youngen married, which wasn't too long after Siobhan's father's death, they moved back to live in the flat above Paddy's fish shop. When Paddy retired, he had the shop renovated back to a house. He left it to Siobhan in his will; Bridget having died before him. Siobhan's asked me to visit her there in April.'

'That'll be great, Rhys. Now. I'm having a family get together on Sunday. It'll be a buffet affair. There are too many of us to sit round my little table. It'll be a farewell do for you.'

'Sounds good to me. I can give you a hand preparing.'

'No need. It's all in hand … what do you think I've been doing with my time while you've been in London?'

'I'd hope something rather more exciting.'

'I wish.

CHAPTER 57

Two Thousand and Ten
Rhys Jones Aged 60

A Whole New Landscape

Rhys stayed with Siobhan at her home in Ballywalter. Siobhan was keen for him to see the harbour, so they went the way she and her mother would have taken many times before. The harbour itself was instantly recognisable, although the fishing boats were fewer and many of the those that were now moored were larger than in previous decades and ranged from smaller pleasure craft with cabins to more impressive sailing vessels. Siobhan said that the area hadn't changed much at all and remained as she'd known it as a child.

'See that wall? Mam used to sit there and talk to Paddy and if he'd had a good catch, he'd give her fish for our dinner.'

'Which Paddy would that have been?'

'Oh, mostly Paddy Olden. His son would usually be working in their fish shop ... where I live now.'

On the way back from the harbour, Siobhan stopped at the corner and turned towards the house situated there.

'That's the house we lived in,' she said. There was sadness in her voice, and her face became serious. 'That's changed too, but it still has the look I remember from my early childhood. It was quite isolated then, but over the years new houses have joined everything together along the coast road.'

Rhys was beginning to love this place already. Its peacefulness, the lapping of the sea on the shore, the gentle breeze, were all drawing him in. They walked past the little row of cottages depicted in Siobhan's artwork, still there almost unchanged.

Siobhan took Rhys to see the house in Ballyhalbert where he'd been born.

'It's much grander now,' she told him. 'Those extensions weren't there of course. Nor all those posh cars. What incredible progress there's been since the mid twentieth century.'

'It's good to see it, Siobhan. The place I was born in.'

'Not that you were there for long, but nonetheless, that's it. See that window up there,' she said pointing to the second floor. 'That's the room Mam and me had. That's where I gave birth to you.'

Belfast bustled in the sunshine, and the broad accents of natives rang out. It was modern, trees growing amid pedestrian walkways giving it a countryside feel. The warmth had brought people out the day they went, and they joined them at the outdoor seating in front of a cafe, taking their time over coffee and cake. Rhys had been to Belfast many times, but only to shop or take the ferry. Siobhan showed him parts that he'd not been interested in, and when they'd finished at the café, she put her hand on his arm, as if to guide him.

'I want to show you something,' she said, 'but I'm not sure how you'll feel about it.'

'There's only one way to find out.'

Right at the heart of town Siobhan stopped at a large building. For a while she said nothing, just stood there looking. Rhys wanted to say something, but it was as if she was spellbound and he didn't want to break whatever was going on in her head.

'That building,' she finally said, 'is where I left you, Rhys. On those steps there.'

Rhys stared at them. Three patchy grey stone steps that even in the days warmth, looked cold and hard. He tried to imagine a tiny bundle wrapped in that beautiful shawl. Would he have cried? Would he have drawn the attention of people passing by? Might his cries have alerted those within? Everything about the building appeared granite hard, the contrast to a tiny baby's form incongruous.

'It wasn't an office then, of course,' Siobhan said sadly. 'I knew the nuns would take you in ... look after you. I kept turning round as Mam and me walked away ... I wanted to run back ... take you in my arms ... carry you home. I loved you so much.'

They stayed like that for a long time, oblivious of those passing by, until Siobhan said,

'Come on. I didn't want to upset you ... but you know ... I don't want to keep things from you either. This,' she said her arm tracing the building's frontage, 'this is the reality, Rhys.'

The following day, subdued spirits from the evening before had disappeared in slumber. They drove to Ballyferris where Siobhan showed Rhys the home her mother had grown up in. She was animated when she talked about it, relating stories of how her mother and grandfather sang and the times her mother and Cora had with their parents. From there she took Rhys back south to Strangford Loch, just west of Greyabby, a short distance from Ballywalter. They sat by the bank and watched while Bonny ran through the grass; laughed as she tried to snap at anything that ventured too close.

'This is salt water,' Siobhan said, 'the inlet from the Irish sea is south of here,' and she pointed in case Rhys had lost his bearings. 'It's full of spectacular wildlife and it's a good place for me to come and draw. I often come here out of season. Fewer people makes for better concentration, but then sometimes I find I'm not drawing, but watching and listening,' she said laughing.

Rhys found it impossible not to smile ... at her enthusiasm ... her wistfulness when she spoke about Ireland ... the way her eyes wrinkled when she laughed.

'It is truly beautiful,' he said. 'I knew I was falling in love with this country, but you've shown me so much more of myself here that I already feel it's my home.'

CHAPTER 58

Two Thousand and Ten
Rhys Jones Aged 60

Torn From a Pad

After another wonderful day in the countryside late sun shone through the west facing window as they ate the last of the evening meal. Wine flowed, even though neither of them were great drinkers. They sat comfortably on the settee and Rhys began to feel the effects of the drink. A little ache began behind his eyes, and he felt very sleepy.

In that dreamy state, Rhys's thoughts turned from pleasing images to brooding issues. Before he knew it, the first feelings of resentment came to the fore, and with them a sense of injustice that Siobhan flatly refused to say who his father was. At first, he didn't realise he was on his feet, pacing the floor, fidgeting, and as though it wasn't him speaking he heard himself say,

'Siobhan! Tell me who my father was! You knew him didn't you? Did you go out with him?' She looked at Rhys, startled, even a little afraid perhaps, but when she spoke her voice remained calm.

'I'm not ready, Rhys.'

'Damn it, Siobhan. Don't I have a right to know? How hard can it be? Was he a murderer … a terrorist? Did he spend his life in prison?' Siobhan leant her head against the back of the settee, closed her eyes and beathed deeply.

'He was none of those things, but in a way he was worse than them all.'

'What do you mean? How can anyone be worse than that? I have to know.'

'Why, Rhys? Why are you so desperate to know?'

'Don't you see? Whoever he is, he's fifty percent of me, and I don't know who I really am until I know who he was.'

Rhys was aware that he wasn't being entirely reasonable, but didn't seem able to stop. Siobhan got up and left the room … left him thinking that was it … she would not be moved, but a moment later she returned with something, and held it face down on her lap.

'This is the moment I've been afraid of since the day you were born, Rhys. Maybe now you'll begin to unders … to understand why I gave you up. Why I had … had to protect you.'

Siobhan sat there, tears flowing unchecked, and Rhys felt a pang of something ... without knowing what it was, whether it was anger at himself for putting Siobhan through this, or a feeling of such tangled emotions he found too difficult to wade through.

He held out his hand for the paper, but Siobhan made no attempt to pass it over. Rhys was confused. Was she going to tell him?

'What can possibly be so awful, Siobhan?' He watched as she lifted the paper, still face down, and held it out. Rhys had to stretch to touch it, but even then Siobhan wouldn't let go. When she did, Rhys was almost afraid to look, yet he couldn't imagine why. Wasn't this what he wanted ... to know who his father was. The page had been torn from a pad and close up it was clear that it was old, yellowed and curled at the edges.

Slowly, Rhys turned it over. He stared at the image there, his body beginning to shake. 'Jack.' The picture was not altogether clear, as though Siobhan had drawn it that way deliberately, but there was no mistaking the image of Jack he'd carried with him throughout life, with one difference. The eyes. Jack had never had eyes. Now Rhys could see them ... unnatural eyes.

'What?' Siobhan said weakly.

'What's his name? Who is he?' Rhys was shouting, rage getting the better of him. 'This man's old. Who is he?'

'I can't tell you.'

'You won't tell me, you mean.'

'That's right. I will not … ever … tell you his name. He raped me Rhys.'

'You knew him, didn't you? He wasn't just some stranger … like this was a random thing.'

'Yes. I knew him.' He watched the agony on her face … and he had caused it. He could not bear to think he had hurt her. He had to get out.

CHAPTER 59

Two Thousand and Ten
Rhys Jones Aged 60

Run Rhys Run

Run, Rhys. Run. Along the road, the sound of shoes slapping on the pavement ... past the cottages, Harbour Road, the new houses. Blind to where his feet were taking him, Run. After all, hadn't he outrun Jack many times before. Surely, he could do it again.

Jack Daw ... his father ... inside his head for nigh on sixty years. Yes, he knew who his father was; knew why Siobhan would not tell him. Had he inherited Jack? Could he still become him?

The surface below changed to pebbles. An unmade road full of potholes, but it didn't matter. Run. He ran, alongside the sea, towards the cliffs where the evening sun had disappeared, leaving way for a full moon. On top, a burning desire to throw his body into the water below took hold, but as he looked down at the balls of his feet hanging over its edge, he discovered his own spinelessness. What if he didn't die? What if he ended up brain damaged ... in a wheelchair? The man in the moon mocked him. 'Don't you dare,' he cried out.

Utterly distraught, and beginning to feel the night's coolness, he lay in a ball almost hoping he could somehow fall from this cliff by some force other than his own. His body rocked uncontrollably, and his head burst with that knowledge he'd wanted so much, but which was now breaking him apart. Who was he? A monster, that's who. Rhys Jones on the outside ... a monster inside. Why, oh why did they not destroy those documents, if they knew they were never going to tell him?

Without thinking Rhys undressed, lay his naked body on the cold cliff. All he'd ever wanted was to be loved, to know where he came from. Now he knew.

'I should have been born out of love,' he shouted, 'not some sordid unnatural sex forced on my mother. Not some grubby event. I want to start over ... to be born again ...'

His eyes closed and for a while he slept. He dreamed of them, not clearly at first, not focused. Not even all of them, just their faces. Al, Beth, and John, and in front of them Katie. His beautiful Katie, who would never know her family. Never grow into an amazing woman.

They were smiling. Looking at him, and then John's voice so clear, it was as though he were sitting right there beside him.

'It's all right, Rhys. It's time to stop the struggle, to stop fighting. You'll be OK. You can be who you want to be. Go ahead. Make the decision. We'll always be here with you.'

When Rhys opened his eyes it was to a dark sky, the moon on its journey westward, leaving the stars sparkling. He thought about the dream. Wondered how his mind could conjure up such stark images. He wanted it to end. He wanted to disappear, to be anything other than a man within a man. He sat up, shivered; remembered the bottle of pills in his pocket. Slowly, two at a time, he threw them to the back of his throat, swallowed as best as he could without any liquid. They stuck, made him reach, but determination spurred him to continue. Soon with most of the tablets gone, his head felt heavy; his eyes drooped, and a mild dizziness came over him.

The sun began to appear on the eastern horizon, and with his poor taught body beginning to relax, he watched the gulls, listened to the surf against the bottom of the cliff, and became aware of a distinct transformation in his head. Without thinking of who might be about at this hour, and still naked, he lay on the stony ground and thought about life; his life and all those who had inhabited it, while tears for them all ran towards the earth, soaked into the soil and became at one with Ireland.

The sun was well up in the sky when he sat up, his pile of discarded clothes still there. Rhys Jones looked at them carefully, studied each item and then turned them all inside out. He stood on the cliff, looked out towards the Irish Sea and with a new found belief, put them back on.

He didn't hurry on the walk north. His legs were uncooperative, his brain fuzzy and yet inexplicably sharp. He watched the same scenery pass by on his right. Heard the same splashing of waves, noticed the same homes and streets. It was all different though now. He was looking with different eyes. Seeing with clarity.

Her front door was open, Siobhan standing at the far end of the hall as if she'd been there all night, and Bonny by her feet. Her eyes were red with crying. Rhys took a step over the threshold.

'I've come home, Mam.'

AFTERWORD

For some of you this may have been a difficult read, but then it wasn't an easy book to write. The themes are dark and disturbing, and perhaps beg the question, 'why write it'.

The answer is that such themes are not fictional. They are all around us, the stuff of so many people's lives. I have been told that these are taboo subjects and should not be written about. I disagree. I believe that is enough reason for authors to embrace them, for authors are in a position to show that there is always hope; that there is always a path to recovery.

Thank you,

Sue

ACKNOWLEDGEMENTS

As always there are many to thank for their support, and it is not possible to mention all those who have been part of the making of this novel.

The inspiration for this work came from a BBC Podcast, so my thanks to the corporation for providing such rich listening material.

I also acknowledge the work of Joseph Campbell [1881 - 1944] for the use of "My Lagan love", published in 1905.

I wish to thank Sophie Robert, for her help and support in providing expertise where I have none. She has been an invaluable part of this journey.

My family, whose encouragement and advice I could not manage without, are integral to any success this novel may bring. They have my whole hearted thanks.

ABOUT THE AUTHOR

Sue Robertson Danells

Thirty years ago I started researching our family history. One ancestor's story, a man who vanished from the records, captured me completely. What began as curiosity became something I couldn't let go. And slowly, it became 'When Darkness Falls', my debut novel.

I published it at 71. And believe me, I had so much to learn, publishing, formatting, finding a cover. But I did it. Because the story mattered. Because I wanted my 95-year-old mother to hold it in her hands. And because, deep down, I needed to prove to myself that it's never too late, to do something brave.

So if you've ever thought, 'I'd love to write a book, but it's too late for me,' I want to gently say: No, it's not. You don't need permission. You just need a story that won't let you go.

You can find Sue on:
facebook.com/suerobertsondanells
instagram.com/danellssuerobertson

messenger com/suerobertsondanells
email: srobertsondanells@gmail.com

BOOKS BY THIS AUTHOR

When Darkness Falls

'Our book club devoured this. The themes of shame, identity, and hope sparked some unforgettable conversations. Highly recommend for thoughtful readers.'
Reviewed by Daryl Franklin

The Long Game

'A gripping British detective mystery with a strong female lead, "The Long Game" is the first novel in a thrilling new series featuring DI Maggie Dent.'

The Pledge

The Pledge
(A Revised Edition of When Darkness Falls)

A Victorian family saga.
Inspired by a true story of promises and hope for Alfred Maurice Tyler.
But even new beginnings could not avert his tragic path of destiny.

Loss
Secrets
a broken promise and ultimately
tragedy in the small town of Brighton.

Alfred Maurice Tyler had a difficult but blameless
life until he broke

The Pledge.